ALSO BY SARRA MANNING

Guitar Girl

Pretty Things

Pretty Things

sarra manning

DUTTON BOOKS

DUTTON BOOKS

A member of Penguin Group (USA) Inc.

Published by the Penguin Group

Penguin Group (USA) Inc., 375 Hudson Street, New York, New York 10014, U.S.A.

Penguin Group (Canada), 10 Alcorn Avenue, Toronto, Ontario, Canada M4V 3B2 (a division of

Pearson Penguin Canada Inc.) • Penguin Books Ltd, 80 Strand, London WC2R 0RL, England

Penguin Ireland, 25 St Stephen's Green, Dublin 2, Ireland (a division of Penguin Books Ltd)

Penguin Group (Australia), 250 Camberwell Road, Camberwell, Victoria 3124, Australia (a

division of Pearson Australia Group Pty Ltd) • Penguin Books India Pvt Ltd, 11 Community

Centre, Panchsheel Park, New Delhi - 110 017, India • Penguin Group (NZ), Cnr Airborne and

Rosedale Roads, Albany, Auckland 1310, New Zealand (a division of Pearson New Zealand Ltd)

Penguin Books (South Africa) (Pty) Ltd, 24 Sturdee Avenue, Rosebank, Johannesburg 2196,

South Africa • Penguin Books Ltd, Registered Offices: 80 Strand, London WC2R 0RL, England

CIP Data is available.

First published in Great Britain 2005 by Hodder Children's Books, London

Published in the United States 2005 by Dutton Books,
a member of Penguin Group (USA) Inc.
345 Hudson Street, New York, New York 10014
www.penguin.com/youngreaders

Designed by Beth Herzog

Printed in USA
ISBN 0-525-47522-2
1 3 5 7 9 10 8 6 4 2

*This book would be a pretty sorry state of affairs
if it weren't for the sterling work of my editor,
Emily Thomas, who plied me with copious amounts
of Diet Coke in swank London cafés,
wrestled my tense issues into some semblance of order,
and kept mostly calm during The Edit From Hell.*

Pretty Things

"She's my best friend, certainly not the average girl."

Charlie

I think I've spent roughly one third of my entire life in Brie's bedroom. I've seen her walls covered in Paddington Bear wallpaper. I've seen the walls covered in pictures of Westlife (which, quite frankly, I still have nightmares about), and I helped paint the walls the current fetching shade of Pink Sequin Editions Indian Summer Flat Matte, which isn't as garish as it sounds. It was also my idea to paint the ceiling midnight blue with lots of little stars sprinkled all over it. I spend a lot of time lying in, on, or around Brie's bed, so I like having something pretty to look at.

I like sleeping with Brie; she never hogs the covers and she keeps her elbows to herself. I even have a drawer here full of T-shirts and clean pants and a spare jar of moisturizer, which simples things up so much.

Brie was snoring very gently and delicately when I woke up

3

this morning. And when I got back from the bathroom, she was still asleep. Which wasn't a huge surprise. Loves her sleep, does Brie. I pulled on my Belle and Sebastian T-shirt, walked across the room, and looked out of the window.

The pavement was already glistening; bumblebees, fat and stupid from too much pollen, buzzed lazily around the lavender bush in her front garden. It was going to be another of those hot summer days when the air seems to shimmer with possibilities. So I didn't know why Brie was wrapped around her flowery duvet like it was the dead of winter.

I tugged gently on the chocolate-brown hair that was all that was visible of her.

"Hey! Sleepy girl! You need to get your arse out of bed," I whispered, leaning down to uncover her ear. "If we're late for the first day, I'm going to claim ownership of the iPod for the whole week."

She gave a tiny, delicate moan and burrowed deeper under the duvet.

It was time for Plan B. "Okay, I'm going to rifle through your underwear drawer, find your grungiest knickers, and sell them on eBay."

The covers were sloughed off with an indignant squeak. "Ewww, that's gross," she mumbled. "And I don't have any grungy knickers."

Brie emerging from sleep is like watching a flower slowly unfurl its petals. She stretched slowly, pink tongue poking out of her mouth as she yawned, her hands curled into fists as she batted the air like a playful kitten.

"What color am I?" she asked eagerly, kicking back her duvet and kneeling to investigate.

I looked at the pale thighs emerging from her boxer shorts.

"Well," I said consolingly. "You're a sort of clotted cream color, and yesterday you were more of a semi-skimmed milk. The sheets, on the other hand, are seriously bronzed."

Brie looked up from dismayed contemplation of her legs and stared at the fake-tan stains on the sheets as if she wasn't quite sure how they got there.

"Well, I'm not going to that drama club thingy," she announced simply, lying back down and pulling the duvet back over her head. "I'm meant to have a tan! I can't act if I'm not looking good." The last two sentences were muffled, and then the Brie-shaped hump started shaking slightly, and I knew she was crying.

Sometimes I worry about how Brie will cope when something genuinely catastrophic happens instead of the usual crap that she deems weep-worthy. If Timberlake, her cat, died, or she found out she had six weeks to live, or her hair fell out, she'd probably have to have a Prozac drip installed.

It really wasn't the right time for Brie to be having one of her regularly scheduled weepathons. I'd begged and cajoled and pleaded to get her to sign up for the summer drama workshop that was starting today. Getting her through the auditions, getting her to *pass* her audition, had taken years off my tender, young life. Because no way, no how, was I going to spend another summer watching daytime TV and eating crisps while Brie watched me eating crisps and occasionally snuck one into her mouth when she thought I wasn't looking.

Getting Brie out of bed and in the mood to kick some drama-workshop butt wasn't just a matter of necessity. It was a matter of life and death. Like that bit in a movie when there's a bomb with a ticking clock attached to it, and it's counting down sixty seconds, and the guy who knows whether the red or the blue wire should be cut isn't going to talk. Down-and-dirty tactics was all that I had left.

"Okay, don't come," I said, like I didn't care in the slightest, while bouncing up and down on her bed in a manner that I knew was going to piss her off. "It's not my problem if you have nothing else in life and you fail your certificate in Beauty Therapy Sciences and have to end up pretending that you're between jobs when really you're working in a call center or worse! Yeah! You're working in Burger King, and the grease is clogging up your pores, and you can't afford proper products anymore, so all the shine has gone from your hair because you're using supermarket own-brand shampoo."

It worked. There was an anguished moan from the bedclothes, and then Brie was falling out of bed to shoot me a baleful glare before disappearing into the bathroom.

It would be at least three-quarters of an hour before she was ready, so I turned on her ceramic hair straighteners and headed down to the kitchen.

Brie's house smells of furniture polish and Glade PlugIns with an overpowering topnote of Dunhill International cigarettes and Gucci Rush, courtesy of her mum. The smell is only temporarily relieved when you're in Brie's room, which stinks of fake tan and Anna Sui Sweet Dreams.

Everything in Brie's house is white and gold to match Linda, who vacuums three times a day. You have the audacity to eat a bag of crisps while you're waiting for Brie to get off the telephone, and there she is trying to trip you up with her Dyson.

Linda looked up when I walked into the kitchen and waved

✿ **Charlie**

the coffeepot at me enticingly. "Morning, sweetie. You're looking particularly handsome today. Pity you couldn't find a hairbrush, though." I could tell that Linda had only had one cup of coffee. Usually she's not quite so laid-back.

I kissed her on the cheek, grabbed a mug from the cupboard, and sat down at the kitchen table, where Henry, Brie's angelic-looking younger brother, was shoveling cornflakes into his gaping maw. This prevented him from sticking his tongue out or giving me the finger, which is what I usually get from him by way of a greeting. Little shit.

Mr. Brie, or Dave as I never call him, was cowering behind the *Daily Mail* as usual and giving the appearance of a man on the edge of a nervous breakdown.

"It's Charlie," Linda announced unnecessarily. Mr. Brie moved his paper aside to give me a nod, but Henry didn't even bother to look up from spraying milk and cereal all over the table. He did manage to reach under the table and kick me extra hard on the shin, though.

At least Linda gave me a cup of extra-strong coffee before we embarked on our usual conversation.

"So, how are you, Charlie?" (She has this really annoying habit of saying my name at the end of every sentence like she has to remind herself who she's talking to.)

"I'm fine, Linda. How are you?"

"Well, I wish I could say I was fine, but I'm not, Charlie. How's your mum?"

"She's okay."

"So you and Brie were home very late last night, Charlie. I hope you gave her a chance to meet other boys, because she'll meet someone else, you know, and then you'll be wishing that you'd been more thrusting and dynamic and grabbed her when you had the chance," Linda said brightly, tapping her cigarette into the ashtray, which was nestled next to the milk jug on the kitchen table. Even a hardened smoker like myself winced at Linda's relaxed attitude to smoking near fresh dairy.

Mr. Brie snorted a couple of times at this damning indictment of my girl-getting skills, because his gaydar is far more evolved than his wife's, which is actually quite disturbing when you think about it.

"I'm not really into girls, Linda." Which she knew damn well. "But if I was, then I'm sure me and Brie would be picking out china patterns and saving for our honeymoon. And anyway you must be secretly relieved that I don't have dishonorable intentions toward your daughter."

"Hmm, you say that, Charlie, but I'm sure if the right girl were to come along, you'd stop all this nonsense. It's just a shame that Brie isn't pretty enough to change your mind."

Which of course was Brie's cue to trip into the kitchen just in time to hear her mother's judgment on her looks.

For a second her face collapsed. Her perfect little smudge of a nose wrinkled up, and her green eyes went cloudy. There was even a slight lip tremble until her features righted themselves into their eternal loveliness. I didn't know what Linda was on because, really, Brie is ridiculously gorgeous.

Brie shook her newly straightened hair out of her eyes, blinked a couple of times, and then sidled nearer so she could give me a good-morning kiss.

"I don't suppose you woke me up too early 'cause I haven't had breakfast yet, you know?" She was already moving past me to investigate the contents of the fridge.

"No, I'm on time, and you're late. Again. Can we go?"

But was Brie concerned with being hideously late for our

first day of drama group? Yeah, right! In the Brie-verse, there were far more important things to worry about.

"There's no bacon or eggs or sausages," she whined at Linda with a wounded look on her face. "I have to have a fry-up for breakfast. You know I'm not doing carbs."

Linda tapped out another cigarette from the packet and knocked the filter tip against her frosted pink talons. "You shouldn't eat all that fatty food, you'll get porky. I'm sure you've put on weight since last week."

And then Brie looked down in horror at her thin little legs in their Diesel jeans, and Linda's work here was done.

I got up—careful not to scrape back my chair on the newly waxed kitchen floor—then grabbed my bag and Brie.

"Get something to eat now, and then we're going," I said in my most "don't mess with me, bitch" voice, the one I use exclusively to chivvy Brie along.

There was a sorrowful sigh, which would have made a lesser being break down in tears. I just gave her a flinty-eyed look and waved my watch in her face until she grabbed a bag of salt-and-vinegar crisps from the cupboard and a can of Diet Coke from the fridge.

"Well, bye bye, sweetie," Linda said, and I wasn't entirely sure which one of us she was speaking to. "Break a leg or something."

Brie muttered something that may or may not have been "bitch" under her breath and picked up her Louis Vuitton Murakami Cherry Blossom bag from the stairs as I followed her out.

We stepped out into the blinding sunlight and simultaneously reached for our sunglasses. Brie was studying the nutritional information on the back of the crisps packet, her lips moving as she sounded out the words. "Seventeen point three grams of carbs," I heard her mutter. "I should be able to digest them by seven tonight."

I reached around to give her waist a comforting squeeze. "Linda has issues on her issues, right? And she only says mean stuff about you because she can't handle that you're cute and hot and she's thundering toward menopause."

Brie tucked her arm into mine and pulled her Von Dutch baseball cap down so she wouldn't freckle. "But, Charlie, you would tell me if I was fat, wouldn't you?"

Brie was wearing tight, low-rider jeans, which showed off her practically concave stomach to its best advantage. Then there was the floaty, gauzy top, which may have been a pocket handkerchief in another life. "Brie, you are not fat. You are as far from fat as it's possible to be. Now shut the fuck up because this conversation is getting really boring." And there was a God because she shut up and actually started walking, giving us an outside chance of catching the bus and getting to Camden before ten.

"We haven't had the postmortem about last night," I reminded her as we got to the bus stop, and she squinted up at the indicator board to see how long it would be before the bus chugged into view.

Brie didn't answer for a while because she was digging around in her bag. But eventually she pulled out her Lancôme Juicy Tube in Marshmallow, slicked it over her lips, and answered me. "There wasn't a single guy in there who knew how to dress." Pause, while she gave me a Significant Look from under her lashes. "Not like you."

"That's because I'm gay, sweetie. Being a style icon is all part of my genetic coding."

"I wish you weren't gay."

"I wish that you didn't wish that I wasn't gay."

Brie and I have this conversation at least five times every day. I love her, she's my best friend, but even if I *was* straight or she was a boy, I'm not entirely sure that we'd go out or ever have one frenzied night of passion on her Calvin Klein bed linen.

I'm an indie/emo hybrid. All my T-shirts have faded in the wash, and I cut my hair with nail scissors and bleach the ends when I get bored. I own three pairs of Converse All Star low-tops, each one more battered than the last, and I bite my nails. Though I do have an incredibly chiseled jawline, if you happened to be comparing me to, say, someone who didn't have a jawline at all. And if I was straight, which I'm not, the kind of girl I'd want to fall wildly and passionately and madly in love with would be Brody from the Distillers.

Brie, meanwhile, is a pastel-colored princess who'd love to get me into Gucci anything and has offered many times to actually pay for me to get my hair properly highlighted. She also has a disturbing tendency to dress like a Desperate Housewife.

Which is not to say she doesn't appreciate my not-so-inconsiderable charms. I'm very pretty, in a manly kind of way.

"Ooooh, Charlie, you have the longest, fluffiest boylashes I've ever seen," she's fond of saying, before getting huffy because she has to apply two coats of Eyelure Kiss Me Mascara to get the same effect.

As we got on the bus and I gave the driver two tickets because Brie never manages to get it together to buy the pre-paid books, she turned to me, mouthed an apology, and smiled.

"I don't know what I'd do without you," she murmured,

before heading for the stairs, and I realized that even though she annoyed the hell out of me and there was no reason for our friendship whatsoever, I couldn't think of another person in this world that I'd want to be my best friend.

The ride into Camden was pretty uneventful. Mostly we hoped that the fat goth boy who'd stunk of patchouli oil and glommed on to us when we'd auditioned, hadn't made the final cut.

"It took me forever to get the stink out of my hair," Brie remembered with a shudder. "I hope everyone's nice. And cute. I need cute boys this summer. Lots of them."

"I hear you," I said feelingly. "One cute boy for you and one for me. We could double-date." I rubbed her shoulder. "So, honey, you ready for your close-up?"

Brie suddenly squinched up her face as if she was in great pain. "Shit!" she exclaimed. "I forgot about the whole acting thing. That weird woman in charge, she's going to expect us to act, isn't she?"

I nodded gravely. "'Fraid so. I think it's pretty much a pre-requisite of a drama group."

"Don't use long words, they give me a headache." Brie looked at her half-eaten bag of crisps and then violently threw them down the bus, earning her glares from a couple of grannies who didn't appreciate getting crisp crumbs in their blue rinses. "Oh God, I feel sick. I don't want everyone star-ing at me. Why did I let you talk me into this?"

Knowing very well that she's the biggest drama queen this side of wherever Paris Hilton lives, I didn't really waste much time consoling Brie. Instead I clasped her hand in mine and gave it a little shake.

"Listen, Brie," I said urgently. "We're going to make a pact."

"What kind of pact? I'm not spitting on your hand or nothing 'cause that's really unhygienic."

I swear to God, I have the patience of a saint. "We are going to swear on our iPod that we will do everything in our power, short of illegal acts, to score the lead roles in whatever lame play we end up spending our entire summer working on. Okay?"

"But what if—"

"Brie! Do Beyoncé or Christina or whichever lame MTV diva you're mostly admiring this week waste their time with what-ifs? No, they spend all their energy on looking fabulous and cutting down any bitch that dares get in their way. So, swear on the freakin' iPod."

"You are *so* gay."

"Finally you're on message about that, great. Have we got a pact or not?"

She pouted for precisely five seconds and then solemnly shook my hand. "Okay, we'll do this pact thing, then."

And then I made her get out the iPod that my mum's boyfriend, Merv the Swerve, brought us back from New York. We took an earbud apiece and because it was Monday and I get to have it Monday, Wednesday, Friday, and alternate Sundays, I forced her to listen to The White Stripes all the way to Camden.

"And the rumour is you never go with boys and you are tight."

 **Daisy**

I've been here five minutes and already I know that I've made a terrible mistake. And it's not just the smell of disinfectant and sweaty socks that seems to permeate every inch of the Arts Centre—even with all the windows wide open.

I'm clutching my soy-milk caramel macchiato like it's a life raft and wondering whether to be annoyed or relieved that nobody seems to show the least inclination to talk to me.

I mean, I fully expect drama students to be pretentious wankers who wear too much black and quote too much Chekhov, but this bunch?

I'm sitting here in this circle jerk of mediocrity. It's like the auditions for *Pop Idol* or something. I don't think any of these *wannabes* has ever read a play or even been to see one. Instead, they're probably stage school brats. Worse, most of them would like to *be* stage school brats. If they couldn't get into the *Big Brother* house, they'd settle for being in the back row of the chorus of some piss-poor musical revival of *Grease* or doing cabaret on a cruise ship.

I thought this was going to be a serious drama group. I'm serious about it. And not just because I think it will look good on my UCAS form when I try to get into the Performance Art course at Brighton University. I actually care about finding my inner self through artistic endeavor, which obviously makes me some kind of freak within my immediate peer group.

I sat there for at least another ten minutes leafing through my copy of *Hedda Gabler* and praying that I wouldn't actually have to interact with any of these nonentities, when someone finally sat down next to me. Not only that but they said hello.

"Hey, hi . . . Daisy?"

"Oh, it's *you.*"

My joy was now complete. It was Walker. Or Shagger, as he's known throughout North London. I can't even remember whether Walker is his first name or last name. Everyone just calls him Walker, so I guess it's not really that important.

Walker and I were in middle school together. And elementary school before that. We even went to the same nursery. Not like I've given him a moment's thought since I've been at sixth form college, unless I've heard on the vine about another one of his conquests.

Last summer, he managed to work his way through a group of six best friends who all thought that he meant it when he said that she was the one.

And there was the Christmas party at my friend Chloe's house where he ended up caught *flagrante delicto* (Latin for "doing it") with this airhead in the bathroom, and he didn't even stop with the thrusting when someone burst in and puked in the sink. Oh yes, he has all the classiest moves. I'm not even sure what they all see in him. Quite apart from the fact that for someone to get *me* interested, they need to have breasts. Walker is basically a dirty, greasy bit of rockabilly rough. All quiff and leather jacket and these big, bruised lips. Mind you, I'm not surprised his mouth looks like that; it gets plenty of action.

"So, haven't seen you since . . . like . . . when was it?"

Why were we having this conversation? "Since the end-of-year dance at St. Augustine's when you tried to shove your tongue down my throat."

Walker looked utterly hangdog, but I'm the one girl in all the world that's immune to his so-called charms. "Oh yeah, sorry about that."

I gave him a prim look and turned the page. "Don't mention it."

"What are you reading?"

Walker reached out one of his huge hands and had the nerve to turn my book so he could see the cover, which was such an invasion of my personal space that it wasn't even funny. "*Hedda Garbler.* Any good?"

"It's *Gabler*, and I don't know yet." Neither of us said anything for a while after that. Yeah, I was being standoffish, but I really disapprove of guys like Walker. Not just because of the whole gay thing but because I hate the way girls flock around him like he's going out of fashion, all bitchy and competitive when really they should be banding together and kicking his skeevy arse.

Luckily, Walker got the hint that I was way more interested in Henrik Ibsen then I'd ever be in him and dug his phone out of the pocket of his jeans and began to text someone.

❀   **Daisy**

I'd just started to think that maybe I'd died on the way here and this drama group and the endless waiting around among these sorry specimens of some secret inbreeding project was actually the seventh layer of hell when Charlie came in.

I love Charlie. Everyone loves Charlie. He's eminently lovable. He used to go to the same gay youth group as me before he decided it was cramping his style. And the weird thing is that he was so charming about it that no one got offended. And being offended is what my gay youth club spent most of their time doing. Which is understandable really because people are incredibly homophobic, or else they're patronizing and think that being gay is something you're "going through" rather than something you are.

But anyway, even though Charlie was fond of wearing this homemade T-shirt with the word GAYER on it, it was impossible to get pissed off with him.

He looked up, caught my eye, and waved.

I was just about to pat the empty seat next to me when I realized that he wasn't alone. A girl was clinging onto his arm and dragging him firmly toward a couple of spare seats by the window. Why he was appearing to actively enjoy the company of a girl who looked like an extra from *Desperate Housewives* I couldn't begin to imagine. But still, the thought of getting to spend the summer with Charlie made up for the fact that the rest of the drama group looked as if they were suffering from some particularly virulent form of brain disease.

"Ah, children. I hope you're ready to leave the realms of the drab and dreary and enter the magical world of the theater."

Lavinia, who's running this course, is absolutely amazing. She's very old (after my audition I Googled her and discovered that she was a member of the Royal Shakespeare Company at the same time as Sir Laurence Olivier) and very grand. A tiny, imperious thing, she was draped in black lace, tapping an ornately carved walking stick in front of her as she paced up and down. I think that maybe I'd like to be Lavinia when I grow up; she takes no shit.

"I'm Lavinia, but I expect you to call me Miss Mitford," she announced after she'd swept into the room and simply clapped her hands to get everyone's undivided attention. Except one of the boys, who looked like a particularly bad impersonation of a gangsta rapper, forgot to turn off his mobile until it polyphonically announced its presence with the opening intro to "In Da Club."

"You! Young man, you really are *incredibly* rude . . ." she hissed at the homeboy, who blushed bright red and looked at his phone like he wished it had never been invented.

After she'd put the fear of God into everyone—even Walker was sitting up stiff-backed under her scrutiny—Lavinia made us introduce ourselves and say why we were here.

Charlie's limpetlike gal pal had to go first. In this teeny, tiny voice, she squeaked: "I'm Brie—" Brie, like the stinky cheese? Someone really should have had a word with her parents before they filled in the birth certificate. "And . . ." Then she sort of batted up against Charlie—who must be loaning her brain cells—before continuing. "I'm here because, er, well, there aren't any auditions for *Pop Idol* this year." And then she actually looked hurt when the entire room cracked up.

Charlie didn't have any problems, though. He just leaned back in his chair, surveyed the circle of strangers with a glint in his eye, and drawled, "I'm Charlie, and I decided that if I was going to be a drama queen, I might as well do it in front of a paying audience." And everyone began laughing again.

I tuned out most of the others, who all came out with variations on the same theme: They wanted to be famous, and maybe there'd be a record producer or a casting director from *EastEnders* in the house on opening night.

I had to start paying attention when it was nearly my turn. Walker came up with some macho nonsense about wanting to be "a film director. I'm starting a degree in film studies in September, and I thought it would be a good idea to experience what actors go through." He sounded very dubious as to whether he still thought it was a good idea, even though Lavinia seemed quite delighted with his answer.

"Ah, wonderful. Following in the footsteps of such luminaries as Orson Welles and Graham Greene. Very good. And you, dear?"

It was my turn. I took a deep breath and gave her the version that didn't have any off-topic sexual politics. "I want to study performance art and I'm very interested in the physicality of live theater so um, yeah . . ."

I didn't even realize that a strand of hair was in my mouth or that I was attempting to chomp down on it and speak at the same time. It's a nervous habit that leads to bad things like split ends—and Lavinia's look of utter horror.

"Young lady! Take that revolting hank of hair out of your mouth this instant."

I spat out the offensive hair and backtracked furiously. "So, I'm very interested in having the opportunity to experiment with gender . . ." Even though I'm the vice chairperson of the Lesbian and Gay Youth Center, I hate public speaking. What I hear in my head and what actually comes out of my mouth seem to be violently unconnected. Though right then that was the least of my worries. Lavinia had glided over to stand in front of me and was tapping her cane impatiently on the floor.

"Yes, yes, dear," she said without bothering to pretend that she'd been listening to me. "I knew a girl once called Phyllida who chewed on her hair. Revolting habit, especially in a debutante, until she was taken to the hospital with acute stomach pains, and do you know what they found when they cut her open?"

I shook my head, although I had a pretty shrewd idea.

"They found a simply gigantic hairball. As big as an orange it was, and she wasn't able to complete her season and ended up dying penniless and alone. Do you want that to happen to you?"

I shook my head again. It seemed like the easiest option. I also concentrated on sending "get the hell away from me" vibes in Lavinia's direction, but she was so thick-skinned that they just bounced off.

"Girl! What's your name?" Oh God, why didn't someone, somewhere, make her stop?

"Daisy," I said clearly and crisply so I didn't get bawled out for poor diction on top of my hair-chewing crimes.

Lavinia leaned forward and peered at me intently, and though I tried to meet her eyes with a calm, steady gaze, I could feel my face burning a deeper shade of crimson.

But Lavinia was turning slowly away and tutting. "Really, you could be so pretty if you made more of an effort. So feminine, so Rubenesque, and yet you choose to hide it under those frightful clothes. In my day, once a girl was your age it was simply unthinkable even to leave the house without a light dusting of face powder and a little lipstick. Still . . ."

I breathed out slowly as she lost her train of thought and started wittering on about the role of the *actor* in the age of television.

I hate that I look like this buttery, girlie girl. People look at me and think they can walk all over me because my hardness is entirely on the inside. It doesn't matter what I do—all they see is this soft, pillowy lump of a girl. I dye my hair black to get rid of the blond (I mean, who the hell wants to be the butt of all those dumb-blonde jokes) and try to keep my lips in a tight line, but boys, especially, can never take their eyes off my tits and hips and mouth. So I cover up. Today I'm wearing a pair of boys' Carhartt jeans and a Super Lovers hoodie that's a couple of sizes too big. Anything to distract people's attention from my breasts. And then I feel guilty because I'm proud to be a woman, but I just wish that everyone else would leave me alone to be proud and not try to make me feel like I'm a size-twelve freak in a size-four world. Having body issues is very self-defeating and something I need to work on.

Anyway, back to Lavinia, who announced that we'd be performing a play at the end of the six weeks (this course is known in every drama department of every college in North London as Theater Boot Camp) and that we were going to choose a play in a democratic fashion.

"Hands up, children, and when I point at you, you may give me a suggestion."

"*Grease.*"

"*Mamma Mia!*"

"Les Misérables."

If we ended up doing a musical, I was demanding a refund.

"Abigail's Party." That was Charlie's suggestion.

"A Streetcar Named Desire." Walker threw in his choice, and Lavinia practically orgasmed on the spot. What a suck-ass. Seems like someone fancies themselves as quite the matinee idol.

"Pretty Woman." The Brie girl doesn't seem to have grasped the difference between films and plays.

Reluctantly I raised my hand, and Lavinia swung the cane in my direction. "Daisy?"

"Electra?" I said hopefully, because it's this wonderful ancient Greek play about this woman who . . . but Lavinia was having no truck with it.

"A classicist," she commented disdainfully, and moved on to the gangsta rapper.

I didn't know why she bothered asking us because once everyone had made a suggestion, she announced grandly, "Thank you for your interesting contributions. I've decided that we will study one of the Bard's lighter works, *The Taming of the Shrew*. I will assign parts tomorrow once I've had the delightful task of getting better acquainted with you all."

The Taming of the Shrew is the biggest pile of misogynistic wank I've ever come across. And I was not going to spend six weeks of my life getting ready to perform it in front of an audience. Even peace camp in Devon with that other misogynistic git, Aaron the camp leader, had to be better than this.

I could feel Walker hovering somewhere behind me as if we were going-to-get-lunch-together buddies, but Charlie was already coming toward me with the Brie creature clutching his arm and scowling.

"You didn't say nothing about Shakespeare when we signed up," she was hissing at him in a breathy Cockney accent.

"Believe me, honey, no Shakespeare was mentioned in the small print," Charlie said, rolling his eyes.

"He sucks," was her incisive comment, and then, out of a bag that was so tiny it probably didn't have room for anything else in it, she took a tube of lip gloss and smeared it over her lips.

"Hey, Daze." Charlie hugged me hard enough that his arms actually managed to go all the way around me. "It's been forever. You and Claire still a twosome of cuteness?"

Charlie's arm was still around my shoulders as we began to walk out. "She's being cute in Devon at this peace camp," I said, unable to keep the acid from creeping into my voice.

But Charlie just gave me a squeeze and an understanding smile. I love, love, love Charlie.

"I just don't get him. He's dead and boring." Oh God, Brie was still going on about Shakespeare and sounding like Kat Slater on helium. Plus, she was clutching onto Charlie's other arm, which was making spatial awareness a problem as we lurched across the entrance hall like some three-headed mutant. I wriggled out of Charlie's embrace and narrowly avoided skinning my knee on a fire extinguisher.

And as I pulled open the fire door into the unrelenting brightness of the midday sunshine, she started squawking about "fine lines" and pulled a pair of pink sunglasses out of the dolly-size bag. Girls like that do the rest of us no favors.

"But, oh! Hey! You know, *10 Things I Hate About You*?" Charlie suddenly exclaimed, taking the steps two at a time. "With Heath Ledger, and Julia Stiles plays that faux riot grrrl who think she's all down with her bad self just because she wears a muted color palette."

Charlie was so excited that he walked into a lamppost.

"I haven't seen it, and are you planning on getting to the point anytime before we're due back?" I sniped.

Charlie gave a long, low whistle. "God, Daze, I forgot how snarky you can be."

"Yeah, yeah, but my snark is infinitely worse than my bite," I reminded him. "Anyway what's the big deal about this film?"

Charlie snaked an arm around the Brie girl's waist, his skin looking like honey against the milk white of her flat stomach.

"Heath Ledger's cute," she said rather inanely.

"He's beyond cute," Charlie agreed, and I snorted impatiently. She was definitely a bad influence on him. "Okay, okay. *10 Things I Hate About You* is a modern version of *The Taming of the Shrew*! But with leather jackets and tequila shots instead of lutes and doubloons and shit."

"Do you think that Lavinia lady would let us do *10 Things* instead?" Brie piped up.

I couldn't bear it any longer. I fixed her with a glare. "No, because that's a film. We have to do a play." (I tried hard to stick to words of two syllables or less.) "That means we have to perform a piece of work that was written for the stage."

Just below the hum of traffic and the whining of a small dog tied up outside the news agent waiting for its owner, I could hear her brain slowly shifting into gear.

"Oh," she said. "Oh. But was, like, *Pretty Woman* a play before it was a film?"

I groaned, and Charlie laughed. "Give it up, Brie. You're going to have to do Shakespeare, but we can watch *10 Things* tonight if you like."

She shrugged. "Whatever."

And in spite of the fact that Brie is the most stupid person

I've ever met, Charlie is so adept at ignoring her more asinine outbursts and lavishing charm on me that, though I hadn't planned to, I ended up going to Sainsburys with them to get lunch (Brie "didn't do lunch," but she still managed to eat two Kinder Bueno bars and swig down a Diet Coke like it canceled out the calories) and sit by the lock for half an hour. Nothing like watching plastic bags and beer cans float along the canal for a little lunchtime ambience.

And because Charlie is gay and Brie is well, Brie-like, once we'd found a spot by the canal to eat our lunch, I pulled off my hoodie because the sun was fierce and didn't care if my breasts were spilling over the top of my pink tank top like two humongous scoops of ice cream.

I was just investigating my pasta and sun-dried tomato salad when Charlie leaned back on his elbows and whispered, "What's that guy's name?"

I looked up to see Walker perched on one of the lock gates, his leather jacket flung on the ground, all the better so the muscles in his arms could be shown off to their best advantage.

"Oh shit, Walker," I said, dismayed by Charlie's mouth, which was hanging open like Walker was a medium-rare tenderloin steak with a side order of chili fries.

"You mean Shagger," Brie corrected me vaguely, and I noticed that her disapproving gaze was a perfect match with my own. "Don't even go there, Charlie."

"Who says I want to go there?" Charlie stuck out his lower lip and ran a hand through his hair. "And why's he called Shagger?"

"Duh!" Brie scoffed, and even though she was wearing a top that wouldn't even have covered one of my breasts, she still managed to look the epitome of maidenly outrage. "He's a complete slag. He's the guy who did it with Manda at this party, and he wouldn't even stop when someone walked in. He treats girls like shit."

"That was my friend's party," I offered. And even though I don't approve of gossiping, I couldn't help adding: "He tried to get off with me at this dance at my middle school. Ugh!" But Charlie wasn't listening, he was far too busy staring at Walker, his mouth hanging slightly open. Drool seemed a distinct possibility.

"But he's all on his own. We should ask him if he wants to sit with us. Daze! Make him come over."

"Yeah, and why would I want to do that?"

But it was too late. Walker glanced over at us, raised a casual hand, and then jumped off the gate so he could saunter in our direction.

"Hmm, looks like he's coming over anyway," Charlie murmured dreamily. "Hey."

I put a hand over my eyes to shield the glare from the sun as Walker loomed over us.

"Hey, Daisy."

I had no choice but to make the introductions. "Walker, this is Charlie and Brie. They're in our drama group. This is Walker, we used to go to school together."

Brie, who I suddenly didn't actively dislike, merely grunted in his direction and became very interested in her can of Diet Coke, but Charlie was sitting straight up and proffering a hand for Walker to shake. Any minute now he was going to roll onto his back and play dead for the queen. Love him dearly, but, my God, sometimes he has no dignity.

Walker was still standing, and I realized he could see

straight down my top. I grabbed my hoodie and held it in front of me.

"You can join us if you like," I said finally, and even though my voice was the dictionary definition of *bothered*, Walker flung himself down on the ground next to me. I inched slightly away from him and pressed my back against the crumbling, moss-stained wall.

"So, what do you think of that Lavinia woman?" Charlie asked Walker eagerly.

"Terrifying," Walker replied without taking his eyes away from my chest. "She's like a rottweiler disguised as a sweet old lady."

"But she seemed to like you," Charlie said, and I closed my eyes. He was so eager and desperate that it was embarrassing to watch. "I like what you said about why you wanted to join the drama group. That film degree sounds cool."

"Yeah." Walker tucked his hands under his head. "But I'll probably end up directing wedding videos, not critically acclaimed art-house movies."

I'd been waiting for the line about how he was going to be the new Tarantino, so that comment threw me a tiny bit, though Charlie was eating the humble pie up with a spoon.

"Oh no, I'm sure you'll be in Hollywood soon. You know, getting your people to call their people."

"Ordering a skinny, no-froth Frappuccino at the Coffee Bean & Tea Leaf on Sunset . . ." Now Brie had joined Charlie on his all-expenses-paid trip to La La Land.

"Taking meetings by the pool at the Chateau Marmont, and you're just sitting there when Jake Gyllenhaal—"

"Oh my God, Charlie, shut up," I snapped, unable to take their inane wittering any longer. "It's never going to happen, and if Walker" (I didn't so much say his name as spit it out) "was serious about being a film director, he'd never go to Hollywood because it's a corrupt place where commerce means far more than creativity." I finished my speech with an angry intake of breath and realized that the three of them were looking at me like I was insane.

"Hey, I'm just saying." The heat was making me more snippy than usual, but there was also something about Walker that made me want to be offensive and rude until he'd take the hint and stop looking at me like I was put on this planet as his own personal large-breasted *thing*.

And then he had the nerve to touch my elbow lightly as if we were friends. "I get you. Hollywood has sucked all the soul out of filmmaking," he agreed throatily.

"Are you talking to me or my tits?" I asked him sweetly, because his eyes were still staring at my nipples as if they were about to impart the secrets of the universe.

Ha! I totally called him on it, and he knew it. I could tell by the way he went bright red and turned his head.

Charlie was grinning and shaking his head in disbelief, and Brie was just staring at me openmouthed like I was a particularly harrowing episode of *One Tree Hill* and she couldn't follow the story line.

I scrambled to my feet and brushed off the tiny pieces of grit that were clinging to my palms. "We should head back," I said decisively. "I'm really not in the mood for a lecture about timekeeping from Lavinia."

And then I marched on ahead at a furious pace because I was being the angry dyke girl, and Charlie probably thought I was crazy. I didn't wait for the others to catch up to me, but I distinctly heard Walker mutter something in an aggrieved tone about "that time of the month." It didn't really matter what he thought, though. I mean, it wasn't as if we were ever going to be bosom buddies. Pun intended.

We spent the rest of the day pretending to be trees. I think it blew their tiny minds, but I quite enjoyed it. It's a basic meditation exercise really. I imagined that I was a sycamore tree on top of a hill, standing proud over the valleys and dales, swaying slightly in the breeze. My fingers were cool, green leaves, and my legs were a solid trunk that had withstood decades of rain and wind and sun.

I had seriously been contemplating chucking in the course, but after being a tree, I felt centered and calm again, so I decided to stick it out. Because I get to spend all summer doing something I love even if I don't love any of the people doing it with me, except Charlie. Besides, what else am I going to do?

Walker

I knew today was going to be shitty. I opened my eyes, and the sun was streaming in through the chinks in the curtains, and for one second everything felt all right, and then it didn't. I remembered all the reasons why today was going to be as crap as all the days that had gone before it.

For starters, I was woken up by an incoming message on my mobile phone. It was from Nancy: *I want my CDs bk & my bks. BTW, u suk.* Yeah, what she lacks in poetry, she makes up for in venom.

It's not that I'm that bothered that we split up. She was a lousy shag and she never shut up for one second. Being with her was like having a pneumatic drill skewering into my eardrums. "What are you thinking?" "Do you love me?" "You don't think I'm easy, do you?"

Nancy was like every other girl I've ever known. When

30

they're girls that I haven't had, girls that I fancy, girls that I'm chasing, then they're mysterious. They could be anything. They could be neurotic. Or they could be cool. Or they could be so damn sweet that I'd never get enough of them.

But they never are. They're just lips and tits and hips. It's a battle of wills, of compromise and bargaining, to get them into bed, and then they start thinking that it's going to be forever, and I'm already bored and moving on to the next one.

But until that happens, then she's the one girl in all the world for me. And when her secrets are still hers alone, I fall in love with all the things I think she's going to be and get my heart broken when I find out that she's just like all the rest.

And I know what people say about me. I know about the nickname, and maybe I deserve it. I've shagged a lot of girls. I've lost count of just how many. I can't remember all their names, but I remember little details about every single one of them.

There was the girl from Brighton with blond hair who bit her lip so hard when I kissed her neck that she drew blood. There was the tiny little emo chick that I picked up at a Death Cab for Cutie gig who stole thirty quid from my wallet when she left.

There was the brunette from Kosovo who couldn't speak a word of English but smiled and smiled when I asked if I could see her naked.

Oh, and there was Natalie, who I loved longer and sweeter and more than all the others. The first night that we slept together, I showed her the scars on my chest from where I'd had chicken pox when I was a kid, and she painted them all silver with her eye shadow, before she kissed them better.

And now I can feel myself falling all over again. Jesus. I

swear someone should lock me up. Because it's Daisy. Who looks soft but has a hard heart. And she's gay. Oh, and she's the biggest bitch this side of the Equator. She looks down that cute little button nose at me like I'm a piece of shit on the soles of her pink Birkenstocks. Which is probably why I can't stop thinking about her. I can resist anything but girls who can resist me. There's probably a long, complicated name for my condition, or maybe the rumors are right and I'm just a life-support system for my penis.

But Daisy looks like she's just stepped out of the pages of a fifties pinup-girls calendar, and I can see her as October. As Miss Halloween in a sexy witch's outfit that she accessorizes with a scowl and a broomstick. And if I didn't have the deranged desire to have her look at me with an expression that didn't border on utter revulsion, I'd have dropped out of that drama group. Like I drop out of everything. Out of bands and windows and girls' lives. So, binning one poxy drama group doesn't rate too highly on my list of things I should never do.

Things have been pretty shit lately. And mostly it's my fault. I just feel . . . I don't know, like I'm not really here most of the time. That I go through life without ever touching the sides.

At least the girls make me feel as if I'm really here. That if someone's kissing you or texting you or even hating you 'cause you fucked their best friend during the week that they were in Ibiza, then you have to be real.

My thought patterns are a little disjointed. I didn't get much sleep last night. I'd decided to sleep outside. I opened the window and climbed out onto the flat roof so I could lie back and watch the stars while the Decemberists played softly on the stereo. The night was thick and heavy like it wanted to swallow me, and I thought about Daisy. Her skin looked so soft and smooth in that tank top she was wearing yesterday, like if you touched her, your fingers would just skate over the surface of her. And yeah, she has tits I could get lost in . . .

The thought of Daisy's tits had a natural conclusion. I'm eighteen, I'm male, I'm sexually active. I don't really need to spell it out any further. So I turned up at the Arts Centre half an hour late, and you'd have thought that I'd firebombed a kindergarten the way Lavinia flared her nostrils and gave me this whole shitload of aggro.

"Punctuality is the privilege of princes," was just one of the gems.

"I'm not a prince. I take the bus. The bus gets stuck in traffic," I told her.

"And yet everyone else managed to get here on time," she countered, and she pursed her lips. I bet that Lavinia was quite a goer in her time—not that gray hair and saggy skin gets it done for me, thank God—but she gave me this lecture about commitment and art and a whole bunch of other bullshit while shooting me these looks from under her lashes and squeezing my arm, so I gave her what she wanted. Which was a slow smile and a tensing of my muscles so she got to feel some biceps under her postmenopausal fingers.

"Miss Mitford. I'm terribly sorry, it won't happen again, but please, I've got a hangover, and you're just making it worse." I lowered my voice, like it was just the two of us and it was intimate. Like, what I was saying wasn't really what I was saying. 'Cause she might try and pull that grande dame act, but she's still female, and when it comes to females, you just push their buttons according to what you want and they give in. Just like Lavinia did with me.

"You really are dreadfully naughty," she simpered. "Next time you're late I will not be so lenient, I quite assure you."

Another sultry look, and I was free to walk to the vacant chair in the semicircle. Charlie winked at me, and Daisy, who was sitting next to him wearing another baggy top that completely obscured her charms, gave me a sour look like she'd been licking batteries all morning.

I felt the full force of Lavinia's wrath approximately ten minutes later when she read out our assigned parts for *The Taming of the Shrew.* She had me down for the male lead, Petruchio. Which, no. A world of no. And Brie, that desperate housewife chick that Charlie hangs out with, is going to play Katharina, the shrew. Which is a pretty good indication that Lavinia is suffering from Alzheimer's or senile dementia or one of those other mind-addling diseases that old people get because that girl couldn't read out the numbers on her bus ticket, never mind play some ballbusting heroine.

I think Brie felt the same way because her face kinda collapsed in on itself, and she dragged Charlie off for this long conversation full of hand gestures. And that thing that girls do when they're trying not to cry, which involves lots of arm flapping and tipping their heads back while they blink their eyes rapidly.

Meanwhile I worked on Lavinia. First I tried to flirt with her because it had worked before.

"See, this whole film-director gig, it's about observing, not being center stage," I said, when I managed to corner her during the coffee break. She was perched on the stage steps, and I had to sit at her feet so I could look up at her with suitable amounts of admiration. "I really don't see myself as that hands-on."

Then Lavinia looked at my hands in a way that I felt wasn't entirely appropriate for someone old enough to be my grandmother. "Ah, but how can you ever hope to get to the heart of a story if you've never been right at its heart?" she purred. I didn't have a bloody clue what she was on about.

"Huh?"

"How can you ever hope to direct performers if you've never performed yourself? Known what it is to give yourself to the performance? To be the conduit for your character's hopes and fears, triumphs and tragedies . . ."

She went on like that for ages. I think wars must have been declared and fought and lost as she pontificated on how I had to make a complete arse of myself as Petruchio for the sake of my future success as a film director.

I gave up. I couldn't flirt anymore. All that smiling made my face ache.

"I'm not doing it," I said flatly, when she finally paused to take a breath. "I can't do it. I'll screw up and ruin the whole thing."

She reached over and patted my cheek with a wrinkly hand that smelled of violets. *"Courage, mon brave,"* she whispered. And it was so lame and cheesy and like every cliché of every rom com ever made that I smiled. It was smile or vomit.

So, life sucked. I was stuck playing Petruchio, Lavinia clearly thought that I was her besotted swain, and if I thought Daisy was in a bad mood yesterday, then today it was like she was overdosing on PMS.

Lavinia gave her the role of Bianca, and instead of trying to reason or flirt her way out of it like I'd done, she blew up.

"No way! No way," Daisy hissed at Lavinia, who must have

been getting the message by now that her cast list was the source of everything bad. "I am not playing Bianca! She's a simpering idiot. She's archaic. She's a throwback to everything that's wrong with Shakespeare and his misogynistic view of women. God, I'd rather play Katharina! At least she tried to change the status quo!" Her breasts bobbed up and down during all this. Like they wanted to make their protest known, too.

Then Charlie wandered into my line of vision with his Brie-shadow, and I was finally forced to tear my eyes away from the delights of Daisy's chest.

"I'm Lucentio," he said by way of greeting. "I must be the only person here who doesn't want to kill Lavinia. I'm the second male lead; finally someone recognizes my talent."

Charlie was wearing a T-shirt with the word GAYER scrawled across it in Magic Marker, which threw me just a little bit.

"Petruchio's best friend?" I asked quite loudly so he could hear me over the sound of Daisy's diatribe about the patriarchal quagmire of Elizabethan drama.

"Yup, and I guess he would be you. And Brie"—he tried to pull her forward, but she ducked her head and wouldn't look at me, stuck-up cow—"takes her rightful place center stage, and Daisy, when she stops being the stereotypical angry lesbian, plays her best friend. Couldn't have worked out better." Charlie looked genuinely happy, and there was something about him, just the way he breezed through life, that made me like him. I could feel my lips twisting into a vague approximation of a smile.

"Yeah, short of having all our limbs cut off, it couldn't have worked out better."

Charlie gave a short bark of laughter. "Jesus! Why did any of you actually sign up for this, if you didn't want to tread the boards?"

Brie muttered something that I couldn't quite hear, and Charlie turned and nudged her with his hip. "Sweetie, somehow I don't think that Orlando Bloom's people are going to be in the audience on opening night." He turned back to me. "So, fancy doing lunch?"

And that's how the four of us ended up in the beer garden of The Elephant's Head.

Daisy had stopped ranting. She was now doing this thing where she kept looking up at the sky and sighing heavily. I took a swig of my beer and tried hard to think of something, anything, to say to her.

It was a long shot that I was going to get a good return on any investment I made in her, if she really *was* gay. And she certainly seemed to hate all boys, except Charlie, but that didn't necessarily mean that she only got off with girls, the thought, okay, which sent my mind spiraling off into this post-watershed montage of Daisy getting down with other girls. Naked girls. I'm so predictable.

"You're staring at my tits again!"

I came back to the slightly less Sapphic surroundings of the beer garden to be confronted by the icy look on Daisy's face.

She was right, I was. Didn't seem much point in denying it. Or apologizing. She was wearing this oversize man's shirt, which girls always do when they don't want boys to look at them. They don't seem to realize that sometimes what you *can't* see is more of a turn-on than, say, Brie's revealing line of hooker wear.

"So, how come you're in the drama group anyway?" I asked after she'd adjusted the white cotton so it was now clinging even more agreeably to her curves.

She narrowed her eyes. "Because my *girlfriend* is in Devon at this peace camp."

I nodded, even though the word *girlfriend* was either a mortal blow to my heart or the biggest turn-on. I couldn't decide which. "Right. So, what are you into? Like, music and stuff?"

Daisy sighed again and gave me this look like she was doing me a huge favor by humoring me, then reeled off a whole list of angry girl bands.

"So do you go to a lot of gigs?" I was doing that thing. That thing when a girl is giving you a hard time and you're trying desperately to come across as a nice guy who's genuinely interested in her as a *person* and not solely in getting her clothes off, so you start every sentence with *so*.

Daisy shrugged and took a sip of her lemonade. "I guess. With my *girlfriend*."

I tried again. I might not be poetic and steadfast and all those other qualities that are meant to sort the men from the boys, but I'm persistent. I do persistent pretty well.

"So, you must be missing her. Who else do you hang out with? All your mates at this peace camp, too?"

She didn't answer for a while but looked over at Charlie and Brie, who were listening to something on an iPod, sharing an earbud apiece. Finally she turned back to me, put down her glass, and stared me right in the eye.

"It's just . . ." I began, but she held up a hand in the universal signal for "shut the hell up, right now."

"Look, what is this about?" she asked without preamble, her eyes wide and guileless in her pretty, flushed face.

"It's about . . . you and me getting to know each other. Being friends. I'm sorry, is that an alien concept to you?" Embarrassment made me come kicking out of my corner.

But Daisy didn't blink those denim-blue eyes, just stared at me intently, resolute.

"You and me won't be friends," she said decisively. "And you don't want to be. I know all about you, and apart from the fact that we're both into girls, we have nothing in common."

She'd got me there. Pinned me like one of those butterflies under glass that my grandfather used to collect, and I knew only one way to smash through. It was going to piss her off, though.

"It's a start, isn't it?" I drawled, making my voice low, as if we were the only two people in the world that mattered. I stared at her mouth for a moment, then dropped my eyes to her heaving bosom before returning to her bee-stung lips, which were fast flattening out into a thin, annoyed line. "That we both like girls. Maybe we could talk about that."

Daisy took a deep breath, as though inwardly counting to ten and restraining the urge to reach across the table and belt me. "Look, I'm gay. And even if I wasn't, boys like you leave me cold."

Funny how I could feel so shivery when the sun was beating down and making beads of sweat break out on Daisy's forehead, which I wanted to lick away.

"Boys like me?"

"You don't see me, Walker," she said more softly. "You just see a pair of tits with a girl attached to them. You treat girls like shit. You have no concept of decency or fidelity or . . . or . . . or how to talk to us as anything other than sexual objects. So, no, we're not ever going to be friends. I would never have a friend like you."

I traced a damp line through the condensation on my beer bottle with the tip of my finger. "Just so we're clear, then, I shouldn't breathe near you, look at you, and especially not speak to you in case I somehow inadvertently make you forget for more than one second that you're gay? Maybe you should have a sign printed, just so that there's no confusion."

Daisy shook her head like she was trying to clear cobwebs out of her hair. "I don't want to be friends with you, but we should be able to attempt a civil conversation. Well, I can. How about you?"

I knew when I was licked.

"Right, then," she said, and looked at her lemonade pensively.

I turned to Brie and Charlie, who were scrolling down the iPod. "Not The White Stripes." Brie was giggling. "He's such a whiny git."

"The Strokes, then?"

"It's my day to choose, and I wanna listen to Missy Elliott."

" 'Cause you're so down with your bad self."

"It's weird, innit? Like, how she went crap after she lost all that weight. She was way better when she was fat."

I couldn't help it. I turned back to Daisy, to her face, not her breasts, and we both shared looks of utter horror at the sheer and frequent idiocy that is Brie. Maybe we had something in common after all?

The weird thing was that all of Daisy's pissy looks and disapproving gestures, when I rolled in every day at least half an hour late, began to get to me.

Lavinia's lectures about my lack of commitment were nothing new. Just someone else saying the same things in a different voice, but Daisy standing on the stage, tapping her foot impatiently and looking at her watch made me feel almost guilty. What made it worse was her utter lack of surprise when I didn't know my lines or managed to make Lavinia clap her hands and shout, "No, no, no, Mr. Walker!" on an hourly basis. I got the feeling that Daisy would have been disappointed if I hadn't disappointed her.

And Brie was starting to piss me off in this really special way that only my stepmother has ever been able to achieve. I mean, Brie's hot-looking, in a facile kind of way, but her teeny, tiny voice makes me dig my nails into my palms. The way that the only dedication she has to anything is to keeping her lips smooth by repeated applications of lip gloss makes me grit my teeth. And the way that she expects Charlie to be at her beck and call, to fetch her Diet Coke, to hold her mobile phone, to wipe her nose for her (an image that will haunt me for years to come), sets my nerves on the "scream" setting.

'Cause Charlie—well, I just can't help liking him. He's easy to be around, not demanding or threatening or making me smoke dope or shag girls or drink until I vomit, which is the basic group dynamic that exists with my other friends. Charlie is so chilled that he manages to convince you that it's easy to be the same.

When he can give Brie the slip, which isn't often and most of the time she comes with, we sit on the steps outside during scene breaks and smoke.

He's not really gay. I mean he is but he isn't. He's not all nudges and innuendo like Graham Norton on speed. In fact, apart from the GAYER T-shirt, you'd never know it to look at him. But it's not like I care. If he's into blokes, then good luck to him. It's just a relief to be with someone you're not in competition with. That relentless "I had her first," "yeah, well I had her last week" crap that I usually do.

"Lavinia keeps checking me out," Charlie said to me darkly, on Friday morning after our first hellish week of rehearsals. "I think she has designs on me."

"Ew, that's revolting," Brie squeaked, getting up and then standing there, waiting expectantly. "You coming, Charlie?"

Charlie held up his hand with a freshly lit cigarette clutched between his fingers. "Smoking . . ."

She huffed slightly and walked off.

"Lavinia felt me up today," I confessed when we'd both watched Brie crash through the door back into the hall.

Charlie shuddered. "God, no," he said faintly.

I took a drag on my cigarette. "She asked me to shift a piece of scenery, and then she put her hand on my back to guide me, and it slipped down a crucial few inches."

"I bet that's why she does drama groups," Charlie speculated with an evil grin. "So she can get her hands on nubile young boy flesh. Lecherous old witch."

I leaned forward and rested my elbows on my knees. "Must be awful to be old. Like, you still feel young inside, but people look at you and just see this shell of the person you once were."

Charlie gave me a considered look. He really looks at people. He doesn't just glance quickly and look away. "What are you doing tomorrow night?"

"Don't know. Hanging out, smoking some blow, drinking. Why?"

He traced a pattern on the knee of his jeans. "I thought maybe we could go out. I mean, the four of us, Brie and Daisy, too. Like, a group bonding thing, if you and Daisy can share airspace together without having an argument, that is."

And the truth of it is, it's a few hours in Daisy's company when she might forget I'm there for a few minutes and remove the poker that she has jammed up her curvaceous arse. Plus, I really need to change something. Probably me.

"Cool," I said. "Yeah, let's do something."

"They know how to break all the girls like you
And they rob the souls of the girls like you . . ."

Brie

I've just spent forty-seven minutes and thirty-one seconds staring at myself in the mirror.

I'm five foot, five inches and I weigh ninety-five pounds, which is almost below the bottom end of the ideal weight for my height, so I don't know why I'm so freaking fat. If I turn around so I can see my lopsided arse, you can just make out the beginnings of cellulite. I'm seventeen! I'm in for a lifetime of orange-peel thighs.

I started at the top. My hair's okay. It would be better if it was blond, but it's straight and shiny, though I have split ends from using my straighteners so much. My forehead is too big, and I think I've overplucked my eyebrows. My eyes are an all-right color: they're green, but they're too small and close together. My nose is too big, and it has this funny kink to it, which is so my dad's fault. My lips aren't full enough, and my teeth are mostly straight, but they're not Hollywood A-list, glowy white, even though I brush with this Beverly Hills whitening toothpaste three times a day.

I didn't even want to start looking at my body but I forced myself to. I noticed the other day that one of my boobs is definitely bigger than the other one. Freakishly so. And when I grabbed the skin on my tummy, there was flesh to spare. My arse is the size of a small country, and my legs . . .

My thighs wobbled when I moved. I stood there and sort of shook my legs and everything *rippled*. I was crying at this point. But I forced myself to carry on so I could see my knobby knees, which are the only bit of me that is actually bony. My calves have absolutely no shape to them, and the whole ugly mess ends with my feet. There is also something seriously deformed about my toes. They stick out all over the place, and they aren't properly separated.

And now I was orange. That was the worst part. I was bloody orange. Stupid, bloody fake tan. There was nothing in the instructions that said you shouldn't put it on and then do a sun-bed session, too. I was the exact shade of Christina Aguilera. It shouldn't be this hard to be pretty. It's like I'm hungry all the time and worrying about what I'm going to eat next, and I have to check myself in the mirror all the time to make sure that my hair is perfect and my lips are shiny and hold my tummy in for hours at a time and keep my back straight so everything doesn't look like it's sagging toward the floor.

Maybe if I dressed like Daisy in baggy sweaters and stuff, it wouldn't matter so much, but the thing about having nothing else is that you have to make the best of what you've got. I don't want to spend my life in a velour tracksuit, because Juicy Couture doesn't do plus sizes.

And thinking about all of this stuff, 'cause I try not to, just made me feel sadder and sadder. And I wanted a Twix, which would just bring me out in zits. Plus, it would involve a trip downstairs, and the minute Mum heard me open the fridge, she'd be peering over my shoulder to make sure that I was going to get an apple because if I put even the smallest crumb of chocolate in my mouth, she reckons I'd bloat up twenty-five pounds and never get a boyfriend.

I couldn't bear to look at myself any longer. So I curled up on my bed and started to cry (I really needed to take my eye mask out of the freezer so I didn't get puffy eyes) at the thought of having to go out tonight.

I love going out with Charlie. When I'm with Charlie, he does all the work. He's funny and cool enough for both of us, and I don't think anyone notices that I don't speak much. But I don't like Walker or Daisy. They look at me like I'm stupid. And hello! Already knew that.

Also, and I know this sounds really bitchy, it's not going to do me any favors, hanging out with Daisy.

One, she's a lesbian. And two, she looks like a lesbian. So people might think if I'm with her that I'm one, too, and it's hard enough to think of anything to say to boys without them not bothering with me at all 'cause they think I'm gay.

And as for Walker—he's the grossest boy alive. Seriously, like you could probably catch an STD just from being near him, like you can catch them from loo seats. Plus, he looks at me with this permanently snotty expression as if I'm a puppy that's just peed on the carpet, and he thinks someone should rub my nose in it so I never do it again.

· · ·

And back in my bedroom, where I was basically orange and crying, I needed Charlie. Charlie would make everything all right.

"Charlie, you *have* to come round *now*," I said when he answered his mobile.

"But I'm in the middle of something."

"What? What are you doing? Why can't you come round? It's an emergency!"

There was a thud like he'd just dropped something. "What could possibly be so urgent that I have to drop everything and rush around to rescue you?"

"I'm orange and I've put on half a pound and I feel like shit," I said and started crying again, not that I ever really stopped. "Do we have to go out tonight? Can't we stay in and watch *10 Things I Hate About You* so I get my motivation right?"

"Brie, you know I love you, right? Can we please have a night out without you having a grade-one existential crisis first?" Charlie is so smart.

"What's an exist . . . existen . . . What you just said, what is that?"

"It means that every aspect of your life becomes like an episode of *EastEnders*." His voice sounded sharp. I hate it when it does that.

"You mad at me?"

"No."

"Would you be mad at me if I said that I'm not going out tonight unless you come round here now and sort me out?"

"I'll be there in ten, put the bloody kettle on."

Great! So now Charlie was pissed off with me. Sometimes I think that Charlie is the only good thing about me. I've known him since forever, but it's not like we're brother or sister. 'Cause then I wouldn't be able to love him the way I do.

I love him because he's kind and sweet, and he'd be really hot if he didn't have such crap hair and wear all those stupid emo-y clothes. He smells nice, too. Like limes and Play-Doh and fabric softener. He never tells me that I'm thick (even if he thinks it). And apart from having a really fast metabolism and waking up one morning to find out that I've turned into Reese Witherspoon overnight, the one thing I want more than anything in the world is for Charlie to not be gay.

It would be the best thing ever. One day he'd just look at me, and he'd stop being gay. Or else he'd realize that he never was actually gay at all, he just hasn't had a girlfriend, which is not the same thing. Anyway, he wakes up, and he's like, straight.

So he comes over to my house, and I open the door, and I'm wearing these Dolce & Gabbana jeans I saw in *Vogue* and a little pink halter top, and it's really sunny, so for a moment I can't see too well. And I shield my eyes, and when I take my hand away, Charlie's still standing on the doorstep, and it's like he's seeing me for the very first time. Really seeing me. And *boom*! He loves me, and we're the perfect boyfriend and girlfriend. A scenester couple. And he throws out all his tatty T-shirts and those hideous low-top Converses because they look like they've been chewed up and spat out by a rubbish truck, and I dress him up in slim-cut Prada suits, and he always wears sunglasses, and, yup, in this perfect-boyfriend world, Charlie is blond.

But Charlie is not blond. And when he turned up, he was still wearing his tattiest sneakers and a Bathing Ape T-shirt.

Plus he had a really pissy expression on his face as he stomped into my room and flung himself on the bed.

"Right. What's up?"

I gulped nervously. I thought that I might have been overplaying the orange on the phone, 'cause sometimes I get worked up about stuff and then an hour later I can't understand why I got so upset.

But Charlie stopped scowling long enough to look at me. (And because he's GAY, I was parading about in low-rider panties and one of my cute little tank tops from The Gap with a built-in bra.)

"Oh my God! You've been Tangoed!"

My heart sank to the bottom of the garden. I could feel the tears prickling at the back of my eyes again. "Is it really that bad? What if I stand over here?"

"What did you *do*?" Charlie was really trying not to laugh now 'cause he realized I didn't find anything funny about this situation. But he kept kinda snorting.

"I used a whole bottle of this sunless, self-tanning lotion, and then I went on a sun bed for half an hour, and I came out looking like *this*!"

"You're such a dozy cow sometimes."

"Yeah, I know, and thanks for the reminder."

"Well, I didn't mean that quite as harshly as it sounded," Charlie said. "C'mere." He patted the bed and indicated that I should lift my leg up, and when I did, he smoothed his hand down my calf. All I could think was that I was glad I got my legs waxed, and the feeling of Charlie's large, warm hand running down my smooth skin made me have all these tingly feelings. Feelings that I'm never going to have for anyone else.

"Okay, we're gonna fix this," he said decisively. "Have you tried washing it off?"

"I've been in the shower *all* morning!"

"Have you tried Ajax?"

"No, I want to get rid of the *fake tan,* not the top five layers of my skin."

Charlie looked up to the ceiling and pursed his lips. It's his thinking face. It also makes his cheekbones look all kinds of yummy.

"Your cleanser," he said at last. "That really expensive cleanser that your mum bought you that cleanses and tones and exfoliates and takes all your makeup off that you never use because it smells funny. Where is it?"

I rummaged through all the bottles and jars in my bathroom cabinet. There were cleansers and toners and moisturizers. Facial scrubs and rescue masks. There was night cream and day cream. Glittery body gel and scented hand lotion. And none of it actually seemed to work. Eventually I found the tub of cleanser.

So I stood in the shower, and Charlie and I rubbed the cleanser into every inch of me, though I made him go back into the bedroom so I could do the bits under my top and knickers. I had to leave it on for twenty minutes, which was pretty boring, but I pulled the shower curtain closed, and Charlie came in and sat on the loo and made me recite my lines to him.

> *"What, will you not suffer me? Nay, now I see*
> *She is your treasure, she must have a husband;*
> *I must dance bare-foot on her wedding day*
> *And for your love to her lead apes in hell.*

*Talk not to me; I will go sit and weep
Till I can find occasion of revenge."*

"What does that actually mean? In plain English?" I asked
Charlie.

He didn't answer straightaway, so I peered around the curtain, and he was squinting at the book. "It means that Katharina's worried that her sister Bianca's going to get married
before her and that their dad likes Bianca more, probably
because she's not an evil bitch monster of death. So then
Katharina has a major snit and goes off to do the Shake-
spearean equivalent of eating loads of ice cream while she
plots her revenge."

"Wow! You're really good at this. So why isn't she going to
wear any shoes when Bianca gets married, and what's the big
deal with the apes in hell thing?"

Charlie peered at the book again. "Haven't got a bloody
clue. But, hey, how come you managed to know all that by
heart already?"

It's true, I did. I have a really good memory, which must be
compensation for being so thick the rest of the time. I only
have to listen to a song once, and it's stuck in my head forever. "Dunno. I just went to the gym and did two hours on the
exercise bike and tried to learn my part. I'm only up to page
fifty-two, though."

Charlie gave a long, low whistle. "You're quite the idiot
savant."

"Piss off!"

"Brie, do you even know what an idiot savant is?"

"Well, no."

"So, there you go, then. I rest my case."

"Charlie . . . don't be mean."

"Oh, stop pouting, princess! Let's wash this gunk off you."

Charlie and me showering together doesn't feature in my perfect-boyfriend-and-girlfriend fantasy: usually he takes me in his arms and kisses me, and then the titles come up. So he chucked me a loofah over the curtain and I turned the shower on the stingray setting and started scrubbing the cleanser off me. I was going to have the babiest soft skin after this. When I was done, I sent Charlie back into the bedroom while I got moisturized and used my brush thing on the back of my thighs to ward off the cellulite.

"How much longer are you going to be?" he finally yelled in exasperation.

"What do you think?" I was back in my undies, and I gave him a twirl.

His eyes narrowed as they swept over every bit of me, even my toes. Somehow, when Charlie's looking at me, I don't get all upset and traumatized like I do when it's me looking at me in the mirror.

"Your legs are a little bit streaky, but you're back to a whiter shade of pale. Could you get some clothes on now so that we're only an *hour* late?"

"You sure I'm not orange? Or even a faint shade of peach, which actually might be okay?"

"You're white and freckly once more, sorry, honey. It's your lot in life."

God, I hoped that wasn't how Charlie saw me. As his white, freckly mate. Or his white, freckly mate who made him wait another hour because I had to decide what I was going to wear and put on my makeup.

Charlie said that I wasn't allowed to wear anything too

Desperate Housewives, which is so not what my look is. We were going to this horrible grungy bar in Camden called Underworld, which pissed me off. I'd never been there, but I'd seen hordes of little punk kids with piercings waiting to get inside when they had bands playing. Obviously they didn't get the memo that goth is, like, totally over.

So we compromised on my black hipster trousers, a black tank top, and my pink kitten heel sandals, which look exactly like Marc Jacobs. Sort of.

Even though I'd snuck down to the kitchen to get him a bag of kettle chips and a full-fat Coke from Mum's secret stash behind the washing powder, Charlie was so bad-moody about me taking ages to get ready that I had to go and whine at my dad so he'd give me twenty quid for a cab.

Luckily we found a taxi right away, 'cause Charlie was having a complete strop about the time. I mean, like, what's the big deal? We were going to some grungy dive with two people who had absolutely nothing in common with either of us. I didn't know why he was getting so freakin' bent out of shape.

"I said I'd meet Walker at eight," he hissed at me. "And it's nine-fifteen now. Jesus, Brie!"

"Can you not have a go at me?" I begged. "Please. I'm only coming out with you because you forced me to."

"Well, I wish I hadn't bothered now," he said with a pout. He was all shoved against the cab door with his shoulders slumped like I'd just told him he had three months to live.

"Charlie . . ."

"Brie, you're working my last gay nerve."

"But Charlie . . . will you promise . . . ? Will you promise not to leave me on my own? Unless you have to go to the loo or something, but even then you have to be superquick."

Charlie gave me this look then. The exact same look my mum gives me when she thinks I've put on weight, or I'm having a bad hair day. Like, there's something seriously wrong with me. But he didn't say anything, just leaned forward and asked the driver if he could smoke. I tried again. "It's just that Shagger—"

"I take it you mean Walker."

"Yeah, whatever. But he's always glaring at me, so can you promise not to leave me out of the conversation? And not leave me alone with him and Daisy?"

Charlie pulled down the window so he could flick out his cigarette ash, then he turned to me. "I think that last one was covered by the whole 'don't leave me alone' clause."

"It's just . . . I'm . . . You know how I get." I stretched out my hand toward him, but then I thought better of it 'cause he was exhaling smoke like a Charlie-shaped dragon. All flared nostrils and glinty eyes.

I looked out of my window, and then I felt Charlie touch my hand.

"I know," he said softly, and squeezed my fingers.

I thought it would help, the whole hand-holding thing. But not so much. By the time we got to Camden, I'd managed to whip myself up into a state of virtual meltdown. I'm the party girl who hates going out. When you go out, you're on display, and people stare at you and judge you and always, *always*, always find you wanting. Like, you know how you can be completely happy with what you're wearing and your makeup's perfect, like J-Lo perfect, and as long as you remember to keep flicking your hair out, it looks good. Then one person, not even someone who's really cool, catches your eye and then glances away with a smirk, and all of a sudden you realize that you're a mess. Or you see one of those girls; one of those gorgeous girls who looks like a model. Worse, she looks like she hasn't even tried to look as beautiful as she does, and then your carefully chosen outfit and all that painstakingly applied makeup and the way you keep tossing your hair over your shoulder doesn't mean shit.

By the time we were queuing to get into Underworld, I was finding it hard to breathe, and I had to remind myself that Charlie was there, and he wouldn't let anything bad happen to me. I think my muscles had seized up because I couldn't have taken my hand off his arm, even if I'd wanted to, which I didn't.

"You promised, remember?" I reminded Charlie as we paid the cover price and we held out our hands to be stamped. I don't know why I bothered slathering my hands in Aveda Hand Relief cream only to have some idiot put ink all over them.

"It will be cool. Frosty cool," he assured me, but it wasn't, because the moment we got down the stairs, Daisy was there and getting in our faces. Plus, she was wearing this top with a cartoon girl on it that was straining against her huge bosoms. Talk about fashion backward. No one should be allowed to wear clothing with cartoons on it once they get past the age of six.

"You're so unbelievably late," she started. "It's almost ten! I've had to hang out with Walker all this time!"

And then the horrible glary boy was there himself. "Ta ever so," he muttered to Daisy, and then nodded at Charlie. I didn't know whether to be pissed off that he didn't even bother saying hello to me or relieved that he wasn't going to give me the evil eye.

"Sorry. Brie had a fake-tan emergency. It was touch and go for a while, wasn't it, hon?"

I nodded. But I wished that Charlie hadn't brought it up because I didn't want either of them running their eyes up and down my tan-free body. It's not like either of them was any great shakes when it came to personal grooming.

"We want to go and get food," Daisy stated, like someone died and made her boss of us.

"Yeah, I'm starving," Walker agreed. "You don't mind, do you?"

I did mind actually, 'cause we'd just paid a fiver each, but Charlie was beaming and acting like he hadn't eaten for days, even though he'd scarfed down an entire bag of kettle chips earlier.

"No. God, no. Food sounds good. Okay, let's get out of here."

It wasn't like I wanted to stay. Not when the place reeked of patchouli oil and stale beer and cigarette smoke. Plus, you know, everyone there was like into emo or goth or nu metal and I felt more out of place than I normally do. 'Cept it didn't really matter 'cause it wasn't like I was going to see any of these freaks again. But would it have killed any of them, especially Walker, to ask me what *I* wanted to do?

And then I didn't get asked my opinion on where we should go. Not like I can really eat anything in front of people who aren't Charlie, but still, it would've been nice. Or like the decent thing.

So then we had to dodge the tramps and the revolting scum punks with their dogs on string and their cans of Special Brew to get to this naff pasta place on Parkway, which just about made me spit. I was so mad that I actually managed to come out with an entire sentence once we were seated—practically in the kitchen and on a table so small that Walker and I *bumped knees*! Ugh. I'm so going to have to disinfect my trousers when I get home.

"I can't eat carbs after seven," I said bluntly without looking at the menu because I didn't need to. We were in a sodding Italian restaurant. It was all pasta and pizza and other evil things laden with complex carbs that my body just refuses to digest.

But Charlie had to go one better. "Yeah, and I can't do dairy," he confided to Walker and Daisy. "I'm lactose intolerant."

Sometimes when I look at Charlie I don't see a heartbreakingly beautiful boy with bad hair and scruffy clothes. I just see a boy who's really mean to me.

"That's because it makes you break out in zits," I blurted out, and then regretted it. Charlie had sworn me to secrecy about that.

He turned to me with a smirk that registered a ten on the evil scale.

"Brie, sweetie," he said in a voice that dripped acid. "Do you remember how we had that talk about things that we don't say in front of other people? 'Cause this is one of those times."

I couldn't see what he was so bothered about. It was only Daisy and Walker. But even so, he didn't have to treat me like I was a complete idiot. Not in front of *them*.

My tummy felt weird, and I couldn't eat. Didn't stop Daisy, though. She ordered garlic bread and a massive bowl of pasta. No wonder she's so fat—she must be, like, at least a size twelve.

After that it was easy. I just drank white wine 'cause it has less calories than red and let them stuff their faces with pasta and bang on and on about the stupid play and all the stupid bands they liked, the ones that hurt when you listen to them.

It was so boring that I drifted off to my special place where girls with long, brown hair and almost flat stomachs are treated like goddesses. And all the boys look like David Beckham, but they'd never cheat on a girl or send obscene text messages. And you can eat as much chocolate as you like and never put on weight, but it wouldn't matter if you did because there are no mothers there to make you eat nothing but carrots if you put on as much as, like, one gram, and anyway all the David Beckham–alikes are panting over you anyway. And it's always sunny, and they have beaches where the sand is silky under your toes and never gets into your bikini bott—

"Oh God, sorry. She does this. She doesn't eat and then she goes all glassy-eyed."

"What?"

"Hey there, hon. Enjoy your little trip away with the fairies?"

Charlie, Walker, and Daisy were sitting staring at me.

"What?" I said again, and touched my face to make sure I didn't have snot coming out of my nose or anything.

"We thought you'd gone into a hypoglycemic coma," Daisy said disapprovingly. "You really shouldn't drink on an empty stomach."

I didn't know what a hypoglywhatever coma was, but I wasn't going to let *her* know that. I just took another slug of my wine and wished they'd all stop looking at me.

"So is it true?" Walker asked in a tone of voice that suggested he thought it wasn't.

"Huh?"

"Charlie reckons you've got the first fifty-two pages of *The Taming of the Shrew* memorized."

"Well, yeah," I muttered. "So?"

You should have seen the way Daisy and Walker looked at me like I was having them on.

"Go on, Brie," Charlie murmured, giving me a nudge. "Do the bit about the mad-brain rudesby . . ."

"Yeah, Brie, go on . . ." Daisy said with this kind of bitchy smile.

I slammed my glass down on the table. "Fine, whatever." I took a deep breath:

> *"No shame but mine: I must, forsooth, be forced*
> *To give my hand, opposed against my heart,*
> *Unto a mad-brain rudesby, full of spleen,*
> *Who woo'd in haste and means to wed at leisure.*
> *I told you, I, he was a frantic fool,*
> *Hiding his bitter jests in blunt behavior:*
> *And to be noted for a merry man,*
> *He'll woo a thousand, 'point the day of marriage . . ."*

I stopped and picked up my glass again. The way they were goggling, you'd think I'd jumped on the table and given them all a lap dance. Like, they wished.

"Happy now?" I asked.

"That was amazing," Daisy breathed. "How do you do that?"

I shrugged. "Dunno. Just got a good memory is all."

"And she knows the fat, calorie, and carb content of any food in the world," Charlie added. "I'm thinking of hiring her out to a traveling freak show."

Then they all laughed like a bunch of dumb hyenas or something. And I wished I had a time machine so I could whiz myself a few hours forward to being in bed fast asleep and miles away from here.

"I'm going to powder my nose," I said with as much dignity as I could muster, and stood up.

Daisy scraped her chair back, too. "And I'm dying for a piss."

I wished Daisy hadn't come to the loo with me, 'cause I don't like having to pee with someone I know in the next cubicle. Luckily there was piped music.

Then she insisted on waiting for me while I put on more makeup. "You didn't eat anything," she said, like it was this big deal.

I didn't answer 'cause I was trying to redo my lip line without smudging it.

"You're really thin," she went on, like it's a bad thing. "You know, we're at this age when it's really important that we get lots of vitamins and minerals from our food."

Bor-ing! "I know," I said, stretching my mouth so I could reapply my lipstick. "But I'd kill myself if I couldn't get into a size six."

I don't think she liked that. 'Cause then she went into this massive rant about stuff. There were lots of long words in it like *patriarchy* and *hegemony*, and as far as I could work out, being a lesbian is kinda cool as you can eat what the hell you like 'cause other lesbians don't mind if you're a chubster.

Almost makes me wish I were a big, fat lesbian.

Ooops. I didn't realize that I'd said it out loud—and just how much had I drunk?—until Daisy had me pinned against the counter and was screaming at me. Actually screaming!

"My God! I don't know if you're the most offensive person I've ever met or just the most stupid!" She was breathing garlic all over me and *touching* me. Her hands were gripping my shoulders, and she was shaking me.

"Get off me!"

"I get that you have self-image issues, which have turned you into a rampant body fascist, but I don't get how you can hang out with Charlie when you're so *homophobic*."

"Charlie isn't really gay, it's just a phase he's going through," I tried to explain, watching Daisy turn from really red to really pale. She had shocking open pores, I noticed, as her face got nearer and nearer to mine again, and she shoved me against the mirror.

"Don't touch me!" I yelped, and tried to push her off. "Leave me alone!"

Daisy was crying. Proper crying with snot and stuff. Some of it had gotten on my tank top. Maybe that's why I was shaking.

Then she suddenly let me go and scrubbed her eyes with her fists before she started washing her hands like she wanted to get the feel of me off her. I hovered next to her. I didn't know what to do. Like, I was the one who'd just been attacked, but she was acting as if I'd done something terrible.

"Does Charlie know that you hate gay people?" she suddenly asked me, and I stared at her with my mouth hanging open.

"I don't hate gay people. I just hate Charlie being gay, it's a whole other thing."

She shook her head and muttered something under her breath.

I tried to think of something to do or say that would make

things not so bad between us. Not like we were friends or anything but . . . the situation had just gone from nought to hideous and it was giving me a headache.

"Do you want to borrow some lip gloss?" I offered.

"Look, Brie, no offense or anything, but could you just piss off?"

To be honest, I couldn't wait to get away from her. I marched back to the table and was wondering how to tell Charlie that we had to go home now. Maybe I could even just text him from the bus stop or something. But when I opened the door that led back to the restaurant, he was still sitting there with Walker and a whole bunch of guys that I didn't know.

Having to deal with a load of other people, with *boys*, just wasn't on my list of things I wanted to do right then. No wonder I've never had a boyfriend. I just don't know how to talk to anyone with boy parts who isn't Charlie.

"Brie!" And then Charlie called my name, and his whole face lit up like I meant the world to him. "Get your pert little rear end over here."

Which was kinda embarrassing that he'd drawn attention to my butt, but at least it was flattering, so I walked over and tried not to tug at my clothing and fidget because all the boys were staring at me. They weren't my type, though. They were all skatey rocker boys, but it was okay, I didn't have to sit anywhere near them 'cause Charlie pulled me down on his lap.

"You okay, hon?" he murmured in my ear, and wrapped his arms around my waist and squeezed me. It was perfect. We were perfect. It was like I was wrapped up in Charlie. I leaned back and could feel his chest and the tight muscles in his arms. I could smell the Kiehl's aftershave balm that I got him for his birthday.

Charlie started introducing me to Walker's mates, who all had posh boys' names like Alfie, Rowan, and Fred, as Daisy came back from the toilet.

"I'm going now," she announced, snatching up her bag, which had another stupid cartoon character on it. She shot me a filthy look, and I shrank back against Charlie, who kissed the top of my shoulder.

"See ya, then," I said.

Walker jumped up. "I'll walk you to your bus stop, if you like," he offered.

Daisy looked freaked out, and I didn't blame her. Walking a girl to a bus stop is Walker-speak for shagging her in the nearest dark alley. Everyone knows that.

"I'm fine, I'm going to get a cab," she shot back.

There was this whole debate about unlicensed minicabs, but finally she left, only she took Charlie with her! Charlie was just as likely to get beaten up by a horde of beer monsters as Daisy was, but when I tried to tell him that, he just hissed at me to get up and started fussing over Daisy like she was some delicate little girlie girl and not the great, fat bruiser who'd nearly beaten me up.

So I was left alone with Walker and his friends. But actually, it wasn't so bad. We ordered two more bottles of wine, and Rowan grabbed me another chair when I said I didn't want to sit on his lap.

Rowan isn't Charlie, but he is sort of cute. He has loads of curly dark hair and the deepest tan, a bit like an Italian Orlando Bloom. I wasn't that into him or anything, but when Charlie came back and I remembered how I was mad at him for going with Daisy, I carried on talking to Rowan. 'Cause my mum says that sometimes it doesn't hurt boys to have a bit of friendly competition.

I think I was quite drunk. My teeth had gone numb, and everything was blurred and soft focus. It made the candles on the table look so pretty. And the best thing about Rowan was that he seemed to be totally into me—which, like, never happens. He asked me loads of stuff about myself and kept touching my knee. Like, he was helping me because I'm really crap at talking to boys who aren't Charlie 'cause I'm not really that interesting.

My head felt really heavy, and Rowan was really sweet when I rested my head against his shoulder. But Charlie was too busy talking to Walker to even notice. And he was trying to be all clever about football when the only thing he knows is that David Beckham plays for Reál Madrid.

"So what music you into, Brie?" Rowan patted my knee again really encouragingly.

Luckily I wasn't so pissed that I forgot that boys don't get that Britney is actually quite good and that her songs contain a lot of pain from her split with Justin.

"Loads of stuff," I said.

"Yeah? Like what?"

I blinked and looked groggily at Rowan's chest. Hmm, nice chest.

"The White Stripes," I murmured, because he had one of their T-shirts on and some of their stuff is okay.

"Yeah, right. You like The White Stripes?" I looked up to see Walker sneering at me. One day he's totally going to stick like that. In fact, I think he already has.

"Leave it, Walker." Rowan took his hand off my knee and punched Walker lightly on the arm.

"I hate it when girls pretend they like stuff just to impress a guy."

"Oh, come on, that's not fair," Charlie protested. "She does like some of their stuff, don't you?"

I nodded 'cause talking was getting really hard, and I didn't even wanna waste the effort on Walker. But he wouldn't shut his stupid, fat gob.

"Go on, if you like them so much, sing one of their songs. Just one." He smirked.

Everyone was looking at me again. And I remembered that they were all boys and I was just a girl, and they probably thought I was dumb.

I tugged on Charlie's sleeve. "I think we should go now, Charlie. I'm not having fun anymore."

Charlie leaned over so he could hiss in my ear: "Just sing one line from one of their bloody songs, and then I promise I'll get you home."

I thought about it for a second. Singing in public to a bunch of posh boys was beyond humiliating. It was right up there with these nightmares I have about appearing on *Pop Idol* wearing only a bra and a pair of flippers.

Then again, Charlie would so owe me one. Maybe even as much as three.

"If I do it, you have to let me have the iPod for a whole week," I whispered back.

"No way!"

"I'm not going to do it otherwise. I'm going to sing "Beautiful" by Christina Aguilera and make a show of you." Which I so wasn't, but Charlie didn't know that.

"You telling her the words, Charlie?" Walker interrupted with his dumb, smug voice. "That's cheating."

Charlie and I straightened up, and all of a sudden I didn't

feel scared anymore. 'Cause Walker thought he'd fronted me, and I'd had enough to drink that I wasn't in the mood to be messed with.

I pulled my shoulders back and gave Charlie the look. He knows what *the* look means. Which is why he started shaking his head and giggling.

"I do, too, like The White Stripes," I announced to Walker, who just arched an eyebrow and blew smoke in my face, which everybody knows gives you wrinkles.

"Well, it's true that we love one another
I love Charlie Black like a little brother."

I didn't even need to look at Charlie because I knew he was going to sing the next bit. He had to. It was our song.

"Well, Brie, I love you, too, but there's
Just so much that I don't know about you."

I'd have done the whole song—I really would have, just to wipe that dumb grin off Walker's face, but I didn't even have to 'cause he started clapping.

"Okay, Brie." He reached across the table and grabbed my hand, even though I *euwwwwed* and tried to snatch it back.

"I'm very sorry for doubting your love of The White Stripes. I hope you can find it in your heart to forgive me."

"Whatever, you freak," I said, and then I turned to Charlie. "Can we *please* go home now? I need to eat something really soon."

Charlie looked at me. Then he looked at Walker and then turned and grabbed his jacket off the back of the chair.

"All right, don't get hissy, missy. Let's get you home before you die of starvation."

Of course, by the time we got back to my house, which involved a really unpleasant night-bus experience where some hatchet-faced girl with a Croydon face-lift hairdo threatened to beat Charlie up because he tripped over her feet when we got on, it was really late.

And by the time I'd eaten a cereal bar really slowly so it would digest quicker, it was even later, so Charlie had to stay over. He didn't want to.

"Just once, Brie, I wanna sleep in my own bed," he protested. "I need some space."

Which is so lame because I give him plenty of space, and he's the one who hogs the duvet.

"But I might choke on my own vomit and die," I pointed out because I had had a huge amount to drink. "I am feeling a little bit sick now, come to think of it."

Charlie fell for it. And when I got out of the bathroom half an hour later after taking my makeup off and doing my medium-intense skincare regime, he was all snuggled under my quilt, and when I got in, he rolled over so I could curl up against his back.

"You didn't have a bad time tonight, did you, hon?" he asked sleepily.

"It was all right, but Daisy and Walker hate me."

"No, they don't!"

"Yeah, they really do, but, hey, bothered!"

"Brie . . ."

"I don't want to talk about them anymore. I'm going to buy a new top tomorrow."

"Are you? Hmm. Where from?"

"FCUK. It's really cute, like a little camisole top with pink ribbon threaded around the neckline."

"Sounds bloody adorable. Do you think I should rebleach my bleachy bits?"

"Oooh! We could bleach all of it. Aw, I could give you highlights all the way through. It would look way cool." Charlie stiffened in my arms. "I don't want highlights, but will you help me with the bleach 'cause you're good at that."

And it doesn't really matter about the times that Charlie pisses me off because we have times where we're cuddled up in bed together and talking about clothes and hair, and I just feel like everything's all right in my world. I love him—it's as simple as that really.

*"We don't need reason and we don't need logic
'Cause we've got feeling and we're damn proud of it."*

Charlie

Two things occurred to me when I woke up the next morning. The first was that I had an erection. And the second was that my erection was pressed against Brie's thigh.

It was nothing to do with rampant lust at the touch of her waxed, moisturized, formerly fake-tanned skin. It was just simple biology. The pressure of urine in my bladder. Or there's even a school of thought that thinks it may be a result of dreams that happened during REM sleep, add in some early-morning-enhanced testosterone, and you're good to go. Or not.

All I knew was that I was packing wood in Brie's bed, and I was a very, very bad boy.

Of course, the minute I started shifting away from her and trying to disentangle my arms from around her waist, Brie gave a little snort and rolled over, so Mr. Stiffy was pressing against her stomach to say, "Good morning, little lady, how you doing?"

"Brie, hon, I gotta get up."

She grunted in a very un-Brie-like manner and nestled in tighter, which made the situation far more uncomfortable/embarrassing/potentially disastrous (delete where applicable) than it had been thirty seconds earlier.

Millimeter by millimeter I edged away from the many-limbed Brie beast, but she kept following me across the mattress. I know she's clingy, but this was verging on the freaking ridiculous.

"Charlie," she murmured sleepily. "What's that thing digging into my tummy?"

I took a deep breath. "Now, sweetie, no need to be alarmed, nothing to worry about, but that would be my penis."

There were a couple of snuffly noises in response, and then she sat bolt upright with an unearthly shrieking noise that must have set every dog in the neighborhood on full alert.

"*Euwwww! Euwwwww!*" she screeched, scrambling away from me like I was carrying the Ebola virus. "Get it away from me! That's gross! *Euwwww!*"

You'd have thought that Brie's obvious repulsion at my morning erection would have quelled its perkiness, but oh no! The little critter was here to stay.

"Brie, I'm going to get up now, and you've got one of two choices, okay?"

She cringed. She actually *cringed* when I spoke and sat on the edge of the bed, cowering. "What?"

"You need to close your eyes so I can get to the bathroom and deal with my penis—"

"Stop saying that word!"

"—or I'm going to have to grab one of your pillows and hold it in front of my . . . erm . . . *it*. Your call."

Her entire face squinched up like she'd just swallowed a vat of yogurt that was a week past its sell-by date. "Oh my God! I'm closing my eyes. Go to the bathroom now."

She didn't just close her eyes, no; little Miss Drama Queen had to pull the duvet cover right up over her face.

When I got back from the longest-ever pee in the world, Brie had actually stripped the linen off her bed and was glaring at me with this very accusatory look on her face.

"I'm going to have a shower now," she said snottily. "And I never want to talk about this again but . . . but . . ."

"But?" I prompted, hunting around for the T-shirt that I'd flung on the floor last night.

"How did you deal with it? You didn't . . . I mean . . . Not in my shower, did you?"

"How did I what the huh with who?" I knew damn well what she was getting at, but I decided to let her sweat it out. After all, this was way more humiliating for me than it was for her.

She looked up at the ceiling and folded her arms as she moved her lips back and forth like she couldn't quite spit the words out. "Did you . . . ?" Her voice was a hoarse whisper as she leaned in toward me. "You didn't masturbate in my shower did you?"

Needless to say, Brie dropped GCSE Biology.

"No," I said slowly and carefully so even Brie could understand. "I peed. In the loo. And that deflated the problem, as it were."

"Right," she said skeptically.

"You do understand that it had nothing to do with being

overpowered by lust at the close proximity of your silken flesh, Brie? I just really needed to have a piss."

But as she stood there with the light streaming in from the window behind her so it was like she was illuminated by the best cinematographer in Hollywood, it was almost as if I was seeing her for the first time. Sometimes her beauty catches me unaware, so all I can do is gasp and wonder that I'm ever allowed to touch her.

With all the makeup scrubbed off her face and her cheeks creased and pink from where they've been resting on the pillow, her hair static with electricity and flying out in all directions, even as she digs a piece of sleep out of her eyes, she's infinitely more lovely than when she's primped and prettied up.

"You're such a pig, Charlie. Ugh, I hope you didn't leave the loo seat up, 'cause gross . . ."

And then she opens her mouth and ruins everything.

Family of Brie was nowhere to be seen when I headed to the kitchen for coffee, cigarette, and breakfast in that order. Then I remembered that they go to the health club on Sundays in this strange bonding ritual, which I don't understand. I made myself a cup of coffee, snagged a croissant from the bread bin, and opened the back door, which led out into the garden.

It was one of those chalk-bright mornings that sunglasses and SPF 40 sunblock were invented for. The air was scratchy and dry. It made me feel restless.

I sat down in one of the garden chairs and swung my feet up onto the table so I could flash back to the night before. But my thoughts just kept straying in a Walker-y direction. I know he's straight, I know all the reasons why it's never going to happen in a million years. And I know a ton of other reasons, too. But last night my delicious little crush on Walker, that had been nicely percolating all week, boiled over into full-blown lust.

Give it a week and I'll be sad when he's sad, happy when he's happy, and ready to walk across deserts in my bare feet if he should say the word.

And it's not just because he's all my bad-boy fantasies rolled into one pert-buttocked, pouty-lipped package. It's more about the important stuff. That he's arch and knowing. He's got a dry sense of humor and excellent taste in music. And we have this connection that I know is more than just the fact that we're the only two sane people in the drama group. When his fingers brush against mine as he lights my cigarette or he pours more wine into my glass, it feels as if my entire hand has suddenly been plugged into the national grid.

This is so entirely predictable of me to fall for a boy so straight that he's known throughout the entire Western Hemisphere as a serial girl-shagger.

Though maybe he is secretly gay and in denial. And the large number of girls he's slept with was just a futile attempt to try and convince himself that he is straight. Yeah, and Brie is going to be accepted into Mensa any day.

Talking of the Briester, she was finally ready to emerge into the sunlight. She had her not-ready-to-put-on-makeup makeup on and the smuggest smile I've ever seen on her face.

Which reminded me that the two of us needed to have a conversation about the hissy fit that Daisy threw on the way to the bus stop last night.

"Hey missy. Your hangover kicking in yet?"

Brie held up a can of Diet Coke in answer to my question (that would be a yes), dragged a chair over, and then winced at the noise. Up close, I could see the telltale puffiness around her eyes and resisted the urge to point it out or she'd spend the rest of the day with slices of cucumber welded onto her face.

"Why do we drink alcohol when we know that it makes our heads hurt the next day?" she mused. "Like, you're sitting there with a ginormous bottle of wine in front of you and thinking that it's only going to lead to a monster headache, so you pour yourself another glass. What's up with that?"

"I think the alcohol probably deadens the memories of what the alcohol does the next morning," I said, and shifted in my chair so I could reach my pockets and get my cigarettes out.

Out of the corner of my eye, I could see Brie open her can of Diet Coke. She was still wearing that annoying smirky expression like it was this season's Versace.

"Okay, why are you looking so pleased with yourself?"

She smiled faintly and shrugged. "Dunno what you're talking about."

I pushed my shades on top of my head so she could feel the full benefit of my Wrath of God glare. "You're currently meant to be clutching your head and vowing never to drink again, and instead you're acting like you've just got through to the last round of . . . I don't know, some lame TV talent contest."

"It's nothing," she murmured, which made me positive that it was something.

I nudged her with my foot and nearly upended the chair. "C'mon, spill, or I'm going to swap your moisturizer for mayonnaise when you least expect it."

Brie screwed up her face and stuck her tongue out as if she

could already taste the calories by osmosis. "If you did that, I'd wipe all your songs off the iPod, which, by the way, I'm having for the entire week."

She was now on smug overdrive, a gloating smile playing at the corners of her lips, and she had to suffer. With the lightning-quick reflexes that made me a hurdling champion back in the pre–cigarette days, when I thought being good at sports was something to be proud of, I scraped back my chair and grabbed her by the waist. She clutched onto my knees and squealed as I upended her and reached for her armpit with one hand.

"I'm going to tickle you until you tell me why you're being so disgustingly self-satisfied."

She was wriggling like a worm in mud. "Don't! Don't! I'll wet myself!"

I waggled my fingers warningly. "Start talking, little missy."

"Please, Charlie . . ." And then the little minx tried to bite my leg.

I dropped her on the ground—carefully, one more knock on the head might take out her few remaining brain cells—and straddled her, pinning her wrists above her head. This would be her cue to shriek and writhe about like she was having a seizure, but instead she just laughed in my face.

"Ha!" she snorted cryptically.

"Ha what?"

I still wasn't jumping on the clue train. Her wrists felt like they were made of cardboard, and I loosened my grip. She was so fine-boned that you'd think the slightest touch could shatter her into tiny pieces. But this was Brie, and she was tougher than she looked. Way tougher.

"Jeez, Charlie," she exclaimed. "I know you want me! This

whole gay thing was just, like, a mistake, which is why you woke up this morning with an *erection!*" She hissed the word and looked around cautiously as if she expected a horde of policemen to suddenly climb over the hedge and arrest her for public indecency.

I suddenly realized that I was still pressing her against the ground in a manner that could be completely misconstrued by, say, someone who was Brie. I scrambled to my feet and pushed my fingers through my hair so I wasn't tempted to strangle her.

"Oh my God! Are you on monkey crack? I'm gay. I'm a pouf. I'm a fairy. I'm a nancy boy. I'm a big old queen. An arse bandit. A fudge packer. A friend of Dorothy's." I realized that I was shouting now and that Brie was cringing back from me, her hands over her ears. "Why does none of this register with you? Why can't you get it into your thick skull that I'm gay? Capital G. Capital A. Capital Y!"

I stopped. I hadn't paused for breath the whole time, and I was stooped over and panting. It was far too hot for all these histrionics before eleven.

Brie's feet were quivering in her flip-flops. My eyes slowly traveled up her body, and I could tell she'd been practicing in front of a mirror. No one can make their bottom lip tremble so effectively without some rehearsal time.

"But I love you, Charlie," she murmured, her voice catching just so.

"No, you don't," I said, back on the same old boring ground because we have this exchange at least twice a week. "You love shoes and I love boys *because I. Am. Gay.*"

She was pouting now. Brie's pout is way better than her lip tremble. There ain't no weapon forged that can defeat it.

"You're not gay," she insisted, like my heartfelt rant of thirty seconds ago had never happened. "You're just controversial."

"Oh God, I am so bored with always having this conversation with you!" I gave a tiny scream of frustration. "If you don't stop, I'm going to tell everyone that your real name is Brianna because your parents thought they were going to have a boy and wanted to call him BRIAN!"

"I swear to God, if you tell anyone that, I will kill you." Brie's voice was low, her eyes murderous, and she was right; I did love her. Not in a groiny way, more in the way that she was my best friend and she was actually a gay boy trapped in a woman's body. But I didn't tell her that because I liked having kneecaps.

And all this shouting and trying to prove that my gayness was a valid lifestyle choice made me remember the highlights of the conversation I'd had with Daisy as we waited for her bus.

"You know, Brie, this is getting really boring." I flung myself back down in the chair. "Daisy has this theory about why you're not down with the whole gay thing."

"Daisy hates me," Brie said flatly. "And she's totally mental anyway." She crouched down to pick up her can of Diet Coke, which had gone flying when I'd picked her up.

"Well, she reckons that you're completely homophobic," I told her, and wondered why it made me feel sick to even say it. That Brie was not just anti-me-being-gay but anti-everybody-being-gay because she hated gay people.

She traced a pattern with her finger along the side of the can, and I realized that sometimes it was hard to figure out what Brie was thinking. Though it was usually about her hair.

"Okay, I am not homophobic," she said finally. "I like gay people. Well, I don't really know any gay people apart from you. Which doesn't mean that I think you are gay. And I know Daisy, but if I don't like her, it's because she's mean and she treats me like I'm beneath her and she dresses really badly."

Sometimes having a conversation with Brie about anything is like trying to have a discussion about the theory of relativity with a three-year-old.

I shuffled my chair along so our knees were bumping against each other and raised her chin with my hand so I could gaze into her slightly bloodshot eyes and see if there was anyone actually at home.

"Brie, I'm going to say it again. I'm gay. I'm always going to be gay. I'm never gonna wake up one morning and suddenly be straight. So, if that's the only reason why you hang out with me, then we've got way more serious problems than the problems we do have."

She shook her head free of my touch and refused to look at me. "I don't get it, Charlie. 'Cause, like, you're always going on about how loads of straight people are secretly a little bit gay, so how come you're not secretly a little bit straight?"

"I do not!"

"Yeah, you do! You reckon like half of Hollywood and any guy in a boy band is gay. And you also say that the lady who works in the café is and Henry and that lame gangsta-rap boy in the drama group . . . Do you want me to go on?"

My mouth was hanging open, village idiot style. I shut it with a snap. Though I was at pains to admit it, the girl did have a point. A really annoying point but a point nevertheless.

"Don't be bloody stupid," I snarled, more for something to say. "You're clutching at straws! Not even straight straws, no pun intended, but those bendy, twisty ones."

"No, I ain't," she thundered. Really shouted, though it still sounded like a mouse squeaking. "You try and make out that

I hate gay people, which is, like, hurtful, and really you hate straight people."

"What*ever!*"

"You can be a real dickhead sometimes, Charlie."

"And you can be a complete airhead all the time, Brie."

Her lips thinned, and she jumped to her feet so she could fold her arms and glare down at me. "Well, if I'm so bloody stupid and horrible, then you can piss off right now!"

That was my cue to kick the chair back, get up, and storm in the direction of the back door. "Fine! I'm pissing off! See you around."

I'd only gotten as far as the hall when she caught up with me and grabbed my arm.

"Don't go," she pleaded, her eyes glassy with tears. Sometimes fighting with Brie is no fun; she takes everything so seriously. "I thought we were going to spend the day together."

I yanked open the front door at the same time as I shook her hand off. "I don't want to stay around here to contaminate you with my gayness. It might be catching."

"But I was going to dye your hair, and we were going to go shopping and—"

I cut her off midsentence by slamming the door behind me. I half expected her to come running out after me, she usually does, but all I could see was her outline in the frosted glass as I looked over my shoulder. She stood there for a bit, and then she walked away. Just for a second, I felt a tiny pang of guilt, but I refused to give it house room. I heart Brie but one day she is going to send me to my own well-appointed room in the local nuthouse.

. . .

I didn't feel like going home right away. Merv the Swerve is usually hanging around the house on Sundays, wearing nothing but a pair of boxer shorts that show off his hairy back and flabby stomach while he slobbers over my mum. How she can stand it, I don't know. If all guys looked like Merv, I probably *would* be straight.

In the end, I jumped on the tube and went to the National Portrait Gallery to see the Cecil Beaton exhibition. He was probably a mate of Lavinia's back in the day. He used to take pictures of all of these debutantes in the twenties and thirties before ending up in Hollywood and becoming best mates with Audrey Hepburn. I wandered around, staring at the monochrome images of beautiful people and feeling slightly sad. There was something unsettling about looking at people living at the peak of their youth and beauty; moments frozen in time by the click of the camera, and now most of them were dead. If only I had someone with me who'd know what I meant.

It's not the sort of thing I could have done with Brie. She only likes moving pictures on a cinema screen, and she'd have moaned about how she was bored or that her feet were hurting or that she hadn't been able to keep her Diet Coke levels topped up for at least half an hour.

As I crossed over Charing Cross Road in the direction of Borders, I wished that Brie wasn't my only real friend. It's not like I'm some antisocial freak. I'm friendly. I have loads of acquaintances. I can't even walk across a pub without stopping to talk to at least five people I know, but none of them can really see me. Even Brie can't.

She just sees this boy who isn't what she wants him to be. She doesn't look beyond the clothes and the hairstyle that she can't stand and see into my heart.

I used to have lots of friends. When I was twelve and I had my birthday party at this stupid Quasar laser place in Archway, my mum almost had a heart attack because fifty kids wanted to come and she couldn't afford it.

Then two years later I came out, announced to the world that I was here, queer, and they could bloody well get used to it. And all those friends who I used to play football with just dumped me. There was a little bit of name-calling, an incident after school where someone tried to throw me headfirst into the path of an oncoming car, but mostly my big gay announcement was a cue for everyone to move on. Like I was the handrail in a disabled toilet—something that was there but they'd never need. Well, that and I might as well have had a sign painted on my head that I fancied all boys. Even the fat, ugly ones who smelled of stale perspiration. Which, actually, not so much.

But you want to know the really ironic thing about my lonely gay self? I only fancy straight boys, which is kinda limiting. And right at this very moment in time, I only fancy Walker, which is even more limiting.

And it's not for want of trying. Jesus, at one stage I belonged to every gay youth organization in London. I've danced in a tutu at Duckie. I've marched at Pride. I've met a ton of gay boys, and not one of them has rocked my world. It seems that they're just complete scene queens and being gay is all they are. And being gay is not all I am. Why should who you sleep with define you?

Or else they're only about the sex. And the getting of the sex. And then not calling the next day or even offering to walk you to the bus stop.

By the time I got to Borders, I was in need of serious retail therapy and possibly a chocolate brownie. I bought an *Alias* boxed set that was on sale, a couple of music magazines from the States that they'd got in on import, and a copy of *The Perks of Being a Wallflower* 'cause I'd left mine on the train when I was coming back from a gig in Brighton last month.

Then I went and sat in the Starbucks on the first floor even though they're an evil, corporate conglomerate, but I really love their strawberry-and-cream Frappuccinos, so what are you going to do? I was flicking through *Spin* magazine and mentally making a list of all the songs I wanted to download when I became aware of the sound of high-pitched giggling.

I looked up, and there were these two baby goths sitting at the next table staring at me. As I caught their collective and heavily made-up eye, they went bright red under their pan-stick and started nudging each other.

"Is he looking?"

"Stop looking!"

"Is he looking now?"

"Way to make it obvious. He's looking! Turn away now."

That carried on for about ten minutes. Me trying to read an interview with Ryan Adams to the accompaniment of giggles and the whole "Is he looking?"/"Stop looking" gigglefest. It would be so easy to be straight. But sometimes life isn't meant to be easy, so I got up, grabbed my stuff, and as I walked past their table, I winked at them. I don't know why.

Then I took the stairs two at a time so they couldn't run after me and molest me by the self-help books.

It was just getting dark when I got home. I walked down my street and breathed in the scent of ripe flowers and ozone. It was so humid and dense that I felt like I was underwater, my movements slow and awkward. Our windows were still wide open, and I could see my mother curled up on the sofa with a glass of wine in her hand.

"Hi, honey, I'm home," I called as I opened the door.

"Charlie, baby!" At least someone sounded excited to see me. "Hard day at the office?" she asked as I walked into the lounge and flopped down next to her.

"So-so. I think Paul in Accounts is nicking from the petty cash, and the photocopier broke again."

She ruffled my hair and smiled. "Where's Brie?"

I pouted. "We're not joined at the hip, you know. God forbid. I have a whole life that has nothing to do with that whiny-ass, little crybaby."

My mother arched one perfectly plucked eyebrow and tugged lightly on a strand of my hair. "Hey! That's not nice. So you two had another row? You'll make it up, babes. You always do."

She handed me her glass so I could have a sip of the Chardonnay she was drinking. "Brie's meant to be my best friend, but sometimes, oh . . . I *hate* her."

Mum scooted around so I could nestle my head against her shoulder so she could rub the back of my neck. My mum does the best neck rubs in Britain. Maybe even the world.

"Don't be so hard on her," she said mildly. "She's a fragile soul is our Brie. And she worships the ground you walk on, though God knows why 'cause you can be a moody little sod."

"Hey!" I said indignantly.

"I'm just sayin', Charlie. That girl has got a thin skin, and sometimes you break her heart without even realizing it."

"Oh, stop being so intuitive, you know I hate it," I muttered grumpily, and refused to give her back her glass. "If I was straight, then I still wouldn't shag Brie. I've told her a million times, but she has this selective hearing disability that makes me want to rip her head off and use it as a football."

"What a nice, sweet boy I've raised," Mum mused, and then stood up. "I'm going to get another glass. Do you want anything while I'm on my feet? Crisps? Chocolate? Some Prozac?"

"Crisps, salt-and-vinegar. And bring the bottle."

My beautiful, fantastic mother made me who I am today. If you're gay, you're meant to have this whole story about how you did the big coming-out speech to your mother accompanied by weeping and smashed crockery and "Don't you ever darken my doorstep again." Not my mum. She just gave me a careful look, didn't yell at me for waking her up (it was four in the morning), and said softly, "It's okay, babes. I kind of already knew." Then she gave me a hug and said that I had to do what made me happy.

Actually I think she was delighted to have a gay son. Just so there'd be someone to go shopping with her. And Saul, my older brother, is already the black sheep of the family. Mainly for joining the army and getting married to this awful woman called Nikki (two *k*s, two *i*s). Mum says that if they ever get around to having kids and making her a grandmother, she's going to slit her wrists.

She came back from the kitchen and threw a family-size bag of Walkers at me before plonking herself back down.

I clutched a cushion to my chest and groaned. "I just want to find someone to have a relationship with who isn't a complete sex-crazed scene queen. Is that too much to ask? *Ow!* What did you do that for?"

She'd just bopped me on the head with the remote control,

but she looked entirely relentless. "Forgodsake, Charlie. I have exactly the same problems. Now, are you going to shut up and watch *Sex and the City* with me or am I going to have to send you to bed without any crisps?"

Four episodes of Carrie and the girls later, I was mildly drunk and ready for bed.

I was just about to turn out the light and settle down for a very uncharacteristic ten hours of sleep when my mobile started ringing. I grabbed the phone off the nightstand and squinted at the display. It was Brie. She'd managed to go a whole day without calling me. That must be some kind of record.

I was tempted to press the MUTE button, but it was *Brie*. Instead I answered it.

"Hey Brie, what's up?"

"Oh, hey. Nothing."

"So . . . why you calling me, then?"

"You still mad at me, Charlie?"

"Kinda."

"Right."

"Well, if that's all, then I'm going to bed now."

"I'm sorry! All right? I'm sorry that you're mad at me and that I pissed you off."

"Okay, then."

"Charlie! Please, don't use your cold voice on me. I've said I'm sorry. I missed you today. Did you miss me?"

"Maybe. Possibly."

"So are we cool now? You gonna come and pick me up tomorrow?"

"I guess. Yeah, I'll come round for you. Be ready, though."

"I'm always ready!"

"Yeah, yeah, princess. So what did you get up to today?"

"Well, nothing much 'cept . . . You know that guy from last night? Rowan? With the curly hair?"

"Yeah. What about him?"

"He phoned me up and asked if I wanted to go out with him next Friday night to see a film. Like, on a date or something."

"Right. Wow. He didn't seem like he was that into you."

"Oh. Do you think? 'Cause like I thought he was."

"Yeah? Okay, I was probably wrong. That's cool, Brie. I'm really pleased for you."

"Really?"

"Yeah! It's your first date. My little girl's becoming a woman."

"But in a girlish way, right?"

"Right. God, you're a head case. I love you. Good night."

"Love you, too, Charlie. See you tomorrow."

"'Night."

"'Night, then."

"I'm hanging up now, Brie."

"Okay, but I—"

Click.

It was the kindest way. Otherwise we'd be there for another ten minutes saying good-bye.

And I had to spend that long pondering the weirdness that might be Brie with a boyfriend. Nah! I give it three hours before he makes his excuses and leaves.

Daisy

Way back in the day, when things were all medieval and there were crusades and knights and tankards of mead, people really knew how to punish themselves. They'd wear hair shirts under their clothes and let their flesh get so sore that they developed these itchy, weepy welts that were constantly aggravated by the harsh fabric. Mostly they did it to show that they were religious, like Henry VIII's first wife (was it one of the Katherines, I can never remember?) who was incredibly pious and a big fan of the hair shirt, though why God would expect anyone to show their devotion by having a rash is beyond me. But, you know, if I could find one that would actually fit over my gargantuan breasts, I think I'd be in the market for a hair shirt because I'm still reeling from the way I savaged Brie on Saturday night.

In my defense, though, getting angry with her was entirely

reasonable because she was talking absolute offensive drivel about being fat and being gay. But the other reason why I was so furious with her was the way she stood there and offered me her lip gloss like it was, I don't know, the Holy Grail or something. I got swallowed up in this white-hot fury that blinded me to everything else but her standing there with her stupid shampoo-commercial hair, the smooth pale skin of her stomach peeking over the low-rider waistband of her trousers.

And instead of seeing red like you're meant to when you're so angry that getting ten years to life on a manslaughter charge is starting to look like a valid lifestyle choice, I was transfixed by the way the lights hit the sheen on her lips and how her mouth looked like she was pouting even when she wasn't. And that mouth kept moving, showing tiny glimpses of even, white teeth, movie-star teeth. And all the while her words danced around me, pricking against my skin and worming their way right into the heart of me.

I hate her.

I hate her because she'll never, ever know how easy her life is because she looks the way she does. She doesn't just fit in. She's beyond all that. It's like everyone else tries to fit in because we're sprinkled with loser dust. But Brie gets to have it easy because she's beautiful, albeit in a vacuous, brain-dead way. Pretty girls lead these charmed lives of doors being held open for them and drinks being bought for them and young men catching their breath as they walk past. She has all that, and it's still not enough for her.

I mean, Claire is beautiful, but it's not the kind of beauty that's going to make revolting tracksuited boys in souped-up Ford Fiestas slow down so they can catcall out of the window. Claire's beauty is about the half smile that plays along her lips when she's listening to music. And the way her eyes get slumberous and smoky when she knows I want to kiss her. Claire's beauty is more rewarding because it's mostly tucked away, hidden, and you have to work harder to see it. Whereas with Brie, she does exactly what it says on the tin, and the tin has BRAINLESS BIMBO written on it in foot-high letters.

So I was entirely justified in telling Charlie, on our way to the bus stop on Saturday night, what a homophobic bitch his best friend was. It didn't help, though—I was still surfing this tsunami of rage.

It even leaked over into the phone call I made to Claire. We've rationed ourselves to one Sunday-afternoon phone call a week because we're not one of those lame couples who have to live in each other's pockets because we're too tragic to have our own lives.

But I have to say that the banner workshop, which seemed to be all Claire could talk about, isn't a particularly engrossing subject. I guess it was one of those "you just had to be there" deals. As she talked, my mind wandered all over the place, but in particular to this playback in my head of the panicked yelping sound Brie had made when I shoved her against the counter in the ladies'.

"Daze! Are you even listening to me?" Claire cut through my thoughts, exasperation giving her voice a sharp edge.

"Yeah, yeah. Sorry, just the sound of you . . . makes me realize how much I wish you were here." I tried to ignore the pang of conscience that twinged rather unpleasantly.

"I miss you, too. It's not the same without you, Daze. No one to sneak to the pub with, no one to kiss me good night."

"I should think so, too!"

"Aaron's a complete knobhead," she muttered darkly. "He

spends most of his time smoking weed and hitting on all the girls, asking them to come back to his tent so they can see his bong."

"Well, I have Shagger in my drama group," I countered. "I think I'm his project for summer. He's determined to do the dyke girl."

"I wish I'd never . . ." we both said in unison, and laughed.

"Maybe I could come down for a weekend before we get into dress rehearsals. I know we said we wouldn't get all clingy and that spending six weeks apart is a test of our commitment, but—"

"Deep breaths," Claire interrupted, laughing. "Run-on sentences are not our friends. And yeah, I know we said that, but God, what were we thinking?"

"I'll see if I can borrow Mum's car then, and I'll text you."

"Good. Well, I'd better get back to my *Weapons of Mass Destruction Suck* banner."

"Okay, love you."

"I love you, too."

And that throaty way Claire got when she was being affectionate reeled me back in so I could remember that no matter how pretty girls like Brie are, it's the pretty-on-the-inside girls like Claire that are the ones worth knowing.

Talking to Claire had calmed me down. She's like my own personal stress ball. It was a pity that my hard-won feelings of inner peace (well, as inner-peacey as I can get) only lasted up until 10:03 on Monday morning when I dumped my bag on the stage and turned around to see Charlie padding purposefully toward me with a very unwilling Brie tagging along behind him.

She was wearing another skimpy tank top and a cutoff

denim skirt that showed her gawky, pasty legs as she almost fell over her flip-flops.

"Hey, Daze, you get home all right?" Charlie said, leaning over to kiss me on the cheek. Then he grinned. "Such a stupid thing to ask, isn't it? Of course you got home all right. You'd hardly be here if you hadn't. You'd be on a slab in the morgue."

"And thank you for that lovely image." I smirked before I looked over at Brie, who was gazing at the floor and then the ceiling and then the wall. In fact, everywhere that wasn't actually me. I could feel my face settling into tight lines.

Charlie gave her this unsubtle nudge that almost threw her off her feet again. "Brie has something that she wants to say, don't you?"

"I'm sorry for the stuff I said on Saturday night," she whispered in this deadpan way like she'd memorized the entire speech. "I'd had too much to drink, but it was no reason to say things that were offensive, although I didn't realize that they were at the time." She paused and looked at Charlie, who raised his eyebrows in what I think was meant to be an encouraging way. "I need to think more about what I want to say before I say it."

She looked at her feet the whole time. It could have been that she was ashamed—more likely she was checking out her pedicure. But as she reached the last syllable, she glanced at Charlie, then turned the full weight of her limpid green stare right at me. Freeze-frame. For a second, everything seemed to slow down, and I started to imagine that there was a reason that she was so beautiful. Like this big, important reason that would make it okay to find her attractive, but then she blinked and the moment passed.

"Okay, then?" she said to neither one of us, and scurried off.

I sat down on the chair in front of me and pulled out my copy of *The Taming of the Shrew* while Charlie shuffled his feet and was obviously waiting for me to say something about the apology that Brie seemed to have spent the last hour refining.

"Well . . ." I said eventually. "That was kinda . . . well, pathetic actually. I hope she's going to play Katharina with a tad more sincerity, otherwise we're all screwed."

I expected Charlie to nod in agreement, but he tilted his head to the side and then took a deep breath.

"Spit it out, then, Charlie."

He sat down in the empty chair next to mine and then pulled it even closer so he could take my hand. "We need to have a talk about Brie," he said seriously, as if the whole weight of the world was on his shoulders. Which must be what it feels like when you're friends with someone like Brie.

"Yeah, we really do," I said, and he looked surprised, like he hadn't expected me to agree with him. But he hadn't waited for me to finish. "Because I'm still trying to puzzle out what the whole deal is between you two. Do you let her hang around you to make you seem cooler? Because if that's the case, then it's really not working."

Charlie flashed me a quick grin before he realized he was going off-message and went all furrowed brow on me.

"Look, I know she can be a bit thoughtless sometimes . . ."

I raised my eyebrows so high at this understatement that I think I strained a muscle in my forehead.

Charlie sighed. "Okay, she can be a lot thoughtless most of the time, but, Jesus, just give her a break. She's not stupid, you know."

I gave Charlie a look. Then another one. And then one

more—just for luck. He wriggled in the chair uncomfortably.

"Okay, she's not going to win any prizes for general knowledge, but she's shy and she gets awkward around . . . well, just about everyone who isn't me. Then this leads to the whole forgetting-to-think-before-she-speaks situation."

I couldn't bear seeing Charlie squirm about like he was wearing a hair shirt, too. Maybe, and it was a very big maybe, Brie wasn't entirely insensitive and lacking any redeeming qualities if Charlie could bear to be her friend.

"She should have enrolled at charm school rather than a drama group," I couldn't resist saying, then instantly regretted it as Charlie's head sank down. "Okay, okay, I'll go easy on her. But one more fat-lesbian crack and she will get the full force of my wrath."

"I thought you'd already given her that."

"Nope. That was about half the full force of my wrath."

"You're incredibly scary sometimes, you know that?"

"Aw, you say the sweetest things, Charlie."

He shot me a tiny smile and then looked up and started pulling at his T-shirt like he suddenly felt uncomfortable in his own skin.

"You all right?"

He glanced over at me as if he'd forgotten I was there. "What? No, I'm fine. Peachy."

I looked up to see what was making him act so strange, but there was nothing. Just Walker, dressed all in black—even though it was eighty degrees in the shade—strutting in like he owned the place. *Quel poseur.*

So, despite what I may lead people to think, I'm not an entirely unreasonable girl. I just play one ninety percent of the time. I watched Brie over the next few days. It wasn't hard. She's in my face all the time now that we're knee-deep in rehearsals and having to spend all our time onstage together.

Though I use those words lightly. Mostly one of us says a line, and then that's Lavinia's cue to bang her stick on the floor and start screaming at us for "having no poetry in our souls." We don't actually get much done, but sit on the floor while someone else, usually Walker I'm pleased to say, gets bawled out.

It's given me plenty of time to study Brie. Not just the way her hair falls down her back in this sleek sheet of chocolate brown or the knobs of her spine. There's other stuff. Stuff like the way she won't say anything without checking with Charlie first. And the way she ends what she says with a "right, Charlie?"

I know now that underneath the fake acrylic tips, her nails are bitten down to the quick. I've seen her in tears after eating too many Kinder Buenos because she thinks she's just gained ten pounds. And I've seen her in tears after making a tiny mistake in one of her speeches that no one else (not even Lavinia) noticed but Brie is convinced has ruined the whole performance.

It makes me hate her not so much. I'm still getting used to being in close proximity to someone who stands for all the things that I loathe, but then I'm also surprised that someone like Brie is so utterly uncomfortable in her own skin. She could be anything she wanted. Famous, rich, a bloody footballer's wife, and instead she cries and clings onto Charlie like he's going out of fashion.

The weird thing is that she's quite good. At being Katharina, that is. The hissy-fit stuff before she marries Petruchio just means that she gets to be her usual petulant self, though Lavinia keeps screeching, "More fireworks, more passion, more oomph, girl! You are incensed by the injustice of your lot in life, not sulking because you've just missed the bus."

But now we're on to the part where she's married to Petruchio and he's depriving her of sleep and food (have I mentioned lately just how much I hate this play?) and her deadpan, resigned tone is perfect. If I had gotten the part of Katharina, I think I'd have screamed my lines with all the fury of Justin from The Darkness, but Brie just rolls her eyes and sighs and generally lets it be known that Petruchio is a grade-one wanker without overplaying it. Mind you, I think that might have something to do with the fact that Petruchio is being played by Walker, who *is* a grade-one wanker.

On Monday, he spent half an hour staring at my breasts as I helped some of the lads shift scenery.

On Tuesday, he started moaning at Charlie that he hadn't had a "shag for days." Charlie, bless him, looked like one of those wide-eyed seal cubs just before it gets clubbed to death.

Wednesday was a red-letter day. He looked at my tits for twenty-three minutes in the morning, and then in the afternoon when we were rehearsing the last scene, he touched my bum! One minute I'm all "Head and butt! An hasty-witted body" (what*ever*) and trying to pay attention to Lavinia, who's badgering me to move my feet, and I back into Walker, who's looming behind me. The next thing I feel is his hand stroking across the curve of my arse so subtly that at first I thought I'd made a mistake. Then I looked over my shoulder before he'd had a chance to wipe the leer off his face.

I didn't do anything just then. Revenge is a dish best eaten cold, after all. I bided my time. I waited. And waited. I'd had a hideous day anyway. Lavinia had ordered me into an office that she'd commandeered and gave me this melodramatic lecture about my portrayal of Bianca. "Be more like Brie," she kept saying, which will happen the day that Satan turns up for work on ice skates. "Be more womanly. You keep yomping across the stage like you're marching off to war."

By the end of the day, I was in a mood so filthy that I needed to scour my soul with Ajax. I set all my phasers on stun, then went to find Walker.

He'd cornered two of the giggliest, brain-deadiest of the wannabes and was talking to them, his tongue curled behind his front teeth, in a way that he believes is irresistible to any-one with a vagina. I made my move.

His earlobe was pink and tender between my fingertips as I pinched it hard and hissed, "I want a word with you." I didn't let go, and he was forced to scrunch down into a hobble as I walked him up the stage steps, into the wings, and down into the dressing rooms. And I took my sweet time about it, too. Even though he kept up a constant sound track of "Ow!" and "My ear!" and "What are you doing, you crazy cow?"

I finally let go of his ear, which was now a fetching shade of stoplight red as he rubbed it gingerly to get the blood flow back, then I kicked the door shut.

That was his cue to give me a look that was so lecherous, it should have come with an NC-17 rating firmly attached to it.

"Couldn't wait to get me on my own, could you?" he crowed. But the funny thing was that when I invaded Walker's personal space bubble, walked him into the wall, and stayed there, he didn't like it. He twitched and cast long-ing looks toward the door and generally squirmed like he was a butterfly on glass and I'd pinned his wings back just before I went for the thorax.

"It's not much fun, is it, when someone's in your face?" I asked him conversationally. "When they're not respecting you?"

I was so close that my boobs brushed against his chest—an occupational hazard when your boobs are as big as mine—but this time he didn't smirk or gaze at them as if they were one of the eight wonders of the modern world. Instead his eyes were fixed on a point somewhere above my left shoulder, and this little tic thing was doing the samba in his cheek.

"Okay, point taken," he said in a low voice. But he wasn't getting off that lightly. Not when I had the power for once. 'Cause boys like Walker: they're all talk, no action.

Everything's fine and dandy when they want to wreak havoc with all your boundaries, but they don't much like it when you return the favor.

Walker and I both knew that he could get away. He was stronger than me, but I was a girl and it's wrong to shove or push girls. Besides, if he had tried it, I'd have knocked him into the middle of next Wednesday.

"See, I think it's time you and I had another little talk," I told him as he flattened himself into the wall a little bit more.

"Why? What do we need to have a talk about?"

"My tits and my arse and the way you can't leave either of them alone," I purred, and watched in satisfaction as color flared up in his face.

"I don't know what you're talking about."

"Yes, you do. I've told you that I'm gay. I've told you that your Neanderthal behavior is offensive and disrespectful, but you've chosen to ignore it. I'm fed up with you continually shitting on my beliefs and my lifestyle choices . . ."

"It's not like that!" Walker protested, looking bug-eyed with horror. "I was just having some fun, I didn't realize—"

"Didn't realize what? That physically assaulting me with your sweaty little paws is a criminal offense?"

"Now hold on!"

I wasn't going to hold on to *anything* of his. And I was about to continue getting medieval on his skanky arse when I heard a squeaking noise coming from the corner. Walker heard it, too, because he frowned and looked over at the same time as me, to see Brie almost obscured by the Coke machine with her hands clamped over her ears. So, I was showing Walker the error of his ways—didn't mean she had to act like she was reliving every single one of her childhood traumas.

"I didn't know you were here," I said eventually.

"I was . . . yeah . . . erm . . ." she yelped, and started scrabbling in her bag, before holding her lip gloss up triumphantly. "Gloss . . . big mirror."

I couldn't help it. I glanced at Walker, and he looked at me, then he looked at Brie, who was staring in awe at her lip gloss like she couldn't believe anything so utterly wonderful could come in such a handy-size tube, and he smirked. Mind you, I had to bite my bottom lip to stop it from quirking upward, too.

Oh God, the thought that Walker and I might be bonding over Brie's deep and frequent idiocy was too horrific to contemplate.

But now that we'd stopped snarling at each other, Brie took that as her cue to start applying her miraculous gloss with one hand while the other hand was rifling through her bag for more cosmetics. Which was kinda rude because Walker and I were in the middle of something, namely me flaying off the top layer of his skin.

Strangely, Walker seemed to agree with me. The boy must

have a death wish the size of his ego because he turned back to Brie, who was gazing at herself in the mirror now with a dreamy expression on her face.

"Hey Brie," he said casually.

"Yeah, what?"

"Don't take this the wrong way, but could you piss off?"

Yeah, right. He wanted Brie to piss off so I could carry on screaming at him? It made no sense. But Brie's little face gave the impression that she'd been diagnosed with terminal acne and needed to rush off immediately so she could commit suicide.

With shaking hands, she gathered up all the lotions and potions that had spilled out of her bag, her lips quivering like a kite on a windy day.

Then she scuttled for the door, though I'd have sauntered there with my head held high. I might even have managed a flounce. She didn't even slam it behind her; it closed with a gentle click.

I rounded on Walker, who was still slouched against the wall, cigarette clamped between his lips as he fumbled for his lighter.

I snatched the cigarette out of his mouth and stamped it under my foot. As grand gestures go, it was right up there.

"Now what?" Walker asked warily, looking in disbelief at the shredded paper and tobacco on the floor.

"How could you say that to her?" I demanded. "You hurt her feelings. I think she's probably gone off to cry somewhere." Walker seemed very underwhelmed by this news flash. Brie spent a large proportion of her every waking hour in tears after all.

"Like, you even give a toss. You can't stand her!"

"I can stand her perfectly well," I said icily because I'd just had the startling epiphany that I actually *enjoyed* being nasty and mean to Walker and that I might as well run with it while I tried to figure out what it meant. Maybe his sole purpose on this earth is to be used as my own personal punching bag because he represents everything that is inherently wrong about the male species? Or maybe he's just a wanker.

"What*ever*!" He was spluttering now. "She was creeping about and earwigging when any decent person would have let us know they were around."

"And you're embarrassed that she witnessed me treating you like the arsehole that you are?"

"Well, yeah! Where have you been, Daze? Try and keep up."

"She might not be giving Mensa any sleepless nights, but I'm sure Brie has managed to work out all by herself that you are an arrogant, sexist jerk."

There's something about Walker that brings out the queen of mean inside me. His stupid greasy hair; those big raw-boned hands and beady eyes trying to cover every inch of me. The way he looms over me all the time. He was shaking his head and smiling thinly. "Are you this much of a witch with everyone, or am I just honored?"

"It's all for you," I said smugly. "What can I say? You know how to bring out the crazed feminazi in a girl."

"Aw gee, honey, you say the sweetest things."

"Don't call me honey," I bit out, and then turned away so he couldn't see the expression on my face. I was enjoying myself far too much.

He started toward the door.

"Where do you think you're going?"

He whirled around, his eyes flashing. "To get as far away from you as humanly possible."

"Nuh-huh!" I wagged my finger at him. "We're going to go and find Brie, and then you're going to apologize for being so horrible to her."

Walker's hand was already reaching for the door handle. "Yeah, and after that I'm going to find some old ladies to help across the road."

"Cool, I'll bring my camera and some snacks," I said, following him out of the dressing room. "Now, if I was Brie, where would I have scampered off to?"

Walker arched his eyebrow and snorted. "Do I really have to answer that? And, once again, do I have to remind you that you hate her guts?"

"I don't." And as I said it, I realized that I didn't hate her. *Hate* was such a strong word. Maybe I merely despised her.

"You wanna say that once more with feeling?"

Walker was a wasp, constantly buzzing around my head and trying to sting me. Or catch me off guard. It was very wearing. I shrugged. "Okay, I haven't paid my subscription to the Brie fan club lately," I admitted as I trudged across the stage and bent down to jump off the edge. "But I promised Charlie that I'd be nice to her. Apparently she has low-self-esteem issues."

I expected Walker to have some snarky response, but he just did something complicated with his mouth that involved making his lips completely disappear and muttered: "Don't we all?"

It was a rhetorical question. I didn't bother replying. Walker continued, undaunted. "Charlie must have the patience of a saint to put up with that freak."

And before I could help myself, an "I know" popped out of me.

Walker pretended to jump in horror. "Hey! Did you just agree with me?" He peered around the corner furtively. "I hope no one caught that, otherwise your reputation would be shot."

"Yeah, well, you'd know all about that," I said sourly, but he just laughed.

We looked for Brie everywhere. In the loos—where she has a permanent spot in front of the mirror. Under the stairs—because it's her favorite place to slope off and have a cry. Even the boiler room—she's been known to go and have a weep in there, too. But she was nowhere to be found.

I contented myself by threatening Walker with the wrath of Charlie, which actually isn't that scary. I kept up a constant litany of "God, Charlie is gonna be so mad when Brie tells him what you said."

Walker tried to take it in his stride, but after we'd been searching fruitlessly, or even Brie-lessly, for half an hour, he was reduced to swearing at me.

"Sod this!" Walker moaned. We were back where we started, which was slumped on the stage. "I'm going home. Tell Charlie that he can kick my arse tomorrow." Then he collapsed on the floor with a groan that made his T-shirt ride up. I didn't like having to look at what it uncovered, which was muscle and taut skin and this tiny trickle of hair that disappeared under his belt. It was so different from the soft bellies of my girl mates. It was very male.

And also sort of inappropriate.

I stood up and brushed my dusty hands on my jeans. "I'll see you later, loser."

Walker stretched out his arms and gave me one of his patented, self-satisfied smiles. The kind that I itch to burn off his face with a blowtorch. "You know, Daze, this is just the sniping of courtship. You want me!"

"Could you be any more delusional?"

"I don't know. Could you be any more in love with me?"

I jumped off the stage with slightly less grace than I was aiming for and almost managed to lose a Birkenstock in the process, but Walker was at my heels. "I'm going your way," he said breezily. "I'll walk you to the bus stop."

"Fine. As long as that doesn't involve you touching me or looking at my breasts."

"You're no fun. Where's your sense of adventure? Oh, hang on, I know this. It's sharing a flat with your sense of humor."

"Yeah, and your sense of decency has the room upstairs." We were so busy with the snipage that it took a moment for us to realize that Our Great Brie Hunt was over. As I pulled open the double doors that led out onto the street, making sure to clip Walker in the face as I did so, there was Brie, sitting on the wall outside and sucking face with one of the skateboys from the other night.

Strangely enough, she didn't look entirely happy to see us. I turned to Walker with what I hoped was a beatific smile. "Wasn't there something you wanted to say to Brie?"

"Hey little apple blossom
what seems to be the problem
all the ones you tell your troubles to
they don't really care for you."

Walker

Daisy spun me out yesterday. Actually, she didn't just spin me out. She sucked me dry, plucked out my heart, and beat me about the head with it, and now I'm just a husk of the Walker I used to be.

God, there was no part of it that I didn't love. I walked home with her shrill voice shrieking insults still ringing in my ears and a goofy expression on my face.

Finally, I've met a girl who can beat me at my own game. It's not about fancying her because she's got big tits and her sexual orientation presents a challenge to my jaded palate. No. It's gone way beyond that.

Now I want her because she doesn't put up with any of my shit. And because she's so busy scowling that she doesn't even have the time to realize that she's prettier than she would ever want to be. If she did, she'd probably be able to take over the world. Which is quite a frightening thought, really. I mean, how dangerous could Daisy be if she got the support and funding of a few terrorist organizations behind her?

She's all around me now, so I can't think of anything but her. I'll be doing something mundane like making a cup of tea or rolling a spliff, and suddenly all I can see is her face smiling that quixotic half smile of hers, her eyes glinting with mischief, and I'll have to stop what I'm doing and take a few deep breaths.

So I'm out on the flat roof with a bottle of imported beer that I stole out of the fridge, and I'm thinking about how Daisy and I are this double act out of an old black-and-white film or something. The summer before Mum died and she was stuck in bed, she and I watched all these screwball comedies from the forties. They always had Cary Grant or Clark Gable in them and Claudette Colbert or Carole Lombard, and they'd just bitch and bite at each other right until the last frame when the screen would fade out to black and they'd be locked in this Hollywood screen kiss for the rest of eternity. *It Happened One Night* and *His Girl Friday* were Mum's favorites. Like, she could quote every single line.

I felt the damp heat of the night make my T-shirt cling to my skin and thought about how Cary Grant's character was called Walter, which sounds like Walker, without stretching the point too much. In my mind's eye, Daisy morphs into Rosalind Russell, with nipped-in waist and starlet-red lips as she husks "Walker, you're wonderful, in a loathsome sort of way" at me.

If only Lavinia had stuck to typecasting and given the part of Katharina to Daisy instead of Brie, we'd have lit up the first five rows.

I was half thinking about moving so I could get to the art-house video shop before it closed to see if they had any of those old screwball films in, when Rowan stuck his head out of the window.

"Your stepmum let me in," he said, and I grunted in response, which is my usual reaction whenever anyone mentions the Gorgon. "Whatcha doing?"

"Nothing much," I sighed. "Might go and get a couple of DVDs out. What about you? You seeing Brie, or are you giving your tongue a rest?"

Rowan climbed onto the roof and sat down next to me. "Nah! She's seeing that Charlie. If he wasn't gay, I'd be worried."

"Yeah, they're pretty tight."

"But is she, that's the million-dollar question?" Rowan mused. "I thought she'd have given it up by now."

I pulled a face. Talking about sex, especially with Rowan, always makes me feel vaguely dirty. In a really unpleasant way.

"She looks like the kind of girl not known for keeping her thong in place, if you know what I mean," Rowan continued.

"Yeah, I know exactly what you mean," I sniffed. "Subtlety and you, not really on speaking terms."

Rowan shoved me in the shoulder. "Christ, what's eating you?"

"Nothing."

"Well then. So, like, I was saying, she looks like she's a goer, like she has all the moves, but I haven't even seen her tits yet."

I grinned. "Did you ask if you could?"

"Yeah! 'Course I did!"

"See, that's probably where you're going wrong. It's that

whole subtle deal again; girls seem to prefer it. Maybe you should try it."

Rowan looked like he'd just stood downwind of a sewage truck. "Yeah, right. So, anyway, wanna go out, pick up some girls? I need to get laid."

I staggered to my feet and waited for the head rush to pass. "With fancy talk like that, how could Brie ever resist your evil charms?"

Rowan chuckled. "God knows, 'cause I sure as hell don't."

We ended up in this shitty club off Oxford Street to see this shitty band because some girl who Rowan had down as a sure thing texted him to say she was there.

The minute we paid the cover charge, the aforementioned girl was wrapped around him like poison ivy, her tongue swiping into his ear as if she hadn't had a square meal in a decade. Someone should have given them their own slot on the Discovery Channel.

I stood there at the bar, my arm wet from where I'd rested it in a puddle of beer, as they stood blocking everyone's quest to get alcohol and tried to eat each other's faces.

When he started groping her arse with one hand and giving me a thumbs-up with the other, I decided to make my excuses and find some other place to prop myself up. The wall by the Ladies' has always stood me in good stead. I gave up trying not to lean against it, even though the disco dirt was a bitch to get off cotton the next day.

I sipped my lukewarm lager and tried not to listen to the band, who seemed to think that effects pedals were there to disguise the fact that they couldn't play for shit. The lead singer was yelping like he'd been castrated within the last twenty-four hours without the benefit of an anesthetic and kept grabbing at his crotch in a very disconcerting way. In the end, I focused my attention on the constant parade of nubile girls entering and exiting the toilets.

That's where it probably doesn't make much sense. That I can be turned inside out by Daisy but still can't keep my eyes off the curve of a breast peeking out of a camisole top, the jut of aggressive hip bones above the sagging waistband of a pair of low-riders, a wet, pink tongue slicking across candy-flavored lips. I want Daisy, but I can't have her, ever, so someone else will have to do. Tonight that someone was Marta, who sauntered over to me and asked me for a light. Our hands touched as I leaned over and lit the cigarette that she held out to me. Then I straightened up and gave her a lazy smile. She smiled back. We knew this dance, the both of us.

Marta's platinum-blond pigtails glowed white in the flare of the strobes. I ran my eyes over her luminous skin and the tight, fifties waitress dress she was wearing unbuttoned right down to her black, lace bra. She stood there with her hands on her hips, offering herself to me. With cherries on top. It would have been rude to refuse.

"I'm Walker," I shouted in her ear.

"I know." She grinned. "Your reputation has gone before you. I'm Marta. We met at Sally's graduation party." Her hand rested lightly on my arm.

"Did we . . . ?" I asked because she didn't seem like the kind of girl who'd mind me asking, and I really couldn't remember.

She bumped her hip against mine in a coquettish manner. "Oh, you'd have definitely remembered if we had. I'm not the kind of girl you forget."

"That a fact?"

"Hell, yeah. So you gonna buy me a drink? A vodka and Red Bull, ta very much."

After I'd got us both a couple of drinks, I followed her to a bench under the stairwell, and she sat on my lap, her bare legs swinging as she told me about how she was going to study fashion design in Glasgow next year and about the stall she worked on in Camden on the weekend.

". . . it's all right, I guess. We make a killing from selling fake Manics T-shirts to Japanese tourists." She finished her sentence and then smiled at me.

"What?"

She peered at my face. "You've got a spot of glitter right there"—her finger brushed against the corner of my mouth—"it's beginning to bug me."

And then her finger was replaced by her lips, and as people trudged past and a couple of girls shot at passersby with water pistols, we embarked on one of those really heavy make-out sessions that you get involved in when the girl's cute and the girl that you really want is permanently unavailable.

And then you find yourself in the girls' loo, shoving pound coins into the condom machine while the cute girl waits in a cubicle and yells at you to hurry up before someone comes in.

It's like eating a bag of crisps when you're really hungry and you haven't got enough money for anything more substantial. I got the job done, she seemed to have a good time, but it was awkward and the toilet-roll holder was wedged against my back, and at one point I looked down and there were two cigarette butts floating in the toilet bowl, and for some reason, the sight of them made me want to cry.

Afterward, Marta made me go outside while she sorted herself out. I looked around for Rowan, but he was long gone. Probably he had enough sense to do the deed in the relative comfort of his own bed.

Marta came out and knocked her bag against my leg. "So . . . Walker, it's been real."

I ran my hand through my hair and wondered why I couldn't think of anything to say to her. "Yeah, real."

She was already moving toward the stairs. "I'll see you around, okay?"

"Hang on!" I caught up with her and tried to take her hand, but she snatched it away. "Look, I'll walk you to the bus stop or something."

She tugged on one of her pigtails and gave me a pitying smile. "Jeez, I didn't expect you to get all sappy on me. My friends are waiting for me; I have to go. I'm a big girl, I think I can manage the stairs on my own."

"Give me your number, maybe we can hook up or I could . . ."

Marta turned around and rapped her knuckles against my forehead, which actually kinda hurt.

"Yeah, right. You don't do dates, Walker, so I'll save you the trouble of lying and just say that I'll see you around. And, by the way, you certainly live up to that nickname of yours."

Then she patted me on the cheek and sauntered off, leaving me feeling like a little kid who's been caught stealing money out of his mum's purse. Isn't it the girl who's meant to feel used and dirty in this kind of situation?

I caught up with her just as she was greeting her little posse of cackling mates with a shimmy of her hips and a "Guess who I just got lucky with?"

"You can't be serious," I blurted out, and they all giggled.

Marta turned around and glared at me. In the unrelenting glare of the streetlights, she wasn't that hot. "Like a heart attack. Get lost!"

I got lost.

I stayed lost for most of the weekend. It's surprisingly easy. You shut the curtains and you get into bed, with the covers pulled up over your head, and you stay there, only getting up to pee and to go on lightning forays into the kitchen for food and drink when you know that the Gorgon bitch and her husband are off the premises.

And you don't think about anything. It takes a lot of concentration and even more spliff to achieve this Zen-like state where nothing matters because you cease to be anything other than the most insignificant speck of dust in the great, big living of life.

I'd just about morphed into vegetable matter and was planning on staying there when Charlie erupted into my room. I thought I was tripping, seriously tripping, because how the hell did he get in? But then the Gorgon poked her head around the door and said, "For Christ's sake, it smells like a bloody casbah in here. We've told you a million times not to smoke marijuana in the house. And would it kill you to open a window occasionally?"

I was just recovering from these mortal blows when Charlie started in on me. "I want a word with you," he said belligerently, and followed it up with a few vague jabbing motions with his index finger.

"What?" I muttered, and then hit on the genius idea of pulling my pillow over my head so I didn't have to deal with anything.

I could hear Charlie shuffling about, and then he tried tugging the pillow away from me. If he'd been a barely clad seventeen-year-old girl, it would have been fun times.

In the end Charlie gave up, and I felt the mattress give as he sat down on the bed. "We need to talk," he repeated grimly. He wasn't budging. He had a resolute tone to his voice that managed to penetrate even my THC-befuddled synapses. I emerged from the bedclothes, sat up, and reached for my cigarettes.

"Talk," I said, with an expansive hand gesture.

Charlie folded his arms and tried to look stern, but the pout ruined the overall effect. "It's about Brie," he began, and fixed me with a glare.

"I never laid a hand on her!"

"I never said you did!"

"Sorry, it's an automatic reaction, you know? Someone getting in my face about a girl because—"

"For the love of God, please don't finish that sentence," Charlie begged, looking vaguely bilious. He rubbed his hand across his face and sighed. He seemed more crumpled than normal.

"Rough night?" I asked with a grin, because really, Charlie was quite an amusing diversion from my own self-loathing and misanthropy.

"I was up half the night worrying about Brie. We had this totally weird phone call," Charlie said sourly. The prim, disapproving tone was back in his voice. "She told me that you swore at her."

"Yeah, I think the words *piss* and *off* were mentioned. You gonna kick my arse now?"

He shuddered. "Physical violence never solves anything,

and besides, if I tried, you'd probably pluck out my rib cage and make me comb my hair with it."

I shoved the pillow behind my back so I could get more comfortable. "Okay, I swore at Brie and then apologized afterward. What else have I done wrong?"

Charlie was staring at his fingernails. Then he got bored and gazed at my print of *The Death of Chatterton* by Henry Wallis above the bed. "God, that's like, the most depressing painting in the world," he muttered. "No wonder you smoke so much dope."

I glanced up at the poet sprawled out on his deathbed. "Thomas Chatterton, generally regarded as one of the first of the Romantic poets," I supplied. "He wrote these medieval poems but didn't think anyone would believe that he had because he was poor and uneducated, so he pretended that they were by this fifteenth-century priest called Sir Thomas Rowley."

"Then what happened?" Charlie was staring at me like I was the main screen at the local multiplex.

"He didn't have a patron, became depressed that he couldn't claim authorship of his own poems, and, suffering from artistic failure and starvation and, oh yeah, gonorrhea, he ended up drinking arsenic and killing himself when he was eighteen."

"No!"

"And the room in the painting? Henry Wallis went to the very attic in Grays Inn Road where Chatterton killed himself to do the painting."

Charlie's mouth was hanging open. "Get out of here! That's so sad and actually incredibly twisted. Why the hell have you got the picture hanging above your bed, you freak?"

"Chatterton was, like, the first punk, wasn't he? And I don't know, I just like the picture. He looks a bit like you actually."

"He does not!" Charlie bristled. "He's . . . scrawny, and we have entirely different coloring . . . well, a bit. I guess there's worse things to look like than a tortured poet with a dose of the clap." He fingered the end of my duvet, but his gaze kept skittering back to the painting. "Brie," he finally said. "We have to talk about Brie. Brie and Rowan. He's your friend, right?"

"We hang out, yeah."

"Okay, so you won't mind telling him to back off and stay the hell away from her." Charlie had stopped with the nervous hand gestures and was stiff-backed and rigid with fury now that he remembered why he was here.

"They're just having fun," I said cautiously.

"No, they're not!" Charlie insisted. "He's . . . I know what guys like him are . . . I don't trust him. I don't like him. He's putting pressure on her to do stuff that she doesn't want to do, and you need to get him to stop."

I got the feeling that this wasn't some high-octane drama that him and Brie had concocted because the pair of them like to think that their lives are like some particularly angst-ridden episode of *The O.C.* His shoulders were slumped now, and he kept biting his bottom lip and clenching up his fists.

But even so, it wasn't my problem. Wasn't his either, come to that.

"Brie's a big girl. It's about time she learned to take care of herself."

"Well, she can't." He rounded on me. "I look out for her, it's what I do." His eyes were glassy, and I realized that he was this close to bursting into tears.

Why couldn't the world leave me alone to not deal with my own shit instead of dragging me into everyone else's, too?

"Okay," I said reluctantly, and Charlie's head shot up, his expression hopeful. "I'll talk to Rowan. Not sure it will do any good, but I'll give it the old college try."

"Thanks." He stood up, scuffing his toe against a pile of dirty T-shirts on the floor. "Look, I'm sorry for charging in here and interrupting your . . . well, heavy schedule of sleeping and getting stoned." He reached for the door handle.

"Hey, Charlie, you wanna go out and get a few beers?" I didn't even know why I was asking, just that I was sick to death of my own company, and he seemed to be one of the few people I could bear to be around.

He thought about it, his head cocked. "Well, all I had planned was a thrilling afternoon of watching paint dry, so yeah."

He flopped down on the chair by my desk and looked at me expectantly. "Clothes might be a good thing if we're going out. And a shower. You're smelling pretty ripe."

I pulled the covers back and took a discreet whiff of my armpit. "Ripe is putting it mildly, I'm going to go for rank," I agreed, then threw out my hand to encapsulate the skanky confines of my room. "CDs, telly, cigarettes. *Mi casa es tu casa.*"

When I came back from the bathroom with a towel knotted around my waist, Charlie had put on The Strokes, opened the window, and collected all the dirty mugs and plates and cutlery into a teetering pile on the floor. "I think they were trying to establish their own ecosystem," he explained as I rifled through the clean pile of clothes on the chair, which was slightly more fragrant than the dirty pile *under* the chair.

Eventually I found some acceptable boxers and a T-shirt. "Yeah, they're sneaky like that," I said vaguely in reply, and as I dropped the towel, I glanced in the mirror to see Charlie staring at me, color rising in his cheeks before he quickly looked away and started thumbing frantically through my CDs.

"I love that album. And that one. Ugh, they suck . . ." His voice was squeaking, pitched so high that dogs from miles around were probably going into paroxysms.

I wasn't quite sure how I felt about Charlie's reaction to my body. I have a good body, despite the huge amounts of alcohol and junk food I shovel into it. A few visits to the swimming pool every week keeps it all taut. Girls like it; now it seems that boys do, too. Well, I suppose it's good to have options. Then again, maybe not.

I pulled on a pair of jeans and a T-shirt from the Cracker Trailer Park in Milwaukee that I picked up in a charity shop, then sat down on the edge of the bed to sort out my socks and boots.

Charlie was very quiet, swinging aimlessly on the chair and gazing at the ceiling. He came to with a start when I nudged his shoulder.

"C'mon, I'll get the first round in."

We decided to walk up the hill to Hampstead so we could go to this pub, which does really good Thai food. Charlie had come out of his funk and was engrossed in telling me scurrilous stories about some of the girls in the drama group.

"So she never has sex with them, but she does everything else and reckons it doesn't count," he was telling me, waggling his eyebrows. "Her parents are freaky religious types, and she's meant to stay a virgin until her wedding night."

I held the pub door open for him. "Well, that explains a lot. I thought she was just playing hard to get."

"You didn't!"

"Oh yeah. And she might be a virgin, but her mouth sure isn't." I laughed and then wondered whether it was completely appropriate to have this conversation with Charlie, who was gay and reminded me of a doomed poet who'd committed suicide in a garret.

He didn't seem too bothered, though. "And Marissa had her belly button pierced, and it was still all gunky when she pulled this guy, stayed the night, and when she woke up in the morning, all the pus had stuck to his sheets and she couldn't get loose."

I propped my elbows on the bar. "How come you know all this stuff?"

He shrugged. "It's a gay thing. Automatically girls expect me to act like Graham Norton, go shoe shopping with them, and act as confessor for their gruesome sexual secrets." His mouth twisted into a sour smile. "It's stupid. Just because I fancy boys, I'm expected to come with this complete list of gay interests. I hate Kylie. I wouldn't be seen dead in leather trousers, and I have absolutely no desire to get myself up in drag."

I ordered two pints of Stella, grabbed a menu, and followed Charlie out to the beer garden. It was late afternoon by now, but it was still fiercely hot. Charlie had pulled a tube of sunblock out of his pocket and was smothering his face in it.

"It's Brie's negative influence," he confessed. "And really not wanting to get skin cancer."

We worked our way through several pints and two huge bowls of Pad Thai and talked. About stuff that wasn't girls.

Like the films of John Waters, indie guitar bands of the late eighties, monster trucks, and alternate realities all got covered off, and I was buzzed from the alcohol and that special glow you get when you connect with someone new.

Charlie was fun people, and when he'd gone in to get another round, I ignored the two girls on the other side of the garden who'd been eyeing me up, because if I went over to talk to them, then I wouldn't be able to carry on debating the plot holes in every single series of *Alias* with Charlie.

But when he came back with two more pints and a packet of peanuts clamped between his teeth, the two girls got up and sauntered over. Actually they were more women than girls and old enough to know way better than to hit on boys at least a decade younger than them.

"Hey," the first one said. "Mind if we join you?"

Charlie placed the glasses on the table and looked at me uncertainly.

I looked at her and her friend. It wasn't like either of them were my type anyway.

"Sorry," I said. "But you're wasting your time."

Charlie sighed in relief. "I'm gay, and he's—"

"My boyfriend," I finished for him and slipped my arm around his shoulders, which immediately tensed up. "And we're having a drink after being separated all summer."

"Because I'm a marine biologist, and I've been communicating with dolphins in the Cayman Islands."

"And I missed you," I cooed, and landed a sloppy kiss on Charlie's cheek, which he immediately wiped off with the flat of his hand.

"Oh well, can't blame a girl for trying," the second one said, and hauled up her bustier to hide the bony gulch that was her cleavage.

"Better luck next time," Charlie called after them as they tottered back to their table, then wagged his finger at me. "Well, you're pretty secure in your sexuality, aren't you?"

"Are you mad at me?"

"No, just not many guys would out themselves when they didn't need to." Charlie reached across the table and snagged his lighter. "But thanks for, well . . . not abandoning me for the two old dears."

He was hunched over and fiddling with anything he could get his hands on. The cigarettes, the lighter, the beer mat, drawing patterns in the condensation on his glass. In short, he was quietly freaking out about something. I racked my brains for some unknown way in which I'd violated the beginnings of our friendship.

"It's nothing you've done," Charlie said quietly, even though I hadn't asked. "It's me and my dumb-arse problem."

And then I knew what his dumb-arse problem was, didn't even need to ask, but it seemed like the right thing to do. "What dumb-arse problem is that, then?"

Underneath the lightweight exterior, he's got balls of steel has Charlie. Kinda one of the reasons why I like him. He took a deep breath. "I fancy you. And I know you're straight. After Brie, you're like the straightest person I know. I thought I should tell you because it'll get awkward if I don't. Or more awkward than it currently feels at this precise moment."

He stood up and started gathering his stuff together.

I put my hand on his arm, and he flinched away as if I'd hit him.

"Charlie! Where are you going?"

"Home," he said in a "Duh! Where have you been?" voice.

"What? Just because you had the stones to admit that you fancy me?"

"Well, yeah!" He scrunched up his face like it was all too confusing for words.

"Oh, don't be such a wanker," I said, and tugged on his T-shirt. "Sit down and stop getting bent out of shape about it."

"Did you have to use the word *bent*?" He pouted, but he was sitting back down.

"Shit! I'm sorry. I didn't mean . . ."

Charlie smiled into his glass. "I was joking. God, you straight boys are so touchy."

We didn't say anything for a while, but Charlie turned and peered at me. "So . . . you okay with it? It doesn't mean I'm going to jump your bones or anything." He sounded wistful.

"Yeah. I kinda knew, anyway. I am pretty damn hot, after all." Which wasn't what I wanted to say, but Charlie seemed grateful.

"I always think it's best to get these things out in the open," he said solemnly.

"Good policy. Look, if I was gay, I'd probably go for you—"

Charlie put his head in his hands. "Oh God, no. Stop," he hissed. "Please don't say another word."

"I mean, you have that whole Thomas Chatterton thing going on, and your hands . . ."

He held his hands up and looked at them wonderingly. "What about my hands?"

"Charlie. We're gonna be mates, right? I always take the piss out of my mates, so you'd better get used to it."

"O . . . kay. You're very strange, anyone ever tell you that?"

I clinked my glass against Charlie's. "All the time."

"I guess you're used to people fancying you," Charlie continued, leaning unsteadily back on the bench and then realizing that he was going to fall over if he leaned any farther.

. . .

We'd been drinking for four hours straight, and my teeth had gone numb, which was usually a prelude to being really drunk. And now I was drunk enough to just blurt it out loud for the first time. Just to get used to how the words sounded. "I think I'm in love with Daisy."

Charlie was scandalized. "No! But she's *gay*, Walker! If Brie is the straightest person I know, then Daisy is the gayest one. She's like the poster girl for being gay."

"Yeah, I got that, ta very much," I said morosely. The whole concept of maybe being in love with Daisy hadn't sounded any less stupid for actually trying it out on someone else.

"She is *so* gay," Charlie kept muttering. "Boy, could she be any more gay. Gay, gay, gay! What part of that is giving you the problem?"

"Yeah, but I'm straight, but you still fancy me," I pointed out, and Charlie nodded glumly.

"And I'm gay, and Brie claims to be so madly in love with me that it's spoiled her for all other men. Let's not even go there," he added hastily when I opened my mouth to question that statement.

"See, there you go," I said. "It's all just labels and bullshit. It's the person you end up wanting, not what they say they are or aren't. You should know that."

"So, does she fancy you? Do you want to sleep with her?"

"No, I want to sleep *on* her. She's so soft."

"She's so going to send you to hell without a return ticket," Charlie said tartly, and then giggled. "And when that day comes, I'd like to have a front-row seat, please."

*"I'll take the best of your bad moods
and dress them up to make a better you."*

Brie

I must have eight hours of sleep a night. Nine hours would be better. Ten hours would be excellent.

'Cause sleep is like the best beauty product in the world. Seriously! It improves the condition of your skin and hair and stuff. Which is why I'm walking around looking like the girl version of that hunchback guy who lived in the cathedral in Paris. I'm scraping by on six hours of sleep a night because of this stupid play.

I'm sitting here with my Eve Lom Rescue Mask slowly drying up and trying not to pick at it because it's kinda itchy. I only do a face mask on a Sunday 'cause it makes my face go all blotchy afterward, and I never go out on a Sunday night anyway. I usually just hang out with Charlie, but instead I agreed to babysit Henry, which is actually really decent of me. Because I'd have much rather been with Charlie, and in the end he had to go drinking with Walker or Wanker as I call him (in my head), and no one would want to spend any time with Wanker unless he really was the last person in the world.

So I'm looking after Henry because he's been blacklisted by every babysitter in our 'hood, and I didn't even ask for more than twenty quid for doing it, even though he's an evil little sod. Not like Mum's bothered. She thinks the sun shines out of his arse. And I have a lot of stuff to think about, so I've shoved him in front of *Kill Bill* after he promised not to tell and I checked to make sure he didn't have his fingers crossed behind his back the whole time. Henry's pretty violent himself, so it's not like seeing a bit of blood and guts is going to make much difference.

I could hear the sounds of lots of fighting from the living room as I flicked through *The Shrew*. I knew most of my lines now, but just thinking about saying them out loud gave me this icky feeling. No one else was acting like it was a big deal. I think the rest of the group just turn up to socialize and stuff, but I've got the lead role! I'm the shrew, which is a whole other reason why I have severe anxiety and sleepless nights, which in turn leads to dark shadows under my eyes and really dry skin. I'm getting through truckloads of Elizabeth Arden Eight Hour Cream at the moment.

It was all very well Charlie running his mouth off to everyone about how I'm an idiot savant (I looked it up in the dictionary, and I'm still ticked off about the *idiot* part) when it comes to learning my lines, but what if they disappeared out of my brain as mysteriously as they got in there? Then what? It was going to be me stuck on the stage in some completely unflattering costume (I've told Lavinia that maroon does nothing for my skin tone, but she ignored me) getting laughed at. Like my nightmare *Pop Idol,* except worse this time: I walk out onstage wearing Scooby-Doo knickers, and Simon Cowell tells me that he really liked me and thought I had star quality until he saw my cellulite.

Apart from that, I don't get Katharina. She's so angry about everything, like her PMS is less pre and more all the freaking time. She's so negative, and I don't think that's a good place for me to be right now. In fact, it's hard to see what her childhood trauma is.

I'd washed off the face mask and was just painting my nails when Henry ran in and hurled himself at me, which sent my very expensive bottle of Hard Candy in Retro flying all over the bathroom floor. Turned out that there were assassins getting their arms hacked off, and it was too much even for him. But did I yell about the fact that there was glittery pink nail polish all over the place? No. Instead I sat him down and gave him a huge bowl of Ben & Jerry's Chocolate Chip Cookie Dough ice cream with McVitie's chocolate digestives crumbled into it, even though Henry's sugar highs can get pretty ugly.

And five minutes later, the little git is running around the house, shrieking, "Brie smells of wee" and whacking me with *my* flip-flops, just as Mum and Dad come back.

Of course Henry ratted me out because I've already covered the part where he's an evil little bastard, but all that Mum did when she came into the kitchen just in time to see me put one spoonful of Chocolate Chip Cookie Dough ice cream in my mouth—not even a spoonful but maybe half of one—was to click her tongue in disapproval.

Then she took the spoon from me and said, "You'll get fat, darling, and then no one will want you."

And Dad was standing right behind her, but he didn't say anything because he never does. It's like he's not even here most of the time. He's just this guy who lives here and pays the bills.

When I was little, me and Dad were close. I'd stand on the windowsill waiting for him to come home from work every day, and as soon as I saw him unlatch the gate and walk down the garden path, I'd run to the front door, and when he got in, he'd put down his briefcase and pick me up and throw me in the air, till Mum came out of the kitchen and told him to stop it before I was sick.

I don't know when he stopped loving me. Or why.

Anyway, to go back to what Mum said before, it's not true. 'Cause someone *does* want me. Rowan wants me. Which is why when he phoned five minutes later and asked if I wanted to come over, I said yes. I think the fact that I was prepared to let him see me with post-extraction facial blemishes was very girlfriendly behavior.

After Rowan picked me up in his Jeep, we drove to the liquor store to get some Bacardi Breezers, and then we went back to his house. What I really wanted to do was maybe go up to the Heath and have a moonlight stroll because it would be romantic and stuff. But Rowan said that he wanted to show me something.

Turned out the something was this bong he'd made out of an empty Coke bottle, which wasn't all that exciting, especially as I would never smoke dope because it's a gateway drug, and then you become a heroin addict. And also smoking gives you little tiny lines around your mouth.

I know it sounds paranoid, but I wondered whether the

bong was just an excuse to get me in his room. I never realized having a boyfriend would mean so much kissing. I thought there'd be more present-buying and hand-holding.

I perched on the edge of Rowan's bed while he showed me how amazing his new bong was.

"I completely modified the water levels in it," he said while I tried not to look at the half-eaten apple wedged into a skanky coffee mug on his bedside table.

"Cool," I said, to show that I was being supportive, and then Rowan looked at me, like up and down and side to side in a way that didn't make me feel very comfortable, and then he crawled across the carpet to me.

He put his hands on my knees and kissed me. Well, actually, he did what he always does, which is kiss me four times on the mouth, and then he puts his tongue in. Like, there's some unwritten rule that boys have passed down that four kisses are a suitable number of kisses before the tongue stuff happens.

He did that for a while and tried to get me to lie down, but I was determined stay upright. Sometime during all this tussling, he took his T-shirt off, and I ran my hands up and down his back in what I hoped was a seductive but not slutty way. Why? Then he tried to get me to touch his nipples. I'm not sure why exactly.

But that was better than him trying to touch mine. So far, I've let him have a feel over the clothes, but he's not going under them. Like, ever. I'm pretty sure he knows that I have those chicken-fillet things stuffed into my bra anyway. But I'm certainly not letting him know for real.

Also he didn't shut up the whole time that he was doing stuff to me. "You're so hot. You make me feel really horny. Just touch it. Just move your hand down. Please, baby. Uh, uh, uh. Oh. Come on."

We'd been at it for about half an hour, and he'd managed to get me flat on my back and was grinding against me, until I was thinking that maybe he'd worn down my hip bones to a fine powder, when my mobile started beeping. I'd been expecting a call from Charlie, so I made Rowan get off me so I could answer it.

It *was* Charlie. He wanted to know if I had his copy of this dumb book of his, which was just stupid because he knows I don't read books.

"You sound weird," he said. Rowan was sitting on the end of the bed, huffing slightly and not looking very happy.

"I kind of can't talk right now," I whispered, even though Rowan could hear me.

"Why? Where are you? Are you with him?"

"Um, yeah."

"Oh my God! Are you doing something, Brie? What the hell are you doing?"

"Charlie! Don't."

"You're not sleeping with him, are you? You'd have told me, right? Because we should talk about this stuff."

"Can we just not? Please, Charlie."

"Are you sure you're okay? Your voice is all scratchy. Is he there?"

"Well, yeah."

"Do you want me to come round and get you? Because I will, if you need me to."

"I have to go now. I'll call you later."

When I got off the phone, Rowan crawled up the bed, and he was breathing really heavily and was all flushed, so I asked him what the matter was.

"You know what the matter is," he panted, and tried to shove his hand up my top.

I pulled his hand away. "No, I don't. Are you okay, 'cause you're, like, looking feverish."

Then I was still holding his hand, and he kinda grabbed it and put it on his *thing* and it was hard, which actually explained what had been digging into me the last few evenings (I thought it was his keys).

"Just stroke it," he begged, but I was all like, *ewwww*. It was a bit of a cheek really 'cause I've known him about a week, and I don't think that's the right amount of time to know someone before you start getting friendly with their bits.

"But why are you all red and stuff?" I asked him as he licked my neck, and I squirmed away because I didn't want him to give me a love bite.

"Are you kidding me? It's because you got me all worked up and hard," he husked in my ear. "Don't play innocent with me."

"I'm not," I protested. He looked really pissed off. "Could we . . . maybe . . . do you want to cuddle me?"

Rowan thought about it for maybe two seconds. "You know, you should probably go home now. You're looking really tired."

I patted my face with my fingertips. My skin did feel quite tight after the face mask. But not enough to get dumped over.

"Are you mad at me? Do I look rough?"

Rowan didn't say anything, he just scooped up the keys to the Jeep and jangled them in my face. "I'll drive you to the bus stop," he said.

I had to wait ages for the bus, which sucked because it meant I had to think about stuff because Charlie had the iPod. I just didn't understand why everything had to be so complicated. Why couldn't I just have a boyfriend who took me nice places and bought me jewelry from Tiffany? Not this . . . it being all about sex.

Just the thought of someone looking at me without my clothes on makes me want to puke. Besides, a guy telling you that you make him "really horny" doesn't exactly mean that he's into you. It makes me wonder what other girls do with their boyfriends.

Like, if I was going out with Charlie, which I'm not BECAUSE HE'S GAY (so freaking bored of that subject, by the way), I think he'd treat me really nicely. Yeah, there would be presents involved, but he'd talk to me about what I did that day or where I wanted to go on the weekend, or he'd tell me that he was feeling down. I'm no good at expressing this stuff, but you know, if it was Charlie, a NOT GAY Charlie, we'd have this connection. We'd be close in a way that wasn't groiny. And then maybe I'd feel more comfortable about at least taking my top off.

The other thing about Rowan is that he thinks I'm kind of experienced. I s'pose it's my fault 'cause I told him I'd had boyfriends before. Not loads because I didn't want him to think I was a slapper but a few so he didn't think I was some kind of unattractive freak.

And automatically if you've had a boyfriend, it means that you've had sex. And like, if you wear clothes that show a teeny amount of flesh, you've had sex. And if you're a girl and you're seventeen and you look like I do, then you've had sex.

That's what Rowan seems to think anyway. Which gets him all narked because I'm not having sex with him.

But at least now I've got a boyfriend, so I guess I shouldn't really complain. And Mum thinks it's wonderful 'cause "you've finally found someone to go out with you."

I just didn't think it would be like this is all.

The next morning when Charlie came to pick me up, I wondered whether I should talk to him about it. But he was in a really bad mood. Or he was hungover because he'd gone out with Wanker in the end and, like, the only way to deal with him is to get drunk.

But Charlie was being all weird. Like, how he was when he phoned. I don't think he likes Rowan much, which is really annoying 'cause Charlie used to spend all his time moaning at how clingy I was and that I didn't make any effort to be friends with other people because I relied on him too much, and now he's doing my head in because he's all about how I don't have any time for him.

So we're on the bus and I'm trying to blend the Touche Éclat in around my eyes when he asks me what I'm doing tonight.

"I dunno. Probably seeing Rowan, why?"

"Why do you have to see him every night? Are you attached by some umbilical cord that I can't actually see?"

"He's my boyfriend, isn't he? So I have to spend time with him."

"I always knew you'd be one of those girls who dumped all her mates the moment some lanky-arsed git came on the scene."

And then he swiveled around to stare out of the bus window and wouldn't talk to me.

Charlie carried on sulking for another ten minutes, even when we got off the bus. I didn't really mind 'cause he was pouting, and it made his cheekbones look even sharper and his bottom lip more kissable than normal. I made sure to brush against him as we walked along so maybe people who passed us would think that we were going out, even though he was wearing his MORE QUEER THAN YOU T-shirt. I don't think he liked me doing that 'cause he started walking really fast, and I couldn't catch up because I had blisters from wearing my new kitten heels the night before.

When we got to the Arts Centre, him *still* not speaking to me and stomping on ahead, Walker popped up like a greasy bad fairy, and they did this lame hand-slapping thing like they were a pair of homies from South Central instead of North London.

Then Walker realized that I actually existed, and he curled the top bit of his lip up while he looked me up and down, before turning away with his really irritating smirk. I wished he would just get run over by a bus and have to spend the rest of his life in constant and agonizing pain. Or possibly just die.

At least things started going my way once we began rehearsals five minutes later. 'Cause Lavinia isn't intimidated by Walker. Not one little bit. In fact, she spends all her time screaming at him about how crap he is. It's great!

"You have no soul," she yelled in her posh voice after ten minutes of him muttering his lines. "You're the descendant of a long line of exalted actors who've played this role, not an extra from an end-of-pier summer extravaganza."

I caught Daisy's eye and she was grinning, and I ended up grinning back, which was odd. But then Walker threw his book down on the stage and pointed at me.

"It's her! She's stepping on all my cues, and she doesn't

give me anything! How am I meant to sodding emote when she's standing there like a block of freaking wood?"

Lavinia went berserk. "How dare you use that language in front of me? Get out! Now! And come back when you're ready to apologize to me, and to Brie."

Walker stormed out and slammed the door behind him. Then Charlie muttered something and scurried out after him. I don't know what he said, but I have a feeling that he didn't defend me like he should have. Anyway Walker came back after fifteen minutes, stinking of pot, and apologized to Lavinia.

"I'm very sorry," he smarmed. "You know what I'm like. Would you like me to write out 'I must try harder' one hundred times, because I will."

Lavinia is such a lightweight. When he kissed her hand she started cooing and ducking her head, then tapped him on his chest and told him to get back on his spot.

I waited for my apology, too, but it never came. Daisy looked at me again, nodded in the direction of Walker, and rolled her eyes.

So after we'd finished working on that morning's scene and Charlie had toddled off after Walker without even asking me if I wanted to go to lunch, I found myself walking out with Daisy.

She was ranting on about what an arsehole Walker is, and I was totally agreeing. 'Cause he totally is. Then she stopped in her tracks so suddenly that I banged into her.

"Hang on a second," she said. "Are we actually on the same page here?"

"Well, yeah," I said. 'Cause we were.

She gave me a sly smile. "We might want to watch all this bonding. Could get weird."

Daisy *is* weird. But she's a girl. Sort of. And I really needed to get a girl's opinion on things, even though she probably isn't the best person to ask on account of her being a lesbian. Jesus! When did everybody go gay?

Also Daisy is really angry all the time. Just like Katharina, so I figure if I spend time with her I can work on what Lavinia calls my motivation.

Daisy wanted to get some noodles, so we went to Wagamama's. I'm definitely not doing carbs this week, but I ordered a salad and some miso soup because otherwise she gets pissed at me for not eating.

Luckily we had Walker to bitch about, or it would have gotten awkward. She really hates him, and she kept going on and on about how he'd told me to piss off the other day.

"Yeah, like I was really bothered," I spluttered into my soup.

"But I thought you were really upset."

"Huh? No!" I insisted. "I was stressed out 'cause I was about to meet Rowan and my hair looked like shit, and you two were being angry and it makes my tummy hurt when I hear people rowing."

"Oh," she said, through a mouthful of ramen. "Oh. I gave him a really hard time about it, too. Never mind; it was fun."

"He's a dickhead."

We didn't say anything for a while, but we were eating our lunch, so that was okay, but then we finished and I decided that there was no one else to talk to about this, so she'd have to do.

"Can I ask you something?"

Daisy looked up from her empty bowl. "Is this anything to do with me being gay?"

She's *so* weird. "No."

"Right, well, go for it, then."

I put back my shoulders and took a deep breath. "Do you think I should have sex with Rowan?"

Daisy, like, spat out her noodles all over the table, which was so gross. I don't think she's really down with the whole straight-people-having-sex thing.

"What?"

I waved a hand in the air. "Look, just forget I said anything, all right? You're totally not the person to ask about this stuff."

Well, then she gets all narked because she thinks she's really good at giving advice because she's a lesbian, and they're meant to be all supportive and stuff.

So I tell her about what's going on with Rowan and what's not going on with Rowan, and how he'd like there to be loads more going on but I'm not sure.

She listened to me talk and she didn't interrupt me, which was good, and when I got to the end, she didn't say anything for a while. She just pressed her hands together and looked at me over the top of them.

"So what do you think I should do, then? Shall I just get drunk and shag him, to get it over with?"

"God, no! Brie! That's the king of bad ideas." Then she reached across the table and patted my arm. "I'm not saying you have to be madly in love, but you should have sex with someone that you care about. Do you care about Rowan?" I wrinkled up my face as I thought about it. Rowan's okay. I don't want anything bad to happen to him, and I'd be really upset if it did, but that's as far as it goes.

"Well, I don't *not* care about him," I admitted. "He's all right, I suppose."

Daisy huffed and puffed, then she folded her arms. "Your first time should be special, and it should be with someone who means more to you than that."

For some reason when she said that, it made me want to cry. I got up and took out my purse to sort out the bill. "I'm going to die a virgin," I said almost under my breath, but Daisy heard me and shook her head.

"Don't be silly. 'Course you won't."

"Well, unless Charlie really does wake up straight one day," I added.

God, that was a stupid thing to say 'cause it just set her off. "You don't just wake up one day and choose a sexual preference," she began, and I tuned out.

"Predetermined . . . blah blah . . . nature not nurture . . . blah blah . . . gender identity . . . blah blah . . ."

She was still banging on as we started walking back to the Arts Centre, and I noticed that she does this thing when she gets mad (which would be, like, ninety-five percent of the time) where she shakes her head, like she can't believe that everyone but her can be so stupid. I'm going to use that. And the whole hand-wringing thing she does.

All I had to do to keep her happy was go "yeah?" and "right" occasionally, and she didn't even notice that I was thinking about more important things. Like, what I was going to wear tonight.

Then she said something that pulled me right away from my totally adorable pink, strapless dress.

"What?" I shrieked.

"Could you not perforate my eardrum, please."

"What the hell was that you just said?" I yelled again.

Daisy gave me a withering look. "I said that Charlie fancies

Walker," she said like I was some thicko who had to be spoken to really slowly. "I mean, *quel* obvious."

"No, he doesn't," I snarled. "Charlie doesn't fancy anyone. He doesn't have sexy feelings."

Daisy snorted and stamped her foot. "You're just being anti-gay again."

I started walking really fast, because I was going to punch her in a minute. "No, I'm being anti-Charlie fancying Walker, who's straight. It doesn't make any sense! Why would he fancy someone who's straight? He's only going to fancy other gay guys, isn't he? And he would never, ever fancy Walker because he's the world's biggest wanker."

Daisy screeched to a halt and grabbed me by my arm. I was going to have bruises tomorrow. She was such a bully. She was all red and panting, kinda like Rowan gets when he has an . . . when his *thing* gets all hard. "So what are you saying? That gay people shouldn't kiss straight people?"

I made a big show of rubbing my arm. "I guess, yeah." I took a step backward 'cause Daisy was pretty mad, and possibly violent, but she was already curling her hands around my shoulder so she could yank me closer and then . . . and then . . . and then . . . *she kissed me!*

No joke! She mashed her mouth against mine. I struggled to get away, but then she cupped the back of my head and she stopped clashing her teeth against mine, and instead her lips were, well, it's kind of hard to say really. I was freaking out, and we were standing in the middle of the High Street, and it was so not what I was expecting.

Like, it's a lot softer than when you kiss a guy. There's no stubble and hard bits against your face. It's just all soft. She tasted of lime and chilis, which was distracting, and her fingers were stroking my hair and . . . when I opened my mouth to tell her to cut it out because I wasn't a lesbian and she was so out of order, Daisy didn't just shove her tongue down my throat like Rowan does. She didn't put it anywhere near me. I didn't kiss her back. I mean, I don't think I did. It's hard to say, really.

I managed to wriggle away. Then I wiped the back of my hand across my mouth. And she just stood there with this smug smile pasted onto her face.

"What was that you were saying? Something about gay people not kissing straight people?" she demanded.

"I can't believe you just did that!" I squawked. "You kissed me! I'm not gay!"

"I know," Daisy said. "But the thing is, my mouth didn't know whether your mouth was gay or straight."

"What the hell are you going on about? You just kissed me!"

"Oh, grow up, Brie." Daisy's smile suddenly fell off her face, so she was back to her usual scowly self. "If you're worried that my gayness is catching, maybe you should go and get some mouthwash on the way back."

Then she stomped off and I went to the news agent and bought a Diet Coke and some of those fresh-breath strips so I could get the taste out of my mouth.

At least I'd decided something, which is really good 'cause usually I'm not good at making my mind up. What I decided was that kissing girls is wrong, and I need to have sex with a boy as soon as possible. If not sooner.

"I'm starting to fashion an idea in my head
where I would impress you
with every single word I said."

 # Charlie

It's finally happened. Brie has inhaled so many fake-tan fumes that she's gone insane. Bonkers. Stark, raving, out-of-her-tree, get-her-a-straitjacket, monkey-shagging mad. What other explanation can there be? Ergo (and I would only use the word *ergo* in the most desperate of circumstances), she has gone mad.

She was in a strange mood, even for her, when she got back from lunch. She was clutching a packet of breath strips like it was a limited-edition Christian Dior necklace. Now, any fool knows that you're meant to let one dissolve on your tongue to get rid of any possible halitosis. Well, Brie necked the whole lot in one go, which could explain the really sour expression on her face for the rest of the afternoon.

What else did she do that was freaksome in the extreme? Well, she has this scene in the play with Daisy where they're meant to be having this big argument, which calls on Brie to hit Daisy. Let's just say that Brie went totally Method on Daisy's arse. Instead of squeaking like a slightly pissed-off mouse, as is her wont, Brie was shouting and yelling and "Minion, thou liest"ing all over the shop while even Lavinia stood there, her mouth dropping floorward like the rest of us. And then when we got to the part where Katharina had to strike Bianca, Daisy took one look at the unhinged expression on Brie's face as she advanced toward her with murder in her eyes and hid behind the pimply kid who's playing Grumio.

"I'm going to hit you now," Brie snarled. "I'm allowed to, it says so!" Lavinia had to bang her stick on the floor and get Brie to work quietly on her motivation in a room all by herself where she couldn't attack anyone.

I had been hoping to go out with Walker afterward because that's what I usually hope these days, but Brie got there first; standing there, glaring at Walker, and bodily preventing me from taking so much as a teeny, tiny step in his direction.

"Charlie, I'm coming home with you," she announced decisively in a very un-Brie-like tone. "I have to talk to you about something."

Somehow I managed to contain my frustration as I shrugged my shoulders and gave Walker a "my best friend's a complete freak show but I have to humor her" smile, but he was already slipping on his leather jacket even though we were in the middle of a sticky heat wave.

"Later," he said, and then he was gone, and really, sometimes I could quite happily strangle Brie.

There was more bizarre behavior on the bus. She kept muttering under her breath and manically reapplying her lip gloss. Actually, scratch that—she does that every day. I should really just cut to the chase. Just like she did when we got back to my house, dumped our bags, and before I could even open the fridge to get her a can of Diet Coke, she came right out with it.

"I want you to have sex with me." She said it like she'd say, "I want you to go to Top Shop with me." Or "I want you to give me a back rub." Or "I want you to paint my toenails."

I actually dropped the can of soda that I'd just grabbed and watched it roll under the table.

"Well, what do you think?" she asked, tapping her foot and trying to behave like this was a regular occurrence. The asking for the sex, not the foot tapping. "Will you do it?"

"No, I will not freaking do it and when did you go insane?" were the words that came hurtling out of my mouth with all the velocity of a speeding train.

Brie calmly retrieved the can, washed it off in the sink— because she's completely germ phobic—then popped the top. "*Daisy* thinks it's a good idea," she said, and took a long drink while staring out of the window into the garden so she couldn't see me gazing longingly at the knives in the sharpening block.

"Well, maybe Daisy's gone mentalist, too," I offered. "Brie, I mean, what the hell are you on?"

She turned away from the window and leaned back against the drain board. "I know it sounds kinda funny, but it makes sense, if you think about it."

Have I mentioned that Brie's logic does not in any way resemble our earth logic?

"Okay, like I haven't said this a gazillion times before—"

"I know you're gay or whatever," she snapped. "But look, Charlie, my first time should be special and with someone I care about, and well, that's you."

For a second, a mere millisecond, the sincerity in her eyes and the catch in her voice moved me, touched me, and for a fraction of a second, I did consider it. And then I realized that the kitchen was only big enough to hold one loony, and that was her.

So, instead of sitting down and reasoning with her like she actually had a working brain cell, I did what anyone would do when they have to put up with Brie on a daily basis. I lost it. I said things, shouted them at top volume if I'm honest, that really I shouldn't have said.

"I'm gay! Not *whatever*, gay!" I screamed so loudly and fiercely that tiny bits of spit came flying out of my mouth and landed on the countertop. "That means that I'm not going to have sex with you. Ever. It means I'm not your boyfriend. It means I don't want to be. And—news flash, sweetheart—even if I *was* straight I wouldn't go out with you, not if you were the last girl on earth."

The color drained out of Brie's face as if she had a contrast button that had suddenly been turned down. She slammed the can of Diet Coke down on the side and opened her mouth, but I hadn't finished. Hadn't even started.

"I don't know why we do this!" I spat. "What is the point of being friends with someone like you? I get nothing out of this arrangement whatsoever, and it just seems like you're hanging on for the mythical day when I turn straight, and, like I just said, you'd be the last girl I'd ever want to fuck if that happened."

I didn't mean a good half of it. I just get so tired of the fact that she won't deal with me being gay. *I* find it hard enough to deal with, but to have this constant battle with the one person who should accept me no matter what—it's exhausting.

But Brie . . . well, she just stood there and looked at me. Then she walked toward me, and I stepped back because there was something so utterly broken about her that I couldn't bear it. Plus she'd already exhibited violent tendencies once today. But she just carried on walking past me in a cloud of hurt and Anna Sui Sweet Dreams, and then I heard the gentle click of the front door as she closed it behind her. I didn't go after her. There didn't seem much point.

And now for the first time in living memory, Brie and I aren't speaking. Not *not speaking* in the way that she's annoyed the hell out of me and I screen her calls for a few hours until I've judged that she's suitably repentant. *She's* not talking to *me*.

She won't take my calls or my texts. The next morning I went around to pick her up, and Linda came to the door and told me that she'd already left.

"I told you she wouldn't wait around forever, Charlie," she said with grim satisfaction. "Got herself a proper boyfriend now, hasn't she?"

And when I cornered Brie by the drinks machine when I got to the Arts Centre, she just stood there with her arms folded and her head hanging down so she wouldn't have to meet my eyes.

"Look, I'm sorry," I said. (And, hello! Since when did I apologize to her?) "I said stuff but you said stuff . . ."

"Fine, whatever," she muttered.

"So we're cool?" Because it seemed like we were a million miles from cool.

She wouldn't answer me. She just wouldn't answer me!

"You're not still mad at me?" I asked incredulously. "C'mon, we have fights all the time."

"Not like that we don't," she said eventually, and then she brushed past me and she was gone.

But whatever. I have Daisy and Walker to hang out with now, so I forbear. And thankfully neither one of them is particularly interested in what went down with me and Brie. Daisy says that Brie is a homophobic hypocrite, and Walker's just amused by the whole thing. Oh, he's so terribly amused all the time, and it makes me feel unbearably excited. Like my new role in life is solely to be there to amuse Walker.

These little sidelong glances he throws me and the upward quirk of his lips when I say something funny (which is practically all the time because, hey, I'm a funny guy) have become as necessary to me as oxygen and Prawn Cocktail Skips.

I thought things might change and get all kinds of awkward between us after my big confession, but they haven't. What has happened is something I would never have predicted: he flirts with me. I don't think he even realizes it—it's an involuntary reaction to someone fancying him. He calls me Charlie-boy in that mocking drawl of his, and he touches me way too much for the good of my heart; a casual arm around my shoulders or a cuff on the cheek if I'm snarking at him. Even, oh God, hair ruffles and, double oh God, this little nudging thing that he does with his hips against mine.

The result of all this touching? I'm so in love with him. I can't think straight, not that *that* would ever happen. It's not exactly the happiest, most snuggliest feeling in the world— probably because every second that I spend with Walker becomes more and more fraught with sexual tension.

No danger of that with Daisy! Nah, my biggest problem with Daisy is that I can't understand half the stuff that comes out of her mouth. We talk sometimes about being gay, which is cool, but for her it's this big, political statement like being a member of the Socialist Workers Party, and for me it's just something I am.

So, this whole Brie-less business has worked out okay. I have Walker (I wish) and Daisy and separately they're a delight, but put them together and I need earplugs and a stun gun and a butterfly net.

This afternoon they had a humdinger of a row because Walker pinched the last crisp out of her packet of McCoys. This was all part of some "sizeist patriarchal plot," apparently. I didn't see it myself.

Walker got so worn down by Daisy endlessly calling him a "cretinous, sexist piece of shit" that he ended up in a foul mood. I know that Walker's laboring under the illusion that he's in love with Daisy, but he's really overdoing the whole unrequited-love thing. Not to mention taking it out on anyone who comes within breathing space of him.

I itched to smooth his frown away with my fingertips, but there wasn't a lot I could do. I just had to try and control my heart rate while he stomped onto the stage and smoldered. I don't think having to act opposite Brie improved things. She does step all over his cues—she steps over everyone's cues—but I think remembering her lines and actually managing to talk at an audible level takes up most of her cognitive thought processes.

In the end, Walker very gently put down his copy of the play and calmly jumped off the stage.

"And *where* do you think you're going, Mr. Walker?" Lavinia asked in her most modulated and icy tone.

Walker turned and sent a sweeping glance around the

assembled company. It was totally Marlon Brando in *A Street-car Named Desire,* especially when he pulled his cigarettes out of his jacket pocket.

"I'm going home before I wring her neck," he said, nodding at Brie, who went a fetching shade of red. "And you can all go and fuck yourselves."

And then he swept out, slamming the door behind him. It was a great exit. If I'd have tried something like that, it would have ended with me tripping over one of my shoelaces. But we were a very subdued company of thespians after that, and in the end Lavinia got so sick of us fumbling our entrances and forgetting our lines that she let us go early.

I walked out with Daisy and wondered what I was going to do until ten the next morning.

Since the whole thing with Brie, I find I have an awful lot of spare time on my hands. Time that's quite hard to fill when there's only me to fill it. But slumped on the wall outside was Walker with a bottle of lager swinging from his fingers and a cigarette clamped between his teeth.

"Hey Charlie-boy," he called when he caught sight of me, and I tried to school my features into an expression that didn't resemble rapturous ecstasy.

"Well, I guess I'll leave you two boys to it," Daisy said drily, poking me painfully in the ribs. Girl does not know her own strength. "Don't do anything I wouldn't." And seeing as how she's a card-carrying lesbian, that left the things she wouldn't do at quite a lot.

Walker gazed kind of weirdly at Daisy as she stomped off, then turned to me as I walked over to him. "I'm going to get really drunk and you're coming with me," he said. It sounded like a plan to me.

. . .

What I hadn't realized was that it would involve going to this really scuzzy pub in Kings Cross. Or that there wouldn't just be pints of beer but that Walker would insist on doing vodka shots between each round.

It wasn't even eight o'clock and I'd already thrown up outside, but Walker was hell-bent on his path of self-destruction and was determined that I should tag along behind. He got me a glass of water, made me down it in one, and then gave me a couple of sticks of chewing gum to get rid of the vomity aftertaste. He's definitely the kind of boy that girls' parents warn them about.

And Walker can be a very maudlin drunk. His chin kept sinking lower and lower, and he went off on this monotone rant about how people thought that he was a user but really he was the usee. All that people ever thought he was good for was a quick shag in the toilets and that no one ever even tried to have a relationship with him.

"How long was your last relationship?" I asked him to show that I was an active participant in the conversation when all I really wanted to do was rest my head in his lap and ask him to wake me up in the morning.

"About three weeks," he mumbled.

"Well, three weeks is a long time," I slurred. "In dog years, it's four months or something."

"But, contrary to popular belief, I'm not a dog, Charlie-boy."

He looked so unhappy. His big, greasy pompadour had wilted in the heat, and he didn't even have the energy to smoosh it back, so I decided to do it for him. But my hand-eye coordination wasn't all that it could be, so I ended up missing his hair and almost poking one of his eyes out.

"Hey!" he yelped. "Watch it!"

"Just . . . your hair." I could feel this sappy smile spreading over my face. I tried to stop it and sit up straight, but flopping against Walker seemed like a far more pleasant activity. In the end I didn't flop so much as collapse on him, and he chuckled softly.

"You're such a lightweight," he drawled. "There's no way you're gonna last until closing time."

I was mesmerized by his lips. They're so full and pouty they look like they hurt. But thinking about how his lips felt wasn't enough, and did I mention how drunk *I* was?

I was drunk. Drunk as a skunk. Drunk as a drunk skunk, and all the crap rhymes in the world can't distract me away from the awful truth: that I had to know what his mouth really felt like. On mine. Kissing mine. And the next thing I knew, I was lunging at Walker.

I didn't manage to connect because Walker turned his head and gently but firmly held me off by placing his hands on my shoulders.

"Oh Charlie-boy, you've had too much to drink. I think I'm gonna have to get you home," he said right into my ear, his breath hot against my neck, and then I was trying to wriggle out of his grasp and he was laughing again. "Really, I'm flattered, but . . ."

And maybe it was the alcohol, or the wanting to die out of sheer embarrassment, or both, 'cause I leaned over and threw up all over my Converses.

I can't really remember much about getting home. There was a whole thing about trying to get a cab and Walker holding me upright and telling me to act sober as he tried to flag down a taxi.

And there was a warm blast of air on my face as Walker

stuck my head out of the window of the cab when I thought I might be sick again. Then there was nothing until I woke up to find the sun streaming in through the open curtains, and I was sprawled out on my bed in my boxer shorts with the wastepaper basket next to me on the pillow. Well, that and the distinct possibility that someone had emptied the contents of a chemical toilet into my mouth while I slept.

As I lay there, trying to ignore the pounding in my head and the sandpapery feel of my throat, parts of the night before kept coming back to me in these hideous Technicolor, surround-sound flashbacks.

"Oh God, I wish I was dead," I said out loud.

There was a rustling on the floor next to me, and then a muffled voice said, "I take it the hangover's kicked in then, Charlie-boy."

"Just kill me now, please," I begged, and shut my eyes. "As a personal favor, could you just put me out of my misery?"

Walker sat up and prodded me in the ribs. Which made me all too painfully aware of the fact that I was half naked and I'd gotten like that because he'd taken my clothes off. Taken them off my scrawny, underdeveloped body.

"Hey, look, you'll be fine," he said. "We'll get a couple of mugs of tea down you, a fry-up, and everything will start to look better."

Him being nice was worse than if he'd, I don't know, just dumped me in a Kings Cross doorway and left me to get mugged and murdered by a gang of crackheads.

"I'm so, so, so sorry," I began. "And being drunk was no excuse for what I did, what I tried to do . . . you must hate me."

I opened my eyes in time to see Walker stand up in all his tight-muscled, bare-chested glory. It really wasn't helping.

"Nah! It was the best night of my life. You were amazing." He grinned, curling his tongue behind his front teeth in a way that had I felt less like dying would have had my heart turning somersaults. "God, that thing you did . . ."

Then I actually tuned in to what he was saying. "Huh? What thing? Did we . . . Did I? . . . Did *you*?"

Walker started laughing, the pig. "Not that I wasn't tempted, but a bit of audience participation always helps." I think I was doing a good impersonation of a puppy with a really sore paw, because he stopped taking the piss. "Relax, Charlie-boy. I managed to keep my hands off you. Though it was touch and go at one point."

"Well, good," I huffed. Then I remembered that Walker was actually the injured party. "Look, I mean it, I'm so sorry . . ."

But Walker just waved a hand in the air. "Everyone tries to get off with me, sooner or later. It's no biggie."

My mother nearly went into cardiac arrest when we trooped downstairs. I could tell that she was dying to hear all the gory details, but instead she contented herself with asking me if I had a headache. When I said that I did, she turned the waste disposal on full blast.

"That's for waking me up when you came in," she said cheerfully as I moaned and clutched my aching temples.

"Now that we've got that out of the way, I think introductions need to be made."

I managed to get it together to percolate some coffee while Mum interrogated Walker to within an inch of his young life. Where did he go to school? What were his future plans? Why did he feel the need to corrupt her youngest son by pouring huge amounts of booze down his throat? That kind of thing.

Walker handled it very well. Even better after I made a huge plate of bacon sandwiches and put them down in front of him. I think him and Mum got on really well, and she's not the easiest person to impress. Doesn't suffer fools gladly. Well, apart from Merv the Swerve.

"You can come round again," she told Walker as she saw us out of the front door. "Possibly with champagne as an apology for last night." And then she kissed us both on the cheek and slammed the door because she knew I had a headache and she can be an evil cow sometimes.

"So. Bus," I said, looking at my watch. Now that I don't have to chivvy Brie along, I'm never late anywhere. It's like a complete revelation.

Walker hunched his shoulders. "Well, so, shall I see you tonight? We could go out and get drunk again. You know, hair of the dog that bit you?"

I shuddered. "I'm never drinking again. Ever."

Walker turned to go. "Whatever, Charlie-boy. I'll see you tonight."

I yanked him back by the sleeve. "Where are you going?"

"Home."

"But what about . . . ?"

"I resigned, remember? Or stormed out in a huff, can't decide which." He smiled, but it looked a little off to me.

"Oh, yeah."

"Lavinia's not gonna have me back after that little per-formance." He sounded . . . well, kind of regretful.

"You *could* say you were sorry," I suggested. "If you wanted to come back."

Walker considered it then shook his head. "Nah. I was way out of line."

But the thought of spending the next few weeks without Walker, in the platonic sense of course, and with Brie not talking to me, leaving only Daisy, was too awful to contemplate. "Walker, you *have* to come back. You're Petruchio and I'll have no one to hang out with except Daisy and she'll keep lecturing me about gender issues. Please, I'm begging you!"

"Charlie-boy . . ." He held up his hands in protest.

"Please! Look, I will pay you to say you're sorry."

"She's not going to let me set one foot on that stage," Walker insisted. "Not even if I offer to give her one."

I waited to see if the bacon sandwich was going to make a reappearance, then glared at him. "That image is going to haunt me for the rest of my life. But I have this fantastic plan to persuade Lavinia to reinstate you."

"Yeah?" I could tell he was wavering, and anyway, it wasn't like he had anything better to do this summer other than bask in the glow of my considerable adoration.

"Yeah! This is foolproof. Better than that, it's Lavinia-proof."

Lavinia loved the bunch of mixed blooms that Walker gave her. She didn't even listen to his hastily prepared speech, just rapped him on the cheek with her knuckles and told him that he was a very bad boy but she'd forgive him just this once.

Brie, on the other hand, wasn't quite so easy. When Walker tried to hand her *her* bunch of flowers (freesias, which are her favorite), she kept her arms by her side and her face stony. "I don't want them," she said in a flat voice. "I've got allergies."

I could tell that Walker was trying not to get exasperated with her, even as I ran my eyes over her. Somehow I felt unsettled without her. Like she was a particularly itchy but snuggly comfort blanket. Just looking at her made me feel a bit more grounded. She was so familiar, and there's something about Brie, about how pretty she is, that makes looking at her . . . well, it's nice. What wasn't nice was the huge and sore-looking love bite on her neck, which she kept prodding with her index finger.

"Look, I'm trying to say sorry." Walker closed his eyes and rubbed his forehead like he was suffering eternal torment.

Brie looked down her little nose at him, which, as he's about a foot taller than her, was quite the achievement. "Well, forget it, and you can fuck off while you're at it."

I never expected her to come out with something like that. Like she'd just grown a pair. Walker nearly spat his gum out of his mouth. I could see him practically counting to ten in his head before he tried another tack.

"Come on, Brie. I know I sometimes give you a hard time, but you're going out with Rowan and we should try and be mates," he said, keeping his voice calm like he was talking to a very small, nervous, and possibly ferocious dog.

Brie snorted. She actually snorted and then she walked off, leaving Walker in midsentence.

He looked at me, then at Brie's departing back, and then at the freesias that he still had clutched in his hand. "Huh?"

I patted him consolingly on the back. "It's probably her time of the month. Don't worry about it."

I decided that I really had to scale back on the Walker-sponsored evening activities. My liver just couldn't take it.

But after a week of staying in and going to bed at a

respectable hour, I was slowly going out of my skull with boredom and too much sleep. I think it must have been the first time in years that my eyes weren't bloodshot. So when Daisy asked me if I wanted to go to this gay club night on the weekend, I thought that maybe it was about time I tried to bond with my chosen people.

Going out with a girl that wasn't Brie was quite a change of pace. I never knew that there were females who could be good to go in less than three hours. Daisy asked me to go around to her house and help her get ready, but all *that* involved was telling her that I wouldn't go out with her if she wore tie-dyed anything (you should have seen this top she answered the door in—it should have come with a government health warning) and making her put on some Christina Aguilera to get us in the going-out mood. Daisy's a lovely girl, but she so needs to lighten up.

A few listens to "Dirrty" seemed to do the trick. Well, that and the bottle of her mother's Bacardi that we nicked. I really am going to give up drinking for another week, starting on Monday. Well, either that or I'll be in the hospital with cirrhosis.

"This is gonna be such fun," Daisy promised as we queued to get into this club in Vauxhall. "Claire and I come here all the time, and it's not all posey and sceney."

I nodded and smiled, but even standing outside, there were boys and they were doing the thing. You know? The checking-me-out thing. Seeing if I lit up all the buttons on their gaydar. Which I never do. My homosexuality is invisible to the human eye.

I moved in a little closer to Daisy because I was getting eyed up by this really tragic-looking queen who was twice my age and wearing blusher. Just then the door opened and the entire queue pushed us forward—Daisy gave a little squeal of excitement. She'd had far too much to drink. In fact, she'd practically hogged the entire bottle of Bacardi, and only my hand on her elbow as we made our way up the steps stopped her going arse over tit. If she threw up anywhere near me, she could sodding well make her own way home.

Inside it was even worse. Like, when I go clubbing with Brie, there are not lots of half-naked boys gyrating their hips in a suggestive manner and groping my arse. Which is something I've always hankered after, but confronted with the reality of it, I just feel like I don't belong. Even if I had a body like Walker's, I can't really see myself shaking my caboose on the podiums.

Everywhere I looked there were people snogging and feeling each other up. The air was heavy with dry ice and the smell of poppers, and everything seemed tinged with this sexual tension. Everyone was here for one thing—to cop off. It was all about sex.

Anyway Daisy buggered off after ten minutes. "Oh, I just need to go and say hello to some people," she shouted over the *thump thump thump* of the techno, and then she was gone.

I had a couple of drinks and then I danced on my own, trying to ignore the errant hands that occasionally strayed a little *too* close to my buttocks, but the music sucked. And the one guy who tried to talk to me wanted to know if I did, too. Even going for a piss was a major obstacle course of dry humping and people trying to eat each other's mouths off their faces. And I knew that whatever I was searching for, it wasn't going to be here.

I looked around for Daisy and found her in one of the chill-out rooms sucking face with either a really butch-looking girl or a very effeminate-looking boy. It must have been the former. 'Cause there ain't enough Bacardi in the world to turn that girl straight.

Watching one of your friends exchanging copious amounts of saliva with some random other that they've just picked up is an etiquette minefield. Should I stand there and wait for her to come up for air so I could tell her I was going home? Or should I just get the hell out of Dodge and send her an apologetic text message from the safety of the night bus? Someone should really write a book about these kinds of social dilemmas.

In the end, I did another complete circuit of the club, during which the love of my life failed to make his presence known. When I got back to the sofa where I'd last seen Daisy, it had been stolen by another snogging couple and she was nowhere to be found.

And I was so heartily sick of watching other people engaged in meaningless clinches that I knew it was time to cut my losses and head back to Muswell Hill.

When I got out of the club, it had started to rain. That really soft, summer rain that tickles your skin and makes everything smell earthy and fresh. I decided to walk home with the sound of Dashboard Confessional on my iPod—because I had no songs left in my heart to sing. I didn't belong anywhere. Not in the straight world, not in the gay world—but in some gray place in between, and I was the only person who lived there.

Not for the first time, I wished that I could just make things easier on myself. That I could be a normal gay boy who liked doing normal gay things like going to gay clubs and getting off with other normal gay boys. Not what I am, which is this freak who's in love with a boy who can't love me back because he just isn't wired that way, or the ex–best friend of a girl who loved me, but I couldn't love her back because I wasn't wired that way.

The really awful thing? Brie. I can't keep pretending that it was her fault. It was *my* fault. I said terrible, hurtful things to her, and she has every right to hate my guts and never speak to me again.

I'm walking home on my own, and she's the only person I want to be around. It doesn't matter that she can't get her head around the gay thing. All that matters is at moments like this when I'm at my lowest ebb, when I'm so down that I can't spiral any further, being in her bed, her hand clutched in mine, and listening to the faint whuffling sound of her breathing as she sleeps, is the only place that I feel like I belong.

Charlie

"Your face reminds me of a flower
Kind of like you're underwater
Hair's too long and in your eyes
Your lips a perfect suck me size."

 # Daisy

I'm not quite sure how it happened, but I'm now in a position to know, from firsthand experience, that sleeping slumped over the kitchen table is not a good idea. I realized this about two seconds after I woke up this morning with my head resting gently in the leftover plate of pasta that I'd passed out in while in the middle of eating.

It took precisely thirty seconds for the freak-out about having congealed marinara sauce in my hair to fade away as I remember what happened last night.

Okay, there was Bacardi involved. A lot of Bacardi. So much Bacardi that it must have short-circuited the lesbian part of my brain, which I'm pretty sure is the only reason why I ended up kissing a boy last night. He was a very girlish-looking boy, and it's possible that I didn't even know when we started kissing that he had boy parts. But about five minutes into the kiss, I was entirely aware of his boy parts, and it didn't really seem like an issue. Possibly because I'm a big skanky ho who can't last three weeks without her girlfriend before I start trying to hump anything with a pulse?

By the time I'd finished washing the gunk out of my hair in the shower, the freak-out had upgraded itself to full-on existential angst. I am the queen of bad girlfriends. I am the worst lesbian in the history of lesbianism. It isn't so much the boy-kissing but the fact that I'd been an active participant in the boy-kissing. I'd *enjoyed* the boy-kissing, encouraged it, reveled in it, stuck my bloody tongue in it. I had to see Claire. I had to go and find Claire and kiss her and purge the XY chromosome right out of my system. I had to borrow my mum's car.

"No way," said Mum incredulously when I phoned her at work.

"But you have to! It's an emergency. I have to drive to Devon now!"

"Yeah, and I have to work all the hours God sends to pay the mortgage and put petrol in the car that you seem to think you have part ownership in, Daisy. Life isn't fair, get used to it."

"Is this because last time I took it out I put a teeny scratch on the bonnet?" There'd been an incident in the Odeon car park, which so hadn't been my fault.

"Yeah, that and the huge dent in the fender that I had to pay to get fixed." I could hear her frowning.

"But I can't afford to get the train. It costs a fortune."

"Tough."

"I hate you!"

"Yeah, I hate you, too, sweetie. If you don't go to Devon, and you find a window in your hectic schedule, could you trouble yourself to take the washing out of the machine and stick it on the line?"

"Fine, whatever. Thanks for being there for me when I need you. I can see your campaign for Mother of the Year has really kicked up another notch."

"Still not letting you have the car, honey."

Which was why half an hour later, with my Stussy messenger bag stuffed to the gills with clean underwear and Body Shop toiletries, I was standing on Walker's doorstep trying to rehearse what I was going to say before I pressed the bell.

"Daisy?" said a voice behind me, and I whirled around to see Walker ambling up the garden path with a gym bag over his shoulder and a bemused expression on his face.

"Oh hi, Walker." I paused. "So, how are you?"

"I'm okay, just been for a swim." He swung his bag at me. I looked at him more closely and realized that his hair was flopping about his face instead of sticking up in a gunky quiff like normal. "Did you want something?"

I just had to come right out with it. Had to beg a favor from a guy who I thought should be sent to the tar pits of some revolting hell dimension for the crimes he'd perpetrated against the rest of girlkind. "Yeah, I kinda want you to lend me your car for the weekend." It didn't sound so bad when I said it out loud.

Walker shook his head slowly. Not in a "saying no" kinda way, more like he still had water in his ears. Then he opened his mouth. "Oh, Daisy, Daisy, Daisy," he said sorrowfully. "You really do know sod all about boys, don't you?" I raised my eyebrows, which seemed to be easier than opening my mouth.

"See, you know how I feel about you, and you think it

makes me a pushover. But you should know that though you may well be the absolute love of my life, I'm still never lending you my car. Not in a million years. Never going to happen. No way. You getting this?"

I was racking my brains for a particularly scathing comeback, as there wasn't a chance in hell that he was going to hand me the keys to his cute little VW Bug, but the tears put in an entirely unexpected appearance before I could start swearing at him.

I was mostly crying because I was so angry. Or confused. Or worried. Or all of the above. But it was actually a masterstroke because Walker shifted uncomfortably from foot to foot and then gingerly patted me on the shoulder.

"There, there," he said hesitantly. "No need to cry."

"Yes, there is," I sobbed, but it was hard to decipher what I was actually saying. Luckily, Walker was very adept at translating weeping girlese. Go figure.

"Look, I'm sorry I was so harsh, but really I can't lend you my car. It's my car! Plus you're not insured and the gearbox does this weird thing when you change down."

"I can only drive an automatic!" I spluttered, and then Walker was pulling a tissue out of his jacket pocket and offering it to me.

"It's okay, it's clean."

"Stop being so fucking nice to me!" I snapped, and shoved him hard, so he almost fell into the hollyhocks. "I have to get to Devon today!"

Walker simultaneously rubbed his arm where I'd pushed him, brushed his hair out of his eyes, and gave me an injured look. "Why do you have to go to Devon?"

"I can't explain. It's complicated, but I need to see Claire."

Walker sneered. He had the insensitivity to sneer in the middle of my meltdown. "You have serious need of my car just because you want to get all lovey-dovey with your girl-friend?" he asked incredulously.

I burst into tears again while he looked like he'd rather be anywhere but here.

"How could you possibly understand?" I wailed. "The whole future of my relationship is at stake."

But Walker is made of the stuff they make cinder blocks from. He shrugged and rummaged in his pocket for his door keys.

I wiped my hand across my face and turned back down the path, wondering if I could buy my train ticket with a check, which would take a few days to bounce.

"Hey! Where are you going?" Walker's hand was on my shoulder.

I shook him off. "To the station," I said curtly.

His fingers curved around my upper arm, gently but firmly, so he could turn me around. "You don't have to do that."

"Why? You going to lend me the car? I could probably fig-ure out the gears. I mean, how hard can it be?"

He winced as if I'd just put his balls in a vise. Then he sighed and I could feel his breath ghost across my face. "Oh, sod it!" he muttered. "Look, I'll drive you to Devon."

"Huh?"

"I said, I'll drive you to Devon. Now. I just need five min-utes to sort out some stuff."

"You have nothing better to do this weekend than chauf-feur me across the country?" Which, okay, sounded pretty churlish considering he was about to do me the daddy of all favors.

Walker, however, thought about my question for precisely one nanosecond.

"No, actually I haven't," he said wonderingly. Then made a small grimace of disgust. "I officially have no life."

I suppose I had a choice, though it was a pretty crappy one. Bankrupt myself to buy a train ticket to somewhere that I wasn't sure even had a station, or spend five hours in a car with Walker. Walker who was staring at my tits.

Rock, hard place, pleased to meet you, my name's Daisy.

"Okay, what's the small print?"

I don't know how he did it, but Walker put on this look of utter hurt like a small kid that's had its favorite toy snatched away. "God, you have such a low opinion of me."

"Not without reason. Don't think that doing me a huge favor means you're getting a reward. Because I'm telling you now that there will be no groping or fondling or inappropriate touching that leads to anything other than my knee in your crotch. And not in a good way. Do I make myself absolutely clear?"

"Ma'am! Yes, ma'am!" Walker clicked his heels together and saluted me, and it took every ounce of inner strength I had not to smile at him.

"Glad to see that we're finally beginning to understand each other," was all I said.

I never thought that I'd end up doing a road trip with Walker, of all people. But actually he was quite good company. He kicked up the minimum of fuss when I needed to stop twice to go to the loo and apologized profusely for the choice of in-flight entertainment.

"It's wedged in there and I can't get it out," he explained as

Magic of the Musicals (the original-cast sound tracks) thundered out when he turned the key in the ignition. "It's my stepmum's. It's not mine. I can't stress that enough. Not mine. Repeat after me."

"It's not yours," I said brightly. "But anyway I love a good show tune."

I didn't love a good show tune after five listens to the tape. Especially when I found myself singing under my breath, *"Jesus Christ, Jesus Christ/Who are you? What did you sacrifice?"*

In the end Walker decided that he was going to drive into the oncoming traffic if I didn't stop, and he turned the volume knob down, which left me free to try and get hold of Claire again.

"So she doesn't know you're coming?" Walker asked me as I got her voice mail for the fifth time in a row.

"Well, no, but she'll be cool. I was planning to spend a weekend with her anyway. It's just that there seems to be like one mobile phone mast in the whole of Devon, so she doesn't always have a signal on her phone."

Walker took one hand off the wheel to light a cigarette. "Might have been better if she knew you were about to descend on her."

"Why? She's my girlfriend. She misses me. I miss her. What's the big deal?"

"No big deal." He shrugged. "Just sometimes people prefer a bit of notice. Like, she might not be there, or she might be in the middle of something, or she might—"

"You're having way too many *mights*," I snapped. "It will be fine. She'll be all kinds of ecstatic to see me." But he'd sown the tiny seeds of doubt in my mind and then shoved a whole bottle of BabyBio on them, too, and I began to worry that maybe Claire'd be less than happy to see me.

"Where's she staying anyway?" Walker asked. "We'll need to get off the motorway soon."

"At a campsite near Croyde," I said vaguely. And Walker sat up straight and gave me a grin of pure delight.

"Croyde! Best surfing in the country," he crowed. "Hey, maybe while you're doing whatever it is you lesbians do"—I pinched his arm at this—"I can hire a board and catch a few waves."

"Really? 'Cause I was planning on letting you watch . . . just to say thanks and all."

He gave me a doubtful look. "You were?"

"Yeah, you wish, sad boy!"

"You know, you're not the uptight, joyless little bitch that I thought you were."

"And you're not the sex-obsessed, insensitive wanker that I thought *you* were. Well, not all the time anyway."

"You're starting to fancy me, aren't you, Daze?"

"Not while there's dogs on the pavement. Now shut up. You need to take the next exit."

"Good thing I dig bossy women."

"Which part of 'Now shut up' didn't you understand?"

We'd been making really good time, probably because Walker did ninety all the way and only slowed down when there were speed cameras looming, but as we wended our way through narrow country lanes, the hedges strewn with buttercups and clematis, we came to a big yellow DIVERSION sign (something to do with a landslide) and had to head in the opposite direction to Croyde.

"It's all right, we'll find a side street and I'll double back," Walker assured me, but we were in the country and there aren't any side streets—just the aforementioned narrow country lanes, which made me wince every time a car came toward us because Walker was still doing a cool ninety miles an hour.

"We're heading toward freaking Cornwall," I screeched after half an hour of aimless high-speed wandering. "Where have all the sodding 'Diversion' signs gone?"

Walker swerved into a hedge to avoid an oncoming tractor. "I hate the country. It sucks," he said fervently. "And the roadkill is upsetting me."

It was true. I'd never seen so many animals flattened in the middle of the road, fur matted and stuck down to the pavement so it was hard to see what it had been before its bad decision to go and play in the traffic. Ugh, just thinking about it made me feel nauseous.

"Right," said Walker, pulling into a rest stop and turning the car around. "We're heading back the way we came, diversion be damned. I'm getting you to Croyde, even if I have to get out of the car and move the rocks one by one."

"Um, thanks."

"Don't mention it. There's only so many dead bunnies scraped across the road that I can handle."

Eventually we got to Croyde, and we even managed to find the campsite after stopping at a surf shack and asking directions. Walker also asked about tides and board hire and acted like he was a great, big, surf-loving puppy dog, which was quite the revelation.

There was just one major problem. When we got to the campsite, the Belsize Park Youth Peace Group wasn't there.

Or rather they'd been forcibly removed for smoking dope, engaging in lewd public displays, and "breaking one of the toilets in the toilet block," as the site manager told us sourly.

"Do you know where they've gone?" I asked politely, trying not to look like the kind of girl who would ever engage in those kinds of activities.

"No, but I'd like to," he said grimly. "Still owe me for that toilet, don't they?"

I strode back to the Bug, my shoulders slumped in the very definition of dejection, to tell Walker the happy news. He took it in very good humor.

"We'll try some pubs or coffee shops, they can't have gone far," he said. "You'll find 'em. Look, I'll even let you listen to *Magic of the Musicals* again if you promise not to sing along."

Though it pained me to admit it, Walker was right. The Belsize Park Youth Peace Group weren't exactly traveling incognito, and the first coffee bar we stopped in and asked if they knew where they were had all the girls behind the counter tittering.

"Oh yeah, we remember them." A blond girl with a nose stud giggled. "Right bunch of hippies. Got kicked off the campsite for being rowdy."

"Where did they go? Are there any other campsites round here?"

Walker was busy eyeing up the prettiest waitress, who was flicking back her hair and looking at him from under her lashes. In short, he was being absolutely no bloody help. "Dunno. They said something about heading down to Westward Ho! That leader guy Aaron reckoned he had friends that were squatting down there."

"Aaron," I sniffed contemptuously.

"Bloody prat he was." Blondie grinned. "Slapped him round the face when he kept trying to pinch my arse."

"If you like I'll slap him again when I see him and tell him it was from you," I offered.

"Yeah. Tell him it's from Sal, and he still owes me two quid for his last cappuccino."

"Cheers. Walker. *Walker!*"

Walker took some time out from his busy schedule of running his eyes up and down Flicky Hair Girl's body to shoot me an annoyed look.

"What?"

"If you can bear to tear yourself away, I have a lead," I told him witheringly.

"I'm with you, Miss Marple—and exactly why are you talking like you're in a cop show?" he complained as he followed me out of the shop.

"And why do *you* have to hit on every girl you meet?"

"You getting jealous?"

I itched to wipe the smirk off his face with the flat of my hand. "Hardly." I opened the car door. "Right, we're going to Westward Ho!"

"The only place in Britain that has an exclamation mark as part of its name," Walker helpfully supplied.

"Jesus! Do you make this stuff up?"

"No, see!" Walker showed me his AA road map, which, yes, had an exclamation mark on the *Ho*.

"Whatever!"

"Oh, don't start getting all stroppy again. I thought I was your knight on a white horse."

"Well, if the white horse is kinda VW-shaped, maybe." I watched the muscles in his forearm flex as he turned the steering wheel and started maneuvering us out of the car park. He did have very guh-making musculature, if you were into that sort of thing. And were able to ignore his less redeeming features, of which there were many. "I am grateful, I am. It just annoys the hell out of me when you treat every girl you meet like your next potential sexual conquest."

"I don't!" he protested. "Oh, don't give me *that* look. I'm just appreciating the beauty of the female form."

"Well, why do you have to do it in such a pervy way? Like you know what color our . . . my knickers are."

Walker closed his eyes and groaned. "Daisy, why do you say things like that?"

"Like what?"

"You know. You might be gay, but you're still a prick tease."

"And once again, I find myself saying, 'You wish!' Just think of me as nature's revenge for all the wrongs you've done to other girls."

"See, about those other girls. You ever think that maybe I was the wronged party?"

"Nope," I said crisply. "You need to go right here."

There were more country lanes that twisted around, like a very twisty thing and I contented myself with pressing down on an imaginary brake and wincing every time Walker took a bend too fast.

Any other time and the pretty, patchwork fields and the chocolate-box cottages with their thatched roofs would have enchanted me. It was all very verdant and picture-postcardy. But all I could think about now was finding Claire and, more importantly, finding her in a welcoming mood. Westward Ho! was tucked away from the outside world like the Devon County Council was trying to keep it secret. As we careered around another hairpin bend, the Atlantic Ocean suddenly stretched out before us. I'd never seen a sea so blue or accessorized with so many miles of golden sand. And when did the sky become so big that it looked hyper-real, as if it was a backdrop straight from the Renaissance; the clouds painted on with just the right amount of cadmium?

"It's so beautiful here." I sighed before I could stop myself.

Walker just nodded. "It really is. Don't suppose you . . . no . . . forget it . . ."

"Was that sentence going to end in some obscene sexual request?"

"And she's back to being a bitch on wheels. Daisy, your continued high opinion of me is the most alluring thing about you. Really, trust me on that."

I rolled my eyes and stuck my tongue out at him before I realized that Walker would probably take the whole tongue thing in the wrong way. In a "rip my clothes off and do depraved things to my naked flesh" wrong way. Plus, he was wearing his little-boy-lost face again.

"Okay, what were you going to say before I cast such cruel aspersions on your character?"

Walker fiddled around with a couple of knobs on the dashboard while I waited with a certain amount of suspense for his answer. He was far more unpredictable than I'd ever given him credit for. Though I was still trying to decide if that was a good or bad thing.

"Do you want to go for a paddle?" he asked bluntly, and then turned his head to stare out of the window so I couldn't see the expression on his face.

Just my luck that I'd say yes and he'd call me out for acting like a big kid. But I'd been stuck in the car for what felt like forever, the sun burning down on us through the windshield and no room to stretch out my legs because the seat wouldn't go back. You spend seven hours with your knees practically touching your chin and the thought of kicking off your Birkenstocks and racing through the surf in your bare feet seems like the best idea that anyone's ever had. Even if the anyone happens to be a sneery-lipped guy who gets under your skin on an hourly basis like a bad case of scabies.

I didn't say anything. I just unclipped my seat belt, opened the car door, and didn't look back. I flew over the gravel, and when I reached the toasted yellow sand, I kicked off my sandals and felt the caress of summer on the soles of my feet as I ran down to the water.

The sea was cold as I let it lap against my toes; the hems of my jeans were getting wet and I bent over to tug the sodden material up to my knees when I felt a hand brush against my back so briefly that I thought I imagined it.

"You didn't wait for *me*," Walker said. And then he smiled at me. This big, doofy grin, quite unlike anything that I'd ever seen flash across his face before. I looked at him, really looked at him, and I saw him for the first time. So all at once, he seemed unfamiliar but the same, like his reflection was staring back at me from one of those distorted, carnival mirrors.

It wasn't about his outside stuff at all. But rather the way he yelped slightly when the ice-cold water splashed against him, the lazy quirk of his lips as he gave in to the primal joy that is wading in the ocean on a hot summer's afternoon. It was, like, I could see his soul.

Then he grabbed my hand. "Come on!" He laughed and he pulled me with him as he ran farther into the sea, so it came up past our knees, and it didn't matter that there were people sprawled out on beach towels a few meters away and swimmers dotted about the waves, their heads bobbing like corks. Because it felt as if me and Walker were the only two people there, but more than that, like we were both part of this great, eternal equation of sea, sky, sun. And at that moment all the stuff I usually feel—the anger and the weirdness that seem to make up me—didn't matter. I squeezed Walker's hand and he returned the pressure.

"This is . . . all of it . . . that stupid car journey and the landslide and everything, it's all worth it because of this," I said, nodding my head at the whole wide world laid out before us.

"I know," he murmured softly.

Then he ruined it. Because his other hand was tracing a pattern against my cheekbone, and he was leaning in, his fingers curling around the back of my neck so he could tug me closer. It would have been easy. It might even have been something I'd wanted if it was some other time and I was some other girl. But it wasn't and I'm not.

"God! What the hell do you think you're doing?" I shrieked, wrenching away from him.

"I thought . . ."

"What? What did you think? That we go paddling together and it becomes a way for you to seduce me? You're a creep, do you know that? You're so lame!"

He closed down. His entire face blanked out, so he was devoid of expression. Just a boy wearing a Walker mask. "Yeah, I'm lame," he echoed. "Didn't you get the memo?"

I was entirely in the right here. And even though the wet sand was shifting underneath my feet, making it hard to stay upright, I was pretty sure that this was moral high ground that I was perched on. Figuratively speaking. So why did the flat way he agreed with me make me feel like I was being an unreasonable bitch?

"Just so we're on the same page," I said anyway.

The walk back to the car was made in icy silence. I scooped up my Birkenstocks from where I'd flung them and trudged up the beach, hating the gritty feel of the sand sticking between my toes and the damp denim clinging to my legs. More for something to do that didn't involve looking at or talking to Walker, who was slumped in the driver's seat with his back to me, I tried Claire's number again.

Bingo!

"Daze? Hey."

"Hey. You'll never guess where I am!"

"Hmm, is this gonna take long, 'cause I'm kinda in the middle of this thing?"

"I'm in Devon—Westward Ho! Big surprise, huh?"

There was silence, then her voice in my ear, sharp, fractious.

"Oh. You're not usually this big with the spontaneity. You could have let me know you were coming."

I was aware of Walker trying to listen to every word. Because he hadn't had the decency to get out of the car and give me some privacy.

"Well, yeah, I would have 'cept you haven't been answering your phone all day."

"So, I guess you need directions. Did you drive down?"

"Kinda. I got a lift with . . . someone. Where are you?"

"Well, actually right now I'm in the middle of a field in this place called Stibbs Cross, but we're going into Holsworthy to get some dinner. I guess you could meet us there."

The whole time Claire was talking I had this internal monologue in my head. A very boring internal monologue that was stuck on one line: *She doesn't want you here; she wishes you'd never come.*

"Where in Holsworthy?"

"Oh, you'll find us, no trouble. There's like one parade of shops in the whole town. We'll be outside the chippie or the Somerfields. Okay?"

"Yeah, sure. I can't wait to see you."

"That's sweet. So, yeah, right . . . In about an hour, then?"

She hung up without even saying good-bye, and the thought of seeing her, which should have made me giddy around the gills with anticipation, left me uneasy and vaguely nauseous.

Walker turned around and reached forward to grab the atlas. I opened my mouth . . . but he held up his hand.

"Holsworthy. I got it, we need the A388."

But I couldn't worry about Walker and his precious, supposedly hurt feelings. I had other things, more important things, to worry about.

By the time we got to Holsworthy, it was evening. Everything seemed soft and glowy without that fiercely lit glare. There was a slight breeze wafting in through the open windows of the car as Walker pulled into the town square. My eyes skittered across the street, and then I saw her. Claire was with a bunch of people standing outside a little supermarket. I knew that all I had to do was get out of the car and go over to her, run my fingers along her arm, and everything would be all right. So why wasn't I moving?

She looked different from how I remembered her. She was tanned and wearing a pair of cutoff jeans and a tank top. But she seemed more remote and untouchable now than she did back in London, dressed from head to toe in black.

Walker unbuckled his seat belt. "I need cigarettes. Then I'm going to sit in that pub over there"—he gestured to the King's Arms on the other side of the square—"and you can come and get me when you want to . . . whatever. You know, drive you . . ." His voice was still devoid of meaning. I really didn't need his prima donna bullshit.

"Fine," I said, and managed to get my brain to pass on a message to my left hand so it would open the door.

Claire had seen me now. She was standing a little distance away from the others and half raised her hand in greeting, then dropped it. Her face twisted up into a frown, and I realized that she was staring at Walker, who gave me a not-so-gentle nudge in her direction.

"Aren't you ready for the touching reunion scene?" he said, sneering.

"Daisy!" Claire was walking toward us now, and I leaned back against the side of the VW because suddenly touching her seemed weird and impossible. "You're here! We wanted to get some chips, and the bloody place closes at eight! So we were going to go to the Chinese, but they just have this skanky wipeboard in the window with the menu on it . . ."

She was talking a lot. Too much. Too fast. Like, the awkward silence of me being there with her had to be filled up as quickly as possible. I tried to smile, but the resolute way she refused to meet my eyes made it slip from my face.

I took her hand and waited for her long fingers to curl around mine, but she shook her wrist gently to free herself. "So, anyway, here you are, and with Shagger, too. Something you want to tell me?"

Walker's expression could have curdled milk. "I'll leave you girls to it." The amount of innuendo in the tone of his voice could have had its own late-night show on Channel Four. And he exited stage left in the direction of the pub.

"You shouldn't call him that," I said, turning back to Claire. "Not to his face anyway. I think you hurt his feelings."

Claire tossed her hair back, the pink faded to the color of candy floss. "Shagger doesn't have any feelings. Apart from the ones in his dick."

That wasn't entirely true. But I hadn't come all this way to defend Walker, who was not really deserving of a character reference.

"You're not mad that I came, are you?" I asked Claire, ignoring the curious stares of the others who were still gathered around the shop doorway. "Things in London . . . they were getting crazy and horrible. I just wanted to see you, you know? Make things better again."

"You make me sound like the Dalai Lama." It was strange, but everything she said sounded as if she'd rehearsed it before. Like she was reciting her lines to an audience, and it was all about the technique and nothing to do with the feeling.

"Come and say hi to everyone," she said, and then, finally, she was touching me, slinging an arm around my shoulders, and leading me across the square.

"Well, if I remain passive and you just want to cuddle
Then we should be ok, and we won't get into trouble."

Walker

Daisy is a piece of work. She's just like every other girl in the world. Doesn't matter that she's one hundred percent dykeadelic, she still uses tears and those little heart-melting half smiles to get what she wants.

Which is why I'm sitting in this pub in some one-horse town in Devon, tearing the coaster to shreds and waiting for her to come back from whatever she's doing so we can go home. Because I'm really not looking forward to driving down lanes so narrow that they might as well be mule paths, in the pitch-black. Like, people who live in the country are too good for streetlights?

And the famous girlfriend? She ain't all that. Or half that. Or even a quarter that. Just your average, dumpy girl who reckons she's a lesbian because she's got nothing going on that a boy would be interested in. She might also want to rethink the supercilious smile and the condescending attitude.

I mean, who the fuck does she think she is? *Shagger?* To my face? I really need to get rebranded.

Daisy might be a snarling, sexually repressed girl who hides her true feelings behind half-baked gender politics most of the time, but really? I've never come across anyone so delusional and unaware. She doesn't see what's going on around her. Especially when it's wearing her girlfriend's spotty face.

I saw the way Claire flinched from the tender handholding, and before that I saw the way she rolled her eyes and nudged her little peacenik pals when she caught sight of Daisy. And I saw the way her hand skinned over the arse of the girl next to her as she started to walk toward us. Like that was where her hand wanted to be.

Which is why, instead of heeding the call of the open road and all that Jack Kerouac bollocks and letting Daisy get the train home, I'm sitting here waiting for her. Waiting to pick up the pieces of her if she manages to get a clue.

Can't even do what I really want to do, which is get hammered and then go somewhere with the little blond barmaid who's been staring at me for the last half an hour like we're on the *Titanic* and I'm in charge of the last lifeboat.

I order a tasteless plate of sausage and chips and make two pints of shandy last for three hours before Daisy comes back.

Did I say come back? My mistake.

What I meant to say was that she staggered through the door, that awful dyed black hair clinging to her flushed cheeks in static wisps, looked wildly around, found me, and then hurried over.

She stood in front of me for a while. Statue still. Then her bottom lip trembled, and then all of her trembled, and then she's hurling herself at me so my arms are full of this beautiful mess of quivering, crying Daisy.

I hate hugging skinny girls. There's something so insubstantial about them, like they're about to snap in two. And you start to wonder how anyone so fragile, so breakable, can be real. But Daisy is solid in my arms, and when my grip tightens around her, she smushes herself against me so her breasts are pressed against my chest and it's easy to plant little kisses in her hair.

"She didn't want me here," Daisy wailed. "She just acted like I was embarrassing her with, like, my very presence."

I rubbed concentric circles on her back, making sure to avoid the whole bra-strap area. "Hey, *hey!*" I said in a soothing voice. "'Course she wanted to see you."

Daisy wriggled in my arms and I had to close my eyes and take deep breaths. If she kept it up, then I'd be keeping it up, too. She disentangled herself, gave a start as she realized that she'd practically straddled me, and shifted so she was sitting on the bench next to me.

"I need a drink," she announced mournfully. "And I've got no money because I gave it to Claire for petrol."

Really decent of her, I noted, especially as she hadn't offered me so much as fifty pence to get a cup of coffee on the drive down.

"What do you fancy?" I stood up and reached into my back pocket for my not-exactly-bulging wallet.

Daisy nibbled her bottom lip as she gave the question serious thought. "Vodka and tonic. Make it a double with ice and lemon. And food. I want some food. I haven't eaten since lunchtime, and that was hours ago."

"I think the kitchen's closed," I told her warily, and

watched her face collapse in on itself again. "It's okay, I'll sort something out."

When I got back from the bar with her drink, a pint of shandy for me, and five bags of crisps in assorted flavors, Daisy was clutching her backpack to her like it was a sick child, tears still trickling down her face.

"What's a communist relationship?" she demanded.

"I have no idea. Maybe it's when you and your, erm, partner both share the same Trotskyite ideology," I said, and chucked the crisps down on the table. "I didn't know what you liked, so I got you one of each."

"Thanks," she said distractedly as she tore into a packet of salt-and-vinegar. "Claire reckons we should have one. I think she's been seeing other people."

I pinched a crisp from the open packet and took an unenthusiastic sip of my shandy. "Define *seeing*. Define *people*."

She wouldn't look at me, just ripped open another bag of crisps, cheddar-cheese-and-chives this time, and shoved a handful into her mouth. I like a girl with a healthy appetite.

"There was this girl," she eventually said through a mouthful of half-masticated potato snack. "And she just glared at me the whole time, and Claire kept pulling her away so they could have these talks. Somehow I don't think they were discussing the banner workshop."

"Huh?" Sometimes Daisy really needs to come with subtitles.

"It's a peace-camp thing. You've broken up a lot of relationships, I imagine."

She was amazing. Did she think that I had no feelings, that I was just a penis with a boy attached?

"Contrary to popular belief, no. I don't go after other guys' girls," I snapped, and fumbled around for my cigarettes. Daisy was having a disastrous effect on my plans to smoke less than twenty a day. "Anyway, why the sudden interest in my sex life? Didn't it used to be at the top of your list of things that sickened you to the pit of your stomach?"

She pouted and pushed her hair out of her eyes so she could fix me with that unwavering, frosty blue stare. "I'm just trying to figure stuff out. Like, if someone was cheating on you if there'd be signs. Or why someone who might be in a happy relationship would suddenly go completely off-topic and kiss a random boy, or girl, in a club."

Her glass was already half empty. Or half full. Whatever. It was ten minutes to last call, so I could just about afford to get another one, if she wanted. She scooped her fingers into her drink, plucked out an ice cube, and crunched it between her teeth. I winced. The sound sent icy fingers marching down my spine before dancing the merengue.

"Sorry," she slurred. "So, what do you think? Why do people cheat?"

"Because I'm the expert?"

"Just answer the question, Walker!"

"People cheat because they're lonely or they're unhappy with their lovers. And sometimes they cheat just because it's being offered to them on a plate, and for that one moment in some dark, smoky club, the way somebody moves to the music, the way their skin looks in the glow of the lights is the most beautiful thing they've ever seen, and they want to be part of that. You know? Just for a little while."

The tip of Daisy's tongue crept out to swipe a path against her lower lip. The air seemed to hum around her. "I think I'd better have another drink," she said after a brief pause that felt as long as an afternoon. "And where the hell are we going to sleep tonight?"

I stubbed out my cigarette. "You're going to sleep in the backseat of the Bug while I drive us back to London."

"I'm not sleeping in the car!" she exclaimed. "It smells like an ashtray, and there's not enough room on the backseat. And, well, you know, you should probably get some sleep, too. You've done a ton of driving today." She shot a disapproving look at my pint glass. "Besides, you've been drinking."

I waved the glass in front of her. "It's shandy."

"If you say so. You're still not driving." She was working her way through the bacon crisps now and looking at her empty glass like she couldn't quite believe that it hadn't replenished itself. "More vodka. Now. Please."

"Daisy!" It was like trying to wade through wet cement. "So where *are* we going to sleep tonight?"

She slumped back against the seat. "Walker, I'm having a really bad day. Could you just sort something out? I can't be expected to do everything."

It wasn't the time to point out that, apart from a few fleeting moments when she'd been utterly adorable, all she'd done all day was bitch and moan and take me for granted.

"Fine. I'll just magic a well-appointed hotel room out of thin air, shall I?"

Her eyes rolled so far back that all I could see were the whites. "They do rooms here. It says so outside. Book one while you're getting my drink. See, that's not so difficult, is it?"

"Okay, give me some money."

"I don't have any money. God, I just said, didn't I? I gave Claire fifty quid for petrol. Haven't you got a credit card?"

I inched away from her so I didn't do anything stupid like pull her head clean off her neck. "You're bloody unbelievable!"

"Can we just not?" she whimpered like I was being completely unreasonable. "And make sure you get two rooms. Oh, and don't forget my ice and lemon."

If I had told Daisy the only room available was a double with a bed in it made just for two, then all kinds of accusations about how I just wanted to take advantage of the emotionally vulnerable, halfway-to-drunk, weepy lesbian would start getting flung around. So I just tossed the key on the tear- and beer-stained table in front of her and plonked down her drink.

"I think my credit card just had a coronary," I commented before taking a good few gulps of full-fat beer and adding the contents of two shot glasses of vodka into my pint. If I was broke, might as well be broke while slightly inebriated.

Daisy just grunted something that might have been "thank you" but was probably, "You're a tosser and I hate you."

I don't know how she does it, though, because just when I've decided to cut my losses and treat her as nothing more than a mildly amusing diversion, she changes. Becomes a girl that I can't get enough of.

She reached across the table so she could clutch at my wrist.

"Look, sorry. I've been acting like a demented harpie. What you've done for me today . . . I really appreciate it. Thank you."

I could feel my face heat up. It had nothing to do with the way her thumb was smoothing across the junction of blue veins. But more to do with how she was looking at me; like I was someone that she was pleased to know. That doesn't happen very often.

"No biggie," I mumbled, and took a huge swig of vodka-enhanced lager.

About the only thing that doesn't actively suck about being stuck in some crap dead end in the country is that they have lock-ins because there's one policeman in town and he's drinking at the bar. By the time Daisy and I were staggering unsteadily up the stairs to Bedfordshire, we'd been drinking for an hour straight after a little bit of haggling with the landlord to put the bill for the drinks on my credit card.

"There was only one room," I got out in a rush, but she seemed supremely unbothered.

"Oh, who cares? It's not like you're going to try anything, and I'm as gay as gay can be," she singsonged as she tried to negotiate putting the key in the lock and opening the door.

I took the key out of her hot little hands, although I didn't have much better hand-eye coordination myself, and managed to get us into the room. Daisy took three small steps over to the bed and sprawled on it in an untidy heap.

The room smelled musty, like some old woman who never washed properly but wore a lot of lavender perfume to disguise the fact, had died in it. The walls were nicotine beige, which contrasted nicely with the orange shagpile and the dried flower arrangements on the chest of drawers.

I tugged the window open and perched on the sill so I could smoke. And if Daisy made one pop about what a disgusting habit it was, I'd kill her.

Instead she propped herself up on one elbow and looked at me uncertainly. "I wish we had something more to drink."

"Yeah, me, too."

"'Cause I should be tired, it's been a pig of a day, but I feel all wired. Like I'm never going to be able to sleep again."

"I could roll a joint if you like." As soon as the words were out of my mouth, I winced in anticipation of a lecture on the evils of certain narcotics and how even dope was a gateway drug, which would lead into a downward shame spiral of heroin addiction and sitting in doorways, drinking cans of Special Brew. But Daisy sat up and nodded.

"Yeah, that'd be good."

Turns out that Daisy's a pretty passive drunk. She watched me make the spliff on the back of a CD case, without saying anything, and as soon as I'd lit it, she reached out her hand and then flopped back on the pillow before taking a huge toke.

I switched off the overhead light so the dim glow of the bedside lamps cast soft shadows on the wall and sat on the end of the bed.

"Here you go," she said, and passed me the joint.

Two joints later, she'd perked up and was giggling feebly about *Magic of the Musicals* again and completely not freaking out that I was lying next to her on the bed.

"Your hair's really soft here," she suddenly said, and reached out to touch the ends of my hair just above the sideburns. "I don't know why you have to put so much gunk in it. It looked sweet when it was all floppy this morning. Quiffs are like, so fifty years ago."

I was too stoned to take offense. "When did you turn into Brie?"

"Ha! I'm twice the woman she is. Quite literally. She must weigh about eighty pounds."

I resisted the urge to rest my head on her breasts and squinted across at her. "Brie looks like she'd snap in half if you touched her."

"Yeah, but some people like that fragile, helpless-little-girl thing, don't they?"

"Do they? Do you?"

I got a warning jab in the ribs for that, but it lacked the usual strength that usually has me checking to see if she's punctured a lung.

"Brie's not my type," Daisy said as decisively as someone as stoned as her could manage.

I rolled over onto my side so I could peer up at her. Her eyes were rimmed red from the joint, and her alcohol-induced flush had paled out. "What is your type, then? I'm not asking because I'm a big, old perv. I genuinely want to know."

It was a perfectly all-right kind of question. In the spirit of being drunk and stoned and getting on better than we normally did. At least, I thought so.

Daisy, not so much. Her entire face crumpled up suddenly as if her foundations had just caved in, and for the third time in twelve hours she was bawling her eyes out. It was one hell of a buzz kill. And you know how some girls look beautiful when they cry? Daisy is not one of them. There's way too much sweaty skin and snot involved.

But then it didn't seem like she was about to read me out any chapters from the Teen Lesbian Handbook condemning my insensitive behavior. She just cried harder and harder, the tears clogging her eyelashes together even as she tried to scrub them away with her balled-up fists.

Really, I was too stoned to do anything but stare at the water stains on the ceiling, but I showed willing. And it wasn't just a get-in-her-pants thing. I don't like to see someone in pain, not someone I care about.

"What? What is it?"

Her sobs reached a new cadence when I spoke, increasing in volume and frequency as she hauled herself into a sitting position so I couldn't see her shiny, tear-soaked face.

"Daisy, c'mon. What's up?" I reached out and let my fingertips just glance across her shoulder like she was a nervous horse that might skitter away if I got too close.

"Everything," she spat out helpfully. "Everything is up."

"I'm sure it isn't," I said weakly because it seemed like the right thing to say.

Daisy's sobs were morphing into dry hiccups that sounded like they hurt. "You wanna know what my type is?" Daisy suddenly shrieked, and I nearly fell off the bed at the sudden moody shift from woe is me to what the fuck? "So do I, 'cause last night my type was boy-shaped!"

There was a short silence while I cursed my bad luck at being someplace that was else while Daisy was hopping on the bus back to Boy Town.

Daisy mistook my silence for stunned disbelief. She crawled across the bed to peer at my face. "Are you shocked?"

And I wasn't. Jealous. Annoyed. Turned on. But not shocked.

"Should I be?" I said finally. "You're obviously going through some *thing*. That's hard. I can see why you've been like, well, how you've been today."

She gave another cry that I think was meant to be a happy one. "God, it's such a relief to be able to talk about this with someone."

So we sat there on the bri-nylon floral bedspread, which was making me itch just from looking at it. And she gave me the whole tired story of the night before and the boy she kissed.

Like, I'm one of her girlie pals and I'm there to be supportive, and afterward we'll braid each other's hair and watch really crap rom coms and eat cookies together.

But at least I got to touch her. Got to wipe away the tears from under her eyes with the tips of my fingers. Got to tuck her damp face against my shoulder as I stroked her back and whispered nonsense words at her.

Then she pulled away and wiped the back of her hand across her face like a tired little girl, and it only took three seconds to fall out of lust and in love with her. She curled up in a ball on the bed and threw me this beseeching look, which tugged at my heart and pulled me toward her, so that I lay down behind her and slid my hands around her waist.

Christ, she was so soft. Her flesh just melted against mine. I couldn't help it. I had to kiss the back of her neck and then stay there a while.

"Are you kissing my hair?" she asked eventually in a small voice.

"No," I said immediately.

"Yeah, you were." She didn't sound as annoyed as she should be. And her, an avowed lesbian, even though she'd kissed some boy who wasn't me the night before. And she wasn't making any move to wriggle away from my hands, which were stroking her skin where her T-shirt had ridden up.

"Thing is, Walker, the worst thing is that the kiss was all right. It was really good, and I'm not sure whether it was just a one-off or . . ." Her voice trailed off, and she didn't seem quite so much the poster girl for gayness anymore.

"Or . . ." My voice was two octaves deeper than normal. She shifted restlessly against me and then turned over so we were lying face-to-face.

"Or maybe it was just a fluke," she whispered. "And to be sure, maybe I should kiss another boy, just to be on the safe side."

"To be on the safe side," I echoed. Though I couldn't help but wonder: *The safe side of what?*

She was inching nearer and nearer to me in a way that was the very definition of wrong touching. "So, do you want to kiss me?"

"Like, as a controlled experiment, you mean?" And even though I knew no good would come of this, I decided there and then to just hop onto this runaway train and see where I ended up.

Daisy frowned and then smiled like one of those praying-mantis girl insects who bite the heads of praying-mantis boy insects after they've had sex with them. "Exactly," she said, and then she kissed me.

She kissed me, and the world and all its woes got swept away in the slipstream.

I never thought that this would happen. Really, I didn't. But it was a chaste kiss. Lips on lips, moving here and there, gently forceful. But when she opened her mouth to sigh, I buried my hands in her hair and tilted her head back. I lost track of the time as I lay flat on my back with Daisy squirming deliciously on top of me. And then it became frantic, less tender. Her tongue was stabbing into my mouth, and I sucked on it, nibbled on it, danced with it, and all the time she made these breathy little noises like I was killing her very gently.

Then she remembered that she had to breathe and

wrenched her mouth away with a gasp, and all I could see was her. Wild hair, pink cheeks, and a mouth swollen from my kisses. I knew then that there'd never be anyone else for me.

"I want to get lost," she murmured, and it was a promise. It was yes.

"I know why you're here, why you're doing this," I said, and I tried to sound stern, but her skin was as soft and as smooth as vanilla ice cream underneath my fingertips.

"Tell me why," she breathed, and reached up to plant hot, frantic kisses along my neck.

"Because you're stoned and because your stupid girlfriend's hurt you and because you want someone to hold you, and I'm here."

"Yeah, that pretty much covers about, hmm, sixty-three percent of it." She smiled and rubbed her cheek against mine. "Wanna know about the other thirty-seven?"

"Are you going to say one of those really wounding, hurtful statements of yours?"

"I'm here because I want to be and because I'm not thinking that you have boy lips and boy hands. You just have lips and hands that I want on me. Because they're *your* lips and hands. And God, yeah, I'm really stoned."

There were more kisses. Wet, languorous kisses that turned the heat up another notch. I could feel her lips curving into a smile as I stroked them with mine. She was all sweet things: sugared almonds and melted chocolate and pink spun sugar from the fair. I'd kissed the tears from her face lifetimes ago, and now her flesh pillowed into my reverent hands. I've never felt anything so heavenly as Daisy's breasts and thighs and the bulge of her belly as I rubbed my cheek against it. She laughed. She actually laughed!

"You're tickling me," she whispered.

"Sorry, baby," I whispered back, although there was just us, and only the moon glinting through the window was witness to the girl and the boy sprawled out on the bed.

"I'm not shagging you! It's nonnegotiable, Walker," she insisted, though she made it sound like the most seductive words ever spoken.

"It's okay," I murmured, and nibbled on her earlobe in a way that made her shudder against me and give a tiny, word-less cry. "We can do other things, okay?"

Daisy smiled at me again from beneath her lashes. Then she nodded.

We spent half the night doing other things. And then she said, "You're sweet," as she fell asleep in my arms. "How come I never realized that?"

When I woke up in the morning, she was gone. Just a dent in the pillow next to me, and the scent of her on my fingertips and all around me.

It would have been stupid of me to imagine that in the morning things would still be the same. But it would have been even more stupid to just pretend that it had been eight hours out of time, when the world tilted off its axis and then righted itself, and we could all just go back to being how we were. Stuff happens in the stillness of the night, and you can't unhappen any of it.

I don't think Daisy realized that.

When I walked out into the bright morning light, my belly full of the breakfast that had been included with the room and that I was damned if I was leaving uneaten, she was lean-ing against the VW. The sun glinted in her hair, turning it every color from jet black to a rich ruby. See, she makes me think in sonnets, even though she is a treacherous bitch who was cuddling up to her girlfriend and whispering softly in her ear as I dragged my lead-heavy feet in their direction.

"Walker," she said coolly, as if she hadn't chanted my name like a mantra a few hours before. "Claire's coming back to London with us. That's okay, isn't it?"

"And you don't have to be his girl
You don't have to be my girl
You can always be your own girl."

Brie

I never thought I'd say this. In a million years. But not speaking to Charlie, like, ever again? It could be a lot worse. To tell you the truth, I kinda think he was holding me back. I'm not sure exactly what from, but without him, life isn't as scary as it was with him.

The first week was awful, and all I wanted to do was call him and send him a million text messages, but then I kept remembering what he'd said, about how he'd never want to go out with me even IF HE WAS NOT GAY and how being friends with me sucked, and I realized that this was it. All this time and he'd secretly hated me. I'd kind of suspected that he might because there were times when we'd be with other people and he'd put me down and stuff. I told myself he was just trying to be funny, that he didn't realize how hurtful it was. But now I knew that each time, he really meant it.

I'm on my own, which was always the thing I was most frightened of.

So by the time seven days had gone by, I was used to getting up really early 'cause I couldn't sleep and spent every night tossing and turning and unattractively sweating underneath my duvet while I reran every mean thing Charlie had ever said to me.

I was at the Arts Centre by nine, and just as I was mooching across the car park and trying not to cry, Lavinia pulled up in her clapped-out car and asked me if I wanted to go to breakfast with her.

Which actually I so did not, but I was too chicken to tell her. She took me to the posh French place on Delancey Street and bullied me into having a proper breakfast, and we talked.

Well, I talked and she listened. I'm not quite sure how it happened. But she kept asking me loads of questions in between nagging at me to eat my croissant. And it all came spilling out. Stuff about the play and why I wasn't cut out for stardom.

Lavinia fixed me with this look. "I think I'll be the judge of that, dear," she said.

"But I sound like an idiot when I'm saying all those strange words," I said.

I expected to get a telling-off about calling Shakespeare's plays "strange words" 'cause she's always banging on about the Bard, but she just smiled faintly and asked me what I thought the play was about.

I panicked for one second because it was like being back at school, but then I knew! I knew what it was about. "It's about hating someone that everyone thinks you should be in love with and then realizing that you are in love with him but you hate the feeling it gives you," I told her, shredding my croissant into flaky crumbs because I was on the brink of a major breakthrough. "Because the guy that she's in love with just wants to control her." And as soon as I'd said it, I was like, Oh my God. It's about me and Charlie, IF HE WASN'T GAY, and we have to get married because I have a younger sister who wants to get shacked up, too, and my dad's being funny about it.

"Very good." Lavinia beamed at me. She was pleased with me 'cause I'd said something intelligent, which was a total first. "And how does that make Katharina feel?"

I didn't even have to think about that. I just held up my thumb and forefinger so there was barely a gap between them. "This big. And really she's cool because she stands up for what she believes in, and she doesn't let people walk all over her just because she hates it when they're angry with her."

Lavinia poured herself another cup of tea. "But she gives in to Petruchio in the end, doesn't she? He tames her?"

And I forgot that this was Lavinia and that she was an old lady and she talked proper, because I just snorted. "Whatever! She just wants Petruchio to think that. I bet the moment that he gets the money from the wager and they go home, she kicks him right to the frickin' curb for being such a wanker."

It was awful! I'd ruined everything by doing what I always do, which is opening my mouth when I don't know what I'm talking about. But Lavinia clapped her hands together and laughed. "Do you know what you've just done?" she asked me.

I hid my face in my hands. "Made a total tit of myself?"

"Language, Brie! No, you've come up with your own unique interpretation of the text. You've found your inner Katharina, and I want you to play her just like that: exasperated and tongue-in-cheek."

"You what?"

She didn't huff or roll her eyes. She just placed her cup gently on the saucer and gave me this look like she could see right inside me. "I want you to play her as you just described. That she's telling Petruchio what she knows he wants to hear, but deep down she doesn't believe a word of it. Can you do that?"

I *so* could do that! I spend my whole life doing that. Letting Charlie see me as stupid and useless so he gets to be the cool one. Letting my mum tell me that I'm fat and ugly and unlovable and never once telling her I'm not because I don't want her to hate me any more than she does.

"Yeah," I said. "I'm pretty much an expert when it comes to telling people what they want to hear."

Then she reached out her wrinkled, liver-spotted hand and patted me gently on the arm. I thought she was going to come out with something dead proud and insightful, but she just said: "Oh, and you might try channeling your intense loathing of Mr. Walker into your role." And then she asked me if I wanted to finish the jug of orange juice.

Something changed then. Though I didn't realize it at the time. Lavinia drove me back to the Arts Centre and I tried to ignore the flippy feeling in my tummy at the thought of having to spend another day on my own because I didn't have anyone to hang out with.

The only empty seat was next to this girl called Tash and her friend Gemma, and when I walked over, they both looked up and gave me a weird look, like I had croissant crumbs all over me.

"Aren't you going to sit with Charlie?" they asked, because he'd just walked in and it was the law that we should be joined at the hip.

"I want to sit here today," I said, and when they looked at me funny, I quickly added: "Is that top from New Look? 'Cause I was thinking of getting one myself."

"Yeah? What color? 'Cause the pink would really make your highlights pop," Tash exclaimed excitedly, and made room for me next to her.

It was that easy! Why did no one ever tell me it was that easy? That you could just go up to people and they wouldn't think you were a total fuckwit? But then I realized. It was easy because Charlie wasn't there telling me that they'd think I was a total fuckwit. Basically, he's been holding me back for years.

So I spent the rest of the day hanging out with Tash and Gemma and some of the other girls. I didn't have to pretend to understand that I knew what they were going on about because I knew what they were going on about. It's all the stuff that I go on about. Like, makeup and clothes and Justin Timberlake. All the stuff that Charlie and Daisy and Wanker think is really shallow. So, I'm shallow. I don't care! Katharina wouldn't care if people thought she was shallow, she'd just bop them one.

I was still coming to terms with how, when I'm just a teeny bit braver and more Katharina-y, people don't treat me like a piece of bubble gum that's stuck to their shoe.

Even when I went around to Rowan's house later, it was all I could think about. I s'pose it's a bit rude to be thinking about other stuff when you're getting off with your boyfriend, but I just couldn't help it. He was yanking at my hand and trying to get me to stroke the bulge in his trousers, which still squicks me out big-time, when suddenly I could feel my face shifting and tightening and getting the pissy expression that I use when I'm all *"I'll see thee hanged on Sunday first."*

"Cut it out," I said sharply. And when he wouldn't, I dug him in the ribs with my elbow. "I said, no!"

Rowan sat up with a jerk. "What's got into you?"

"Well, it certainly ain't gonna be you." Then I clapped my hand over my mouth before more words could pop out, but he wasn't heading for the door and telling me I was a crazy bitch at all.

"Sorry. I got carried away, you get me—"

"Yeah, yeah, I 'get you' but you're going too fast. And you never take me anywhere, and all you want to do is try and take my clothes off and maul me. It's like, totally not respecting me."

There was this silence where all I could hear was this ringing in my ears like the world was about to end. But it didn't end. And we didn't end. I mean, Rowan didn't break up with me or kick me out without driving me home.

Instead he reached out and stroked my hair back from my face, like really gently, as if I was something precious. "I'm sorry," he repeated. "I got the wrong idea, I thought . . . I don't know what I thought. I've been kinda selfish, haven't I?"

"I know I look like I'm . . . well, that I'm all slapperish, but I'm not," I replied firmly.

"You don't!" He looked horrified. "Oh God, you don't think that I think that?"

I nodded. "Well, you treat me like that."

"Oh, baby, honey, sweetheart," he murmured, and then he hugged me. This proper hug that was so sweet; he rubbed my back, and then when we started kissing again, it was really romantic. No tongues, just lots of hair stroking and lip nibbling and he stopped digging his thing into my thigh. And when he drove me all the way home, instead of just driving off before I'd even closed the car door, he turned off the engine and squeezed my hand.

"Maybe we could go away after your play?" Rowan suggested. "For the weekend. My folks have got this time-share in Spain."

"You wanna go on holiday with me?" I squeaked in surprise. 'Cause Charlie used to say that he would *never* go away with me because without regular rest breaks I did his head in. Rowan kissed the tip of my nose and then gave me one of his slow, sexy smiles. "Wouldn't be asking if I didn't, would I?"

I sort of floated into the house on this cloud of happiness, and even Mum shouting from the lounge about whether I'd eaten the last Twix couldn't do anything to make it disappear. Until I got in the shower, looked down, and realized that going on holiday with Rowan would mean that he'd see me in my bikini. The only naked bits of me that he's seen so far are my face and my feet. And Katharina was nowhere to be found when I tried to summon her for a bit of a stern talking-to.

But weekends away together: it means one thing and one thing only. That he doesn't just want to shag me. He wants to have a relationship with me. Like, he wants to make a commitment or something.

Over the next couple of weeks, the rehearsals got really intense. Lavinia expected everyone to know their lines, and if they didn't, she'd go all Linda Blair on them. Without the pig's blood.

I was finding it very easy to be shrewish. All I had to do was look at Wanker or Daisy or Charlie all sitting there together and acting like they were too cool for school, and I automatically felt like a mardy cow. Charlie is just pathetic. He follows Wanker around like a little puppy dog, fetching and carrying. It is so obvious that Wanker is secretly laughing at him. He keeps calling him Charlie-boy, which is so patronizing. If Charlie and I were still friends, I'd totally call Wanker on it 'cause I know he is going to end up hurting Charlie.

And the reason I know it. Well, it was, like, destiny or something. I wasn't sure how it was going to happen, and when Lavinia asked me to get a couple of props from underneath the stage, all I was worried about was getting cobwebs in my hair.

It was all dark and musty down there, so I wasn't sure at first. I thought I could see something moving in the shadows, and I was terrified. 'Cause I'd been out for breakfast again with Lavinia that morning and she'd told me that when she was in rep loads of theaters were haunted by ghosts of girls from the chorus line who took their own lives when they were dumped by the leading man. Or it happened once in this playhouse in Hull.

So I stood there, rooted to the spot, squinting at the corner where I thought I'd seen something and trying to persuade my legs to move and get me the hell out of there. And then I heard sounds. Wet smacking sounds. Kissing sounds. Then the kissing sounds became talking sounds.

"How can you kiss me like that and still reckon that you're gay?" said a voice I knew I'd heard somewhere before. Then there was a laugh and a girl said, "Well, let's call it an experiment to test my sexual boundaries."

Okay, there's only one person I know who says wordy crap like that: Daisy!

Then there were more kissing sounds until he said, "I can't take much more of this. You're killing me. I'm sure Charlie knows that there's something up with us."

It was Wanker!

Wanker and Daisy sitting in a tree, K-I-S-S-I-N-G—and Charlie so didn't make three. And *she* is meant to be a great, big lesbian, and she'd molested me! Which I am so going to need therapy for when I'm older. What a tart. Then she said, "Oh, just shut up and kiss me."

When I got back upstairs without the props, I was dying to tell someone. 'Cause I never have any gossip. I'm, like, the last person to know anything. I looked for Tash and Gemma because if I didn't tell someone, I was going to burst. But as I hunted for them, it suddenly occurred to me that maybe I shouldn't. That it was some seriously wigged-out, private shit between Wanker and Daisy. And deep down, I knew that Charlie would be destroyed, and I didn't want that. We might not be friends anymore, but I didn't want to be responsible for him finding out something that would break his heart.

I did think about texting him, but it wasn't really the sort of thing you can explain using only a hundred and sixty characters. Besides, Rowan and I had this big night planned. He was taking me out to the cinema, and then we were going to a tapas bar. Really, it was our first proper date. So I decided not to do the text thing and thought about date stuff instead.

Rowan was dead romantic. He paid for everything that night and didn't even try and cop a feel during the film. And later, when we were in the restaurant and I was worrying about whether I should eat the salsa because I couldn't remember whether it had carbs in it or not, and it might make my breath all garlicky, he suddenly reached across the table and stroked my hand.

"Y'know, Brie, I'm really glad that we sorted stuff out," he murmured. "You're so cool."

I was just about to deny it but stopped myself, and instead I gave him what I hoped was a mysterious smile.

"Thanks, Ro," I said. "You're pretty cool, too."

There was this strange silence, and he was looking at me so intently that I had to stare at my fajitas instead.

"What?" I asked him in a small voice. "Have I got something in my hair?"

Rowan smiled faintly. "No, your hair looks gorgeous, just like the rest of you . . . Y'know, it's almost our one-month anniversary, we should do something really special."

I beamed at him. He was so the perfect boyfriend. He was romantic and caring and . . . and . . . those were the things that Daisy said were important if you were going to sleep with someone for the first time. And if we were going to go on holiday together, maybe it was a good idea to get it out of the way before we went so I could worry about the whole bikini thing instead.

"And it's the first night of the play," I reminded him. "There's gonna be a party afterward."

"Cool."

"And after that, I was thinking that maybe we could, um, y'know, do it." I said it so quickly that the words kinda ran into each other, and I don't think he understood me. He sat there blinking for a little bit, and then this slow smile crept over his face.

"You wanna have sex? With me?" He raised my hand to his lips and kissed the tips of my fingers, which was so swoony and like something out of a film.

So I nodded firmly. "Yeah, on our anniversary. It will be really romantic."

It takes a lot of preparation for an opening night and losing your virginity. Especially when they're both going to happen in the space of three hours.

I had to fit my bikini waxing and my tanning-booth appointments in around all the extra rehearsals. At one stage, when the hairdresser was running late, I thought I might have to go to the Arts Centre with my low-light foils in. I was glad that I was so busy 'cause it took my mind off the thought of having to stand in front of loads of people in a costume that made me look like the back end of a bus. And then having to take all my clothes off in front of just one person.

It was weird but the week just flew by, and then it was the morning of like, the biggest, scariest day of my life.

Lavinia reckoned that we shouldn't rehearse so we'd be fresh for tonight, but she expected us to get to the Arts Centre on time so we could help set up for the cast party.

Lugging crates of booze about and arranging potato snacks in bowls has never rated highly on my list of fun things to do, plus there was a good possibility that I could break a nail, so I sat under the shade of the big oak tree outside and went over my lines for the millionth time. Until I realized that I didn't need to 'cause they were wedged in my head so hard they'd probably stay there until the day I died.

So, now that I didn't have to worry about the play, it meant I could start freaking out about having sex and whether it would hurt or not.

I was just wondering whether Rowan would think it was really skanky if I bought some condoms, and if I actually had the nerve to go to Boots and buy them, when a shadow fell over me. I looked up to see Daisy hovering in front of me.

"Hey," she said, and then gestured at the book. "You having a last-minute run-through?"

Now, Daisy hadn't spoken to me since the kiss. Not like I'm bothered, so I didn't really get why she'd come out and was trying to make conversation.

I put the book on the ground, then realized it would get dirt and possibly creepy crawlies on it and closed it.

"What's up?" I asked, 'cause she was scuffing the grass with the toe of her revolting trainers and generally acting like she was pissed off about something. Like, hello, what else is new?

"I guess I'm nervous about tonight," she said, and sat down next to me. "And my life has suddenly gotten really complicated."

Complicated is not the word I'd use to describe sneaking off to swap spit with Wanker, but there you go. "Everyone's life is complicated," I said.

Daisy smiled really faintly like she hadn't considered that before and threw herself down on the ground. "I s'pose." She started making a daisy chain, her hands swift and sure as she wove the flowers together. "You know when I kissed you . . . ?"

"When you forced yourself on me, you mean, yeah?" Take that, superbitch!

Daisy pretended that I hadn't said anything. "Did you like it? I mean, just between you and me, was it okay, or did it completely gross you out and make you absolutely positive that you only wanted to kiss boys for the rest of your life?"

Now, if I hadn't caught the whole sucking-facefest with

Wanker, this might all have come as a bit of a shock, but even I could tell what she was really asking. Basically, was she a complete freak because she liked kissing boys *and* girls?

And I could have messed with her head because she so totally deserves it, but all I said was, "I know about you and Walker, and I couldn't give a shit. But if Charlie finds out, it's gonna tear him up, so you might wanna think about that." I felt really pleased with myself, too. Katharina was back! But then I glanced down, and Daisy had stopped making the chain; her hands were folded in her lap, and they were wet with tears. I looked up and her shoulders were shaking, and then she was proper crying. Sobbing, heaving, quite a lot of phlegmy stuff.

I patted her on the back. "Um, er, don't cry."

"Oh God," she hiccuped. "I've made this awful mess. There's Claire and I'm meant to love her, and then there's *him* and he annoys the hell out of me."

"He annoys the hell out of everyone," I pointed out, and Daisy raised her tear-stained face in a halfhearted smile, which you could hardly see because of all the snot coming out of her nose, before resuming her sobfest. "I'm just saying, Daisy—"

"But he's funny, too, and he's really kind," she said almost as if she was talking to herself. "Thoughtful. And the things we do, the things I let him do to me . . . I'm meant to be gay!"

If I had to listen to another word, my head would explode. A few weeks ago she was being all superior because she thought that gay people should be allowed to kiss straight people if they wanted. And it sounded like she was doing way more than kissing Wanker, and she was having freakin' hysterics about it.

"Maybe you're not as gay as you thought you were." This was so not my area of expertise. I just don't get any of this gay business and why it has to be such a big deal. "It's just, like, you're only a little bit gay instead of a lot gay."

"That's the most asinine thing you've ever said," Daisy began, and then stopped. "You can't be a little bit gay, it doesn't make any sense."

"Yeah, and being a lot gay and getting off with Walker does?"

I got to my feet and scooped up my book. "Like I said, if Charlie gets hurt then you're both gonna be really sorry. There might be bitchslapping involved." And while she was processing that, I walked off. Lavinia says it's always best to leave your audience wanting more, and besides, I was so totally ready for my close-up.

I don't remember much about my performance. I remember standing in the wings and scratching my ribs because the bodice of my dress was super-itchy, and then I heard, "Such friends as times in Padua shall beget," which was my cue, and I took a deep breath and walked onstage.

Once I stood under the warm glow of the spotlights, I felt at home. It was fun. I thought that I'd have sweaty palms and I'd want to race through my lines just so I could get offstage as quickly as possible, but it just wasn't the case. It was about being part of a story, and I got totally into the moment, just like Lavinia said I would. It didn't matter that I fluffed a couple of my lines because I was being someone else; getting to live someone else's life for a little while. And I remembered all the stuff that Lavinia and I had talked about. And when Petruchio started acting like a complete sexist pig and wanted me to tell him that it was night when really it was day, I rolled my eyes and sighed and shrugged my shoulders as if to say, *My husband's a complete mentalist, but what can you do?* The audience loved it. Even though it wasn't the end of the play, when we finished that scene, they started clapping.

I even managed to kiss Walker without gagging. I hadn't let him near me in rehearsals, especially since I found out about him and Daisy, but all I had to do was press my lips against his and hold them there for a count of three. I was secretly relieved that I didn't feel one teensy bit of sexual attraction toward him. I'd always wondered whether he had some kind of chemical thingy that he gave off that made girls want him, but I didn't feel anything.

I got a standing ovation when we took to the stage after the show. I clutched this bunch of freesias to my chest so no one could see any possible glimpses of the chicken fillets poking out of the low-cut dress, and listened to the applause and the cheering. It was all for me. I was the center of attention because I'd been good at something. Me! Yeah, I could get used to this.

There's this song on our iPod, one of Charlie's, with this line in it about being the girl with the most cake, and I felt like that. As I stood on the stage and took curtain after curtain, I had a glimpse of this girl that I could be if I wanted to. I was free to be whoever the hell it was that I was meant to be. Not Katharina exactly. And not Brie, but someone in the middle.

And then the curtain fell for the last time, and someone's arms suddenly were around me, and I heard Charlie whisper in my ear, "You rocked, babes!" For a moment, I leaned back, and the feel of him around me was just as good as the applause.

Then I saw Rowan standing in the wings and waving at me, and I wrenched myself free. "You're gay," I hissed. "So stop mauling me!"

I felt horrible about that afterward. But then Mum and Dad were there, and even though *she* couldn't bring herself to say anything other than, "Maroon really isn't your color, sweetheart," Dad gave me a hug! He, like, touched me. "I'm so proud of you," he said. "Really, you were quite remarkable. Maybe we should think about looking into drama schools for you."

I was still reeling from that when someone gave me my first glass of wine. And after that it was a blur of faces and more wine and everyone hugging everyone else and Rowan holding my hand and refusing to let go, even though it made the wine drinking and the flower holding kinda difficult.

Rowan was being very touchy-feely and kept whispering about how he couldn't wait for us to be alone.

"You even look hot in Elizabethan gear," he murmured at one point before trying to lick my ear, and then I got this sinking feeling, as if my stomach had just ended up on the floor. We were going to be having sex. And actually all I wanted was a hot bath and my bed.

There was only one way to get through it, and it wasn't sober. "I need another drink. Now!" I announced, and another glass of wine appeared. And another. It was like that magic pot of porridge from this story I used to read when I was a kid, only with more alcohol.

By the time I went back to the dressing room to get my stuff, I was having trouble doing the little things that I normally take for granted. Like, walking in a straight line and opening doors and putting my clothes on.

I'd just managed to get my new Mango dress over my head when Rowan sidled in. "You too good to knock?" I asked as I tried to pull the dress down so I wasn't flashing my fat thighs at him.

He just smiled. "Alone at last."

And really, I thought, looking at him properly, he could have made more of an effort than a pair of ripped jeans and a T-shirt that had faded in the wash. It was my big opening night, after all. I turned around to hang up my dress and felt him come up behind me.

"I can't wait," he rasped, sliding his hands up my arm.

"Yeah, that's nice," I said absentmindedly as I stretched up to put the hanger on the rail.

"No, I really *can't* wait. Let's do it now." That's when his hands grabbed my tits and his leg shoved in between mine. And it was so not sexy. It was rough, not tender, and then he started sucking on my neck, and instead of freaking out about the chicken fillets and how fat I was under my clothes, I knew that there was no way I was going to do this. Because deep in my heart, I knew that I didn't want to. I just wasn't ready. I might not be ready for, like, another ten years.

"Rowan! Cut it out," I snapped, and tried to wriggle free, but he just kept groping me and pushing at me, so I was pressed up against the wall.

"Stop playing hard to get. You said tonight and I've waited bloody long enough," he hissed. And his hands were all over my arse, trying to yank the skirt of my dress up, and I heard a ripping noise. When I tried to turn around, his hand was there at the small of my back, so I couldn't really move. He was so much bigger than me—which I'd never worried about before, but now it was all I could think about. Didn't matter how many workouts I'd done, it wasn't enough to push him away.

"No!" I said sharply. "I don't want to. Get off me."

"You're such a cocktease!"

"I am not. Get off me!" I was shouting now and bucking my hips to try and dislodge him, but his whole body was leaning into mine, and his hands had my arms pinned to my side.

"I've spent weeks on you." He sounded angry, like he had a right to be. "And I want something back in return."

"Get off! Get off! Get off!" It was funny because when you actually need to scream, it doesn't come out right. It comes out as this choked noise. I felt as if I was underwater. Every time I tried to move, it seemed like I was weighted down, and for one little second, I kinda thought that maybe it would be easier to just let him because I didn't know how to make this stop.

His leg was worming its way between my thighs again, and that's when I'd decided that I'd just about had enough. I went really still and Rowan chuckled. "I knew you'd come round to my way of thinking," he said. Then he relaxed his grip on me and tugged me around by the shoulder so now I could get my arms free, bring my hands up, and scratch my nails down his face. I'd seen Sydney Bristow do it in an episode of *Alias* when the baddies had given her this strength-sapping injection, and it worked pretty well for me, too.

Rowan jumped back and touched his fingers to the bleeding marks on his cheeks. "Ow! You fucking bitch! What the fuck did you do that for?"

"I said no!" I screeched. "What part of *no* don't you understand?"

"Oh, don't make out that I forced myself on you. You wanted it as much as I did," he ranted furiously.

I elbowed him out of the way in my rush to get to the door, but he was there first, his hands grabbing at me, and this time I didn't give him a chance. I picked up the wooden sword that was lying on the bench next to me and whacked him over the head with it.

"You tore my new dress, you stupid bastard," I yelled just as the door opened and Charlie burst in.

"If I wait for the right moment
would you say yes to me?
If all my friends desert me
would you be there for me?"

Charlie

I kicked the door open in this bizarre macho display of aggression just in time to see Brie bashing Rowan over the head with a prop sword, which, being made of plywood, promptly fell to pieces.

"You tore my new dress, you stupid bastard," she was screaming, more furiously than I'd ever thought possible, while he shook shards of wood out of his curls. "And thanks for trying to rape me!"

Well, when I heard that and I saw the scratch marks on his face, I put two and two together and came up with about a gazillion. "Okay, I'm going to kill you," I announced in a deranged voice, and then I punched him, which actually really hurt me.

I'd never noticed how big Rowan is because he wears all these oversize skater clothes, but once he pinned me to the wall by my throat, I began to realize my mistake.

"Um, Ro? Might want to let him go," I heard Walker say behind me.

Rowan bared his teeth in a sharklike smile. "Yeah, I will after I've punched him back."

"Okay, I'll wait for you to do that, and then I'll beat the crap out of you," Walker said reasonably.

Somehow I'd stumbled onto the set of *The Sopranos*, and it was going to end in bloodshed and cement body bags.

Rowan let me go so quickly that I slid down the wall and looked up to see Walker and Daisy standing in the doorway. Brie twisted around so she could mournfully assess the damage to her dress and then crouched down in front of me.

"You all right, Charlie?"

"Am *I* all right? Are *you* all right?"

On a scale of one to ten, I'd have given her smile a very shaky three. "Yeah, I'm fine," she said. "Well, I was fine, and then everything went crappy again."

It wasn't the resigned way she said it, as if things going crappy was inevitable and she'd be stupid to think otherwise, that made me realize why I love Brie. It was the way she'd charged at Rowan like a Valkyrie, wielding that silly sword like she was about to slay a dragon, that made me realize that I hadn't stopped loving her. That I'd probably never stop loving her. Even when we are both old and gray and sitting side by side in the nursing home, dribbling into our bowls of semolina and arguing about what teen movie we want to watch next.

See, I get to see the bits of Brie that no one else ever gets to see. And there's more to her than being pretty with really low self-esteem issues.

Brie's cheek was baby soft as I put my hand out to stroke it, and then yanked it back because I wasn't allowed to touch her anymore because I was a stupid dickhead who'd thrown away my best girl.

"Why are you looking at me like that?" Brie asked. "My hair's gone frizzy, hasn't it?"

"Jesus, Brie, you've just been physically assaulted, and all you can do is worry about your hair," Daisy screeched, yanking Brie up and enveloping her in this full-on hug, which made Brie yelp and squirm to get away.

"Where's Walker?" I asked, because he seemed to have vanished and taken Mr. Date Rapist with him.

Daisy let go of Brie, who shot away from her embrace like she'd just been scalded and went back to fingering the torn back seam of her dress. "He told Rowan to step outside so they could have a little chat," Daisy said, making quotation marks with her fingers. "I have a feeling violence might be involved."

"Well, I don't know why." Brie sounded cross and began stuffing things into her fake Louis Vuitton holdall with a certain amount of savagery. "I was totally dealing with that jerk. I'm not helpless."

Daisy looked like she wanted to argue that point, but I managed to pull myself into a standing position and held my hands out in front of me in protest. "Just don't. There's been enough theatricals for one evening."

"Yeah, and it's not like you're doing such a great job of getting *your* life together," Brie murmured darkly, and I wasn't sure if she was talking to me or Daisy.

Daisy went bright red and opened her mouth to say something no doubt cutting and bitchy, but then thought better of it—for probably the first time in her life. "I should go and find Walker," she said. "Make sure he's okay."

We didn't have a big discussion about it, but I ended up going home with Brie. She was being very calm, apart from the continuous moaning about how Mango dresses didn't grow on trees and how she was going to make Rowan pay for a new frock. She stalked out of the dressing room with her head held high, and all I could do was stumble along behind her.

Walker was standing outside smoking a cigarette and looking at his knuckles like he'd just sent them crashing into Rowan's face. He slowly uncoiled himself as Brie marched past and gently touched her on the arm.

"Rowan says he's sorry," he said, in such a way that I knew Rowan hadn't said anything of the sort.

Brie simply looked at Walker's hand curled loosely around her forearm, until he got the hint and let go.

"Are you okay?"

"I wish people would stop asking me that. I'm fine, but I'm sending him the bill for my dress. Look at it!"

Walker peered over her shoulder. "Hmm, yeah, looks torn and, er, nasty," he said gravely. "So, you two fancy a celebratory drink?"

Brie flared her nostrils. "Are you, like, joking? You know, this was meant to be my big night, and it got totally ruined."

"But you were great, Brie!" I said hastily, in an effort to jolly her out of this strange mood. "Wasn't she, Walker?"

He shot an amused glance in my direction from under his lashes. "You blew everyone else off the stage. You're quite a hard act to follow," he admitted.

"Well, it's about finding your motivation," Brie replied with a secret little smile hovering over her mouth. Then she straightened up. "Anyway, I'm going home now."

"I'll walk with you," I offered.

Brie raised her eyebrows. "Whatever."

"I'm just going to go and find Daisy and see if she needs a lift or . . . something," Walker muttered. *Gotta love the boy for making even a ride home seem like an invitation to depraved sexual acts,* I thought as I followed Brie's majestic sweep out of the main doors.

Brie kept up the Ice Princess routine all the way to the bus stop. It was very unsettling. I know her better than anyone, or I thought I did, but these last few weeks since I ripped us apart have turned her into this unapproachable girl I don't know how to talk to anymore.

I wanted to gather her up in my arms, feel her thin bones underneath my fingers, and just have everything be all right again. Not this. Not sitting next to her on the bus and racking my brains for something to say to her.

Brie didn't seem to notice that I was in complete turmoil. Or maybe she did. Maybe I don't know anything about her. I thought that she'd crumple up and die without me, and instead she managed very well, thank you very much.

When we got to her gate, though, she looked over her shoulder at me. "You coming in then or what?"

Thankfully, Brie's parents seemed to be off the premises as I climbed the stairs to her room. It had only been like three weeks since I was last here, but when I opened the door and had my nostrils assaulted by the familiar smell of expensive skin-care products and the acetone whiff of nail-polish remover, I almost keeled over. And not just because Brie had been heavy-handed with the hair spray.

I sat on her bed, jiggling my feet and wondering what I

could possibly say to her to make it all right again. Sorry might be a good start, but it didn't seem like enough.

"I made tea." Brie padded across the carpet and placed two steaming mugs on the nightstand, then folded her arms. "I know what you're thinking, Charlie. You're trying to come up with some big speech about how I always fuck up when you're not around, but you can just save it, all right?"

I squinted up at her. "Actually I was thinking of going down on my hands and knees and begging your forgiveness," I said hopefully.

"Oh." That was all I got. Just "Oh." And then she reached past me to get her pajamas where they were neatly folded underneath her pillow and went into the bathroom to change.

I gazed at the ceiling. Then I gazed at the spot on the carpet where I'd spilled Diet Dr Pepper. Not for the first time I wished that Brie didn't take so long in the bathroom.

When she came out, pink-faced and slathered in moisturizer, I expected another earful.

Instead she walked over to me, raised her hand, and slapped me around the face. Then she smiled beatifically. "Okay, I feel better now. You staying over?"

I touched my cheek in disbelief. "You just hit me!"

"Well, duh! Look, when I try and say stuff, it always comes out wrong and then I get frustrated and angry. So you hurt me and now I've hurt you, so we're even."

God, I totally love her. Even though she is unhinged. And just then, there was only one thing left to do, which was to yank her down so she was sitting on my lap and put my arms around her.

"I love you, you silly bitch," I murmured into her neck.

"Yeah, well, I love you, too, even though you're mean," she replied, and burrowed against me, her hands stroking the back of my neck.

We sat like that for a while, and then Brie rolled off me and started chucking her vast collection of cuddly toys off the bed. Her bottom wiggled with the effort, and I gave in to the temptation and gave it a good smack.

"You're such a pervert," she hissed, and threw a skanky-looking teddy bear at my head, before tugging back the duvet.

I toed off my sneakers and got rid of my jeans and then crawled in next to her, smooshing against her back and wrapping my arms around her waist.

I think I'd probably been mulling it over ever since the bus ride—the reason why we'd split up, which indirectly had led to that awful scene with Rowan in the dressing room. Even though Brie'd bitchslapped me, it didn't seem like enough to make it all right. It needed some grand, dramatic, and utterly selfless gesture on my part. It was either that or grovel.

"So, do you still want to . . . with me?" My voice sounded incredibly loud in the dim light of her room, and I felt Brie give a start.

"I thought you were GAY," she squeaked, and rolled over.

"I am," I said, sitting up as she turned on the bedside lamp. "I'm so gay, I'm, like, the very gayest of all the gays, but you know, it's what friends are for, and I hate the thought that you'll find another creep like Rowan and do it with him, when your first time should be special."

Brie hugged her knees and frowned at me. "But *your* first time should be special, too. Or, like, have you done it with someone already?"

Just for a second I let my eyes glaze over at the thought of last summer's holiday romance, Pedro. The cabana boy who taught me the ways of the world and then broke my heart, and who would remain a secret that I'd take to my grave because actually he wasn't that cute, but, my goodness, he did things with his tongue . . .

Brie waved her hand in front of my eyes to get my attention, and I realized that I'd zoned off into an Iberian world of cold Sol lager and hot kisses.

"Sorry, I was just—"

"I don't know, Charlie, 'cause I love you and you're gay and if we do it and it's crap I might go off you and if it's really good I might be even more in love with you."

I expected to feel relieved when she turned me down. I didn't expect to feel, well, like I wasn't good enough for her. It wasn't so much that I wanted to have sex with Brie, but I kinda wanted *her* to have sex with me. I mean, she is a girl and she has girl parts, which are as alien to me as life on Mars, but everyone needs a little validation now and again.

"Are you sure?" I asked, unable to keep the huffiness out of my voice, and she had the nerve to giggle and poke her tongue out at me.

"This is like, completely ironic, isn't it?"

"I guess," I said sulkily.

"You asking me to do it with you, and I'm all like, I don't think so, and you getting pissed off."

I narrowed my eyes at her. "I am not pissed off."

She gave me a self-satisfied smile. "Yeah, you are. You love me. You want me. You ain't gonna have me!"

"You're so enjoying this, aren't you?"

"Oh yeah!" Brie nodded and then leaned over and kissed me on the cheek, her hair brushing against my chest. "It meant a lot that you asked, though. I suppose this means that you're my best friend again."

"Well, the offer's there if you change your mind."

Brie snuggled down, her head on my shoulder and her hand clutching mine. "Well, if I'm still a virgin ten years from now, we can talk about it then. Now shut up and go to sleep."

But I couldn't sleep. Before long, Brie was sprawled out on her back making strange little panting noises, and all of a sudden I was scared to touch her. Because I wasn't just relieved that she'd spurned my advances, I was *disappointed*.

I spent ages trying to work out what the hell that was about until my eyelids started dropping downward and refused to stay open.

When I woke up in the morning, Brie was wrapped around me like a blanket, her leg hitched over my thighs and her hand resting on my heart. We'd been in this position a million times before. I'd even had an erection before, but this time it had less to do with needing a pee or what I'd been dreaming about in REM sleep, and more to do with how soft Brie's skin felt against mine and why it made all my nerve endings suddenly itch.

I shifted restlessly underneath her, and Brie opened her eyes and gave me a sleepy smile. "Hey," she husked in a croaky voice. She nibbled her bottom lip between her teeth and frowned. "You look freaked. Have I got bedhead?"

Yup, in her quirky, self-involved way, Brie had hit the nail right on the head. 'Cause, yes, I was absolutely freaked. Because I'm gay, but all of a sudden I want to kiss her more than anything else in the world. But you just can't say stuff like that to your best friend. You can think about it and you can not understand why you're thinking about it, but the last thing you should do is say it or raise your head just far enough so you can find out if her lips taste as sweet as they look.

And then we were kissing. Brie and me were kissing. Lips on lips and my hands tangled in her hair so I could tilt her head back and dip my tongue inside her mouth.

It was like a Hollywood screen kiss, just before the picture fades to black and you know the hero and the heroine are going to ride off into the sunset and live happily ever after. Except this was Brie and me. It was me rolling us over so I could look at her, all pink and glowing, her hair fanned out on the pillow. It was her hands scampering across my chest, stroking and kneading at my flesh like I was her own personal piece of plasticine.

And my hands were creeping under her tank top, and she was letting me, leaning back to give me more room; her breath hitching in her throat. Our limbs tangling together on the tangled sheets . . .

But then the thought popped into my head that I was going to see her naked. Naked Brie! Oh my God! Brie was going to be naked and we used to build sand castles together and I remembered the first day at nursery when she fell over in the playground and burst into tears . . .

"Oh, *ewww! Ewwwww!* Oh, Charlie, *ewwwww!*" Brie was pushing me away so violently that I rolled off the bed with a yelp, a manly yelp, to land on the floor.

She peered down at me, then peered down at herself and grabbed the end of the duvet. "Sorry about that," she squeaked. "Oh God. This is weird and *ewwww*. Like, I don't think I love you in this way, Charlie. It's like trying to have sex with my teddy bear or something. Can we not? I'll just die a virgin, it's okay."

Just like that we went from tawdry teen lust to looking at each other with matching expressions of horror. Brie pulled a face and started making gagging noises. "Ugh! I have Charlie-taste in my mouth."

"Cheers, Brie," I snapped, and then wiped the back of my hand across my lips. "Can I just say that you have the worst morning breath!"

I got a permafrost glare from her, and I couldn't help it, I flopped back onto the carpet and started to laugh. I laughed so hard that the tears streamed down my face and trickled into my ears. I was dimly aware of Brie moving, and then she leaned over me and whapped me over the head with her pillow.

"You're a crap snog." She giggled. "No wonder you're still single."

I snatched the pillow out of her hands, resisting her feeble attempts to do some damage with it and pulled it over my head. "Brie, what the fuck is wrong with me?"

"I don't know, Charlie. Maybe you're having gender issues," she replied seriously, and then frowned. "I think I've spent too much time with Daisy, the big slut."

Huh? I'd forgotten Brie's habit of randomly insulting people for no apparent reason; it's one of the things I've missed most. But then I remembered that I was actually in the middle of a sexual identity crisis.

I grabbed big handfuls of my hair and whimpered. "I don't get it. 'Cause five minutes ago I really fancied, really, *really* fancied you, like you were Orlando Bloom or something." Brie didn't seem too happy to be compared to the lithe star of *The Lord of the Rings*. She peered down at her chest as if to check that her breasts were still attached, and then, assured that they were, she gave me her full attention.

"And then . . . ?" she prompted, curling her legs under her and reaching for her Aveda hand cream.

"And then I didn't. I mean, I don't. And it wasn't like I was just having an experimental fiddle with you . . ."

"Well, gee, that's a nice way to put it . . ."

"Oh, stop pouting, you know what I mean. It was like it was our bodies fancying each other but not our heads."

Brie looked up from rubbing gloop into her palms. "This gay thing is really confusing. There should be a book."

"Or possibly flash cards," I added. "But now I'm back to where I was before, which is being madly in love with Walker, the straightest boy in the 0207 area code."

A small *pfffft*ing noise came from Brie's direction. "Walker," she said by way of explanation.

"Walker what?"

"Just Walker. Really, Charlie, you don't want to go there. Take it from me," she said in a manner that would have been condescending if it was anyone else. But coming from Brie, it just sounded funny, like she was trying on someone else's voice to see if it would fit.

"I can't think about this anymore," I groaned. "Maybe I'm just destined to never understand this whole sex thing. It'll just end up giving me worry lines."

Brie scrambled to her feet and jumped off the end of the bed. "I'm going to have a shower now, and the thing we did before? With the kissing and stuff? I think that we should never, ever mention it again. Okay?"

"A world of yes," I agreed fervently.

I listened to the sounds of Brie showering, then using her electric toothbrush (two minutes for the top row, two minutes for the bottom row). There were a few clonking noises as she chose various bottles and pots of face gunk and even a muffled "shit" when she dropped something on the floor. It was so good to be back.

I crawled across the floor to get to my drawer and pull out clean boxers and a T-shirt. Downstairs, I could hear the family of Brie having breakfast, and outside birds were tweeting and the world was generally getting its shit together on what looked like was going to be another gloriously sunny day. I looked up as Brie walked out of the bathroom. She gave me a smile, but there was something wrong with it. Like, it was an effort to keep it on her face.

"Charlie," she said, and touched me gently on the shoulder. "Charlie, I need to talk to you about Walker. And Daisy."

*"There's no escaping
the fact that you're a girl and he's a boy."*

Daisy

Even though I swore it was never going to happen again, I woke for the fifth morning in a row to the sound of Walker's clock radio tuned to XFM and some shite moperock blaring out.

Walker's arm tightened around my waist. "Turn the bloody thing off," he grunted, rolling over and yanking me close like I was his own personal full-length body pillow.

Last night we finished the performance late, climbed into the Bug, and he announced casually, "Let's go to Southend!"

"Let's not because it's nine o'clock, and we have to get up early tomorrow."

But he was already firing up the ignition. "Oh, come on, it'll take an hour this time of night on the M25. There's this fantastic fish-and-chip shop called Baileys and we can go on the rides."

"But Walker . . . !"

"But Daisy!" he echoed in a stupid impersonation that he thinks sounds like me. "When was the last time you did something you shouldn't?"

That would have been precisely eight hours before, when we'd sneaked back to his house and spent the hour rolling about on his bedroom floor. I looked up, and from the dark glint in his eyes and the way his tongue swiped across his lips, it was clear that he was remembering, too. "Apart from that, I mean," he said throatily, and then he was cupping the back of my head so he could kiss me, and we ended up going to Southend.

He's such a bad influence on me. Before he came along, I had order and lists and an absolute, unshakable belief in who I was. Now? Chaos, self-doubt, and confusion.

It's like I've turned into someone else. When I look in the mirror, I don't recognize the girl I see staring back at me with her kiss-swollen lips and the slightly dreamy look in her eyes. When we'd gotten back to his place at way past midnight, he'd lit candles and put on a CD by some sweet-voiced soul singer and kissed me for hours and hours until I couldn't even have told him my own name.

Funny how different things look in the morning. Like now, when there was a cloud of stale cigarette smoke hovering over me, and all I could see were dustballs and overflowing ashtrays.

I dug my nails into the hand that was currently ghosting toward my breasts, and when he yelped in protest and let go, I scrambled out of bed and then yanked the duvet off him to cover my, oh sweet Jesus, naked body.

"Huh!" he snorted as I dug under his bed to find my bra, then wished that I hadn't as I came face-to-face with a mound of dirty plates.

"Huh what?"

"You've been awake for all of two minutes, and already you've managed to physically attack me before you make plans to run off with your lesbian street cred in tatters. I think that must be some kind of personal best, Daze."

It's very hard to keep a duvet wrapped around you while you struggle into your underwear *and* give Walker a glare that would turn less thick-skinned boys to stone, but I managed it. I've always been good at multitasking.

"I have to meet Claire for breakfast," I hissed, and his face went all squinchy and slitty-eyed.

"Yeah, well, give her my love," he blustered in the lamest comeback of all time.

"Hardly." I sneered. "And just so you know, we will not be doing this again. I think my sanity just returned."

Walker propped himself up on one elbow as I buttoned up my shirt. "You always say that," he pointed out, and his voice had gone gentle and was almost veering toward tender. I hate it when it does that. "But you always come back."

"Not this time," I said firmly. I sounded really resolute. A girl who has made her mind up and then sticks with it.

"If you meant that, it would make things so much easier for both of us," Walker said cryptically.

I didn't have time to bawl him out or get into another argument. "I'll see you at the Arts Centre," I said, opening the door, but he just rolled over so he could quite literally give me the cold shoulder.

Claire seemed to have inherited Walker's filthy mood. Though to be fair, she's been really standoffish since she got back from Devon. Normally I would have been more concerned, but it's just one more thing on my list of things that I don't really want to deal with.

I'd barely sat down and taken a restorative sip of coffee before she started. "I know you've been seeing someone else," she announced flatly, and while I was still reeling from that blow, she continued: "I have a feeling that it started while I was away. Did it?"

"No," I protested, because technically I started seeing someone while I was in the same county as her. Which wasn't really answering the question, but the thing with Walker was just a temporary blip, and there was no point in fessing up over a completely non-relationship. "Why would I be seeing someone else?"

"Oh, fuck off, Daisy. You have the world's biggest love bite on your neck, and I don't recognize the teeth marks."

My hand shot up to cover the bruise that Walker had left last night. I was going to kill him later. Why didn't he just piss up my leg and be done with it?

"I'm not seeing someone," I insisted, and then I plowed on because I never know when to just shut my mouth. "It's just about sex, but I'm sure you know all about that."

Sometimes I think that Claire and I have just been having a continuous argument ever since she got back from Devon. The words change but not the feeling of being furious and scratchy with each other. Right now she was giving me her finest Wrath of God look as she chased a chip around a big splodge of ketchup. "Is this payback?"

"Payback for what?"

"For me going to peace camp without you." She said it really carefully, like she'd deliberately weighed up the words in her head. "For maybe fooling around with a couple of people." The strange thing was that my world didn't cave in when she actually admitted that. Instead I felt like this ginormous load had been lifted from my shoulders. "Oh. You and that girl, the one with the lip piercing?"

Claire squirmed in her seat before she could check the movement. "I just wanted to test the limits of our relationship," she explained primly. "It's important to explore who we are."

"You said people," I suddenly piped up. "People, as in boys and girls. You been fooling around with a *guy*?"

She didn't have to say anything; the disgusted look on her face said it all. "As if! I mean, why would I want to do that? In case you hadn't noticed, I'm a lesbian."

"Just checking." I tried to sound light and breezy, but I wasn't fooling anyone.

"Are you sure that there's nothing you want to tell me?" Claire asked suspiciously. "This other person that you're not seeing, they wouldn't happen to be of the male persuasion, would they?"

I looked down at the plate of slowly congealing egg yolk and cold chips. "Maybe," I replied in a small voice, conveniently forgetting that having an open relationship was meant to be a hypothetical thing. "But I'm just exploring who I am, too."

There was a whistling sound as she took a sharp breath. "Well, aren't you just new all over? I thought you were meant to be the big lesbian warrior."

"I am! I am!"

"So what, like, you're bisexual now? Or were you just trying on being gay for a while because you heard all the cool kids were doing it? Do you still love me? Or am I too—"

I clamped my hands over my ears. "Just stop it! I don't know! I just don't know!"

"Who is he?" I wished she'd just stop with the twenty freakin' questions.

"No one you know," I said too quickly, and her whole expression went sour like she'd sucked the juice out of a bag of lemons. "Just some guy from the play." No way was I telling her it was Walker, who she disliked more intensely than any other person alive. Apart from George Bush. Even Charlie gets her pursed-lipped disapproval because he's "frivolous and that GAYER T-shirt is fucking insulting."

Claire didn't say anything for a while, just picked at the chips. And I started to feel resentful, not because I was expected to entirely validate my sexuality but because she was more annoyed about that than the fact that I'd been seeing someone else behind her back. Like, feel the love, not!

"You'd better sort yourself out, Daze," she informed me fiercely. "Otherwise you're going to have to resign from about half your committees, and that's not gonna look good on your university application, is it? That you have a problem with commitment."

As I stomped up the High Street, already resigned to the fact that I was late for rehearsals, I heard the beep of the Bug's horn and looked around to see Walker driving slowly alongside me and completely ignoring the abuse he was getting from the long trail of cars behind him.

"Get in," he ordered tersely.

I got in, before he became the victim of some random road-rage attack.

"Um, thanks," I mumbled unwillingly, and wished my mother hadn't been so big on instilling manners into me.

"Whatever."

I was saved from having to actually talk to him (when I couldn't even begin to find the words) by my mobile beeping. It was a text from Claire: *Sorry I was such a bitch. I luv U— even tho I don't show it enuf. The boy thing freaked me out but if you can deal so can i. Call me.*

My life seemed to have turned into an episode of *The Jerry Springer Show*. They'd call it "I'm cheating on my lesbian lover with a boy slut." It would have made things easier, taken fifty percent of my choices away, if she'd just messaged me to let me know that I was never to darken her doorstep again.

"No one's forcing you to do this," Walker suddenly bit out, interrupting my unhappy reverie. I glanced over to see his knuckles were white as they gripped the steering wheel. "You might wanna think about why you're getting naked on a daily basis with someone you claim to loathe."

"I never said I loathed you," I pointed out. "Well, not recently, not since . . ."

"Not since you got your hands on my hot, tight body," Walker said succinctly. "Lesbian, shmesbian!"

"I wish I was asexual." I sighed. "Like a plant. It would really simple my life up. All I'd have to worry about was photosynthesizing."

"You want to know why I'm so irresistible to a professional lesbian such as yourself?" Walker continued, cutting through two lines of traffic to make a right, which earned him a chorus of angry car horns.

"Oh, do give me the benefit of your experience," I said with deep sarcasm.

"When it's dark and we're on our own and you've managed to extricate the stick that's usually wedged up your arse, none of that sexual politics crap, which you hide behind because it's easier than actually having to deal with life, matters. I'm just a boy; you're just a girl. We're having a relationship—"

"We are NOT having a relationship," I growled. "It's just a sexual experiment."

Walker turned into the Arts Centre car park, narrowly missing a traffic post in his fury. "Or your dirty little secret. Which is why you won't tell anyone about us."

He'd been like this all week. Wringing his hands about sneaking around behind Charlie's back. Not that it was any of Charlie's business. I felt the familiar clench-unclench of my stomach as I worried for the fiftieth time that morning about whether Brie would have the stones to tell Charlie about catching me and Walker mid-tussle.

"Jesus," Walker muttered angrily, flinging off his seat belt and opening the car door. "We're like sodding Buffy and Spike. Somewhere in this there's a whole metaphor happening where you have me equated with a soulless vampire."

"What the hell are you going on about now?" I asked, shouldering him out of the way because he was just standing there fuming.

"If I didn't love you quite as much as I do, and God knows why I do—"

"Just shut the fuck up!" I upgraded my growling to screeching. "You don't love me! You think you love me because I'm not so much of a pushover as the skanky trolls you usually hang out with."

We were standing outside the main hall now. Walker wedged his hand into my armpit and hauled me into an alcove. "Why are you like this?"

"Because I'm confused about why I seem to prefer spending all my time getting sexual with a boy. Shall I say that again? A *boy* who personifies everything I hate about hetero-sexuality."

That was Walker's cue to mash his mouth against mine. It was a show of dominance and aggression, and I curled my hands into his hair so I could strain against him, deepen the kiss until my knees went trembly, and I was pretty sure that if I opened my eyes, all I'd be able to see in front of me would be twinkling stars. Or possibly God.

Walker broke the kiss off first. We stood there, leaning into each other and panting. Then he gently caressed my bottom lip with his thumb. "That's why I stick around. Doesn't matter how much shit you throw at me, you kiss me like that, Daisy, and it tells me everything I need to know."

I sagged against the wall, his words pricking into my over-sensitized flesh like burning arrows. Walker stooped down to pick up his jacket, which had fallen on the floor during his clinch, and then turned toward the hall again.

"Either you tell Charlie or I do," he said over his shoulder. "I don't like lying to him just because you have issues on your issues."

I had to go and apply lip balm then, painfully aware that I might be morphing into a Brie clone. But even she didn't have as much cause as me to continually smear my abused lips with copious amounts of Vaseline. When I got into the hall, Walker was slumped in a chair, glowering. I sat down next to him, and he scraped his chair, like, two millimeters away from mine.

"You're so immature," I whispered to him, but he wasn't paying any attention, just looking at the doors as Brie and Charlie walked in, her hand tucked into the crook of his arm.

"Well, that's interesting," he mumbled. "Looks like we'll be expected to tender our resignation as Charlie-boy's new best friends."

"Charlie's not like that," I said, but what did I know? Charlie shot a dark look in our direction and then let Brie pull him over to the other side of the room, where her little wannabe brigade was hanging out.

"Oh my God!" I prodded Walker's arm. "He knows! Do you think he knows? I bet she told him!"

Walker turned to me and arched his eyebrow in a manner that makes my toes curl up and I would never admit to anyone. "Hang on, you're saying Brie knows?"

"It's a whole thing," I said vaguely, hoping that it would put him off the scent. "She walked in on us under the stage one time. It's no big deal."

Walker went from nought to huffy in five seconds. "You're unfuckingbelievable," he said.

"Don't be mad at me," I begged, even though I knew he had every right to be. "I'm sorry, it's just all this is—"

"I really don't think I can bear to hear you spout the lesbian manifesto again," he spat at me, and inched his chair even farther away from me.

But that was the least of my worries because just then Lavinia glided in—well, as much as a woman who suffers from arthritis but insists on wearing heels can glide—and proceeded to tear all of us and our performances the night before to shreds.

She reserved her special venom just for me. "I've seen more emotion from a sack of potatoes," she shrilled, banging her cane down on the floor, while I wished that she'd just disappear in a cloud of sulfurous smoke like the witch that she was. "You have no respect for the play, no respect for me, your fellow actors, or yourself, to turn in a performance so singularly lacking in anything noteworthy. At best, you were barely competent. At worst, you were a travesty. The Bard is turning in his grave."

It was too much. I wanted to jump out of my body. My stupid, fat body that seemed to want to spend most of its time wrapped around Walker's. I couldn't bear to be in my own skin anymore.

"Get out!" Lavinia barked at me. "And I don't want to see you until tonight, when you will give me a credible Bianca if it kills you."

She didn't need to tell me twice. I yanked my hoodie off the back of the chair and practically ran out of there.

I ended up walking down by the lock. There's a spot just as the path runs out with a big grassy verge, and I sat on that and didn't look at my copy of the play. Truth be told, I wasn't even sure if I was going to make it to this evening's performance. There really didn't seem to be much point. Then I did start looking at it because I just couldn't bear my own company. I wanted to reach into my head, pull out my brain through my left ear, and then stamp on it so my annoying, querulous voice (pretty much the voice I use whenever I'm saying something to Walker that doesn't involve the words *kiss* and *me*) would just shut the hell up.

I reread Bianca's first speech, even though I already had it committed to memory:

> "Good sister, wrong me not, nor wrong yourself,
> To make a bondmaid and a slave of me.

That I disdain. But for these other gauds,
Unbind my hands, I'll pull them off myself,
Yea, all my raiment, to my petticoat;
Or what you will command me will I do,
So well I know my duty to my elders."

It was so typical of Bianca. That whole selfless, woe-is-me shtick. Never doing what she wanted to do but pleasing other people, like they were more important. Then I read it again. Then I really read it. Then I had this complete epiphany.

That instead of blaming Bianca, I should feel sorry for her because she was a victim of society. She was so used to being an outcast because she was a girl and she lived in girl-unfriendly times that she didn't know how to behave in any other way.

She reminded me of someone who wasn't sitting a million miles away. A stupid girl who was so worried about stepping outside of the lines that she thought were drawn around her that it had soured her and made her bitter and twisted.

What did it matter if I was gay or straight or bisexual? It didn't! It wasn't about getting lustful over bloody gender types. Walker was actually right, and I expected to be struck down by a thunderbolt as soon as I thought that.

It was about being in the dark of his room, slow, sweet music humming out of his stereo, and the way it felt when I touched him and he touched me. I wasn't into boys, I was into just one boy, *him*. The same with the girl thing. I didn't fancy all the girls in the world, I just fancied Claire, though God knows why, because all the characteristics I claim to hate about Walker are evident in her, too.

Maybe I should stop defining myself through the people I

slept with and start trying to work out who the hell I actually am, because I don't have a clue. I'd give anything a try if it means that I can stop hating myself so much. I carried on flicking through the pages as I thought about all the ways I could make it up to Walker for being such a nightmare. Mentally, I started compiling a list in my head.

- Be the one who initiates the kissing, instead of picking a fight with him so he's goaded into initiating the kissing.
- Get the *Magic of the Musicals* tape out of the cassette deck, possibly with a screwdriver and brute force. Then help Walker to make some new mix tapes.
- Stop bringing up his skanky past.
- Stop hitting him every time he says something that I disagree with.
- Stick up for him when other people are putting him down.

I paused. Partly because Bianca had just come out with something so bitchy ("being mad herself, she's madly mated") that I was forced to reevaluate the whole victim thing, and because I'd gotten stuck on the last clause of my list. It wasn't just about Walker and me. It was about me and Claire, too. Because I didn't really want to give her up, either. And then I realized something that was glaringly obvious. Couldn't I have both of them?

*"You're not right in the head
and nor am I
and this is why
this is why I like you."*

Walker

After Daisy's frantic exit, we all sat there in subdued silence while Lavinia issued demands and orders before making us do another complete run-through of the play.

Really, she shouldn't have bothered. We sucked like a nuclear-powered Hoover. Brie announced that she was saving her energy for tonight's performance, and Lavinia practically patted her on the head and shooed her away, while Charlie had to act like he didn't hate my guts. Put it this way, he's not going to be giving Robert De Niro any sleepless nights.

By the time Lavinia stopped screeching at us like a fishwife, it was time to break for lunch. It was too late to save my eardrums, which had been permanently perforated.

Charlie tried to sidle out when my back was turned, but he wasn't quick enough to avoid my hand seizing a handful of his T-shirt and stopping his wild flight out of there.

"Are you mentally deficient?" he asked incredulously as I refused to let go, and he was forced to stop wriggling or end up tearing his vintage DEATH TO THE PIXIES T-shirt.

"Probably, yeah," I admitted. Then started walking in the direction of the door. He had no choice but to come with me, as we were still attached.

"You know, people will start to get the wrong idea," he said sourly. "What with the clutching and the dragging."

"I think my reputation can stand it. Maybe they'll think that I've done all the girls and now I'm working my way through the boys instead."

"I'm sure Daisy would have something to say about that," Charlie bitched, but when I let go of his T-shirt and opened the door, he walked out and waited for me.

Unfortunately, looking like a cross between an avenging angel and Victoria Beckham, Brie was waiting outside for Charlie. She stood with her arms folded and her fake tan glistening in the sunlight.

"Whatever you have to say, you can say it to Brie, too," Charlie demanded, and then loped over to her and whispered something in her ear, which made her shoot me another venomous look.

I had to tail the pair of them to the pub while they walked along, hand in hand, stopping to look in every window of every shop that sold clothes. She is such a bad influence on him.

When we got to the pub, they just stood there, practically tapping their feet in unison and making it clear that lunch and the drinks were on me.

And while they *ummm*ed and *aah*ed about how many carbohydrates there might be in a plate of sausage and chips, I wondered what the hell I was doing there. This is not my usual MO. At the first whiff of trouble or inconvenience, I'm off. I don't stick around. I'm not the long-haul guy.

But here I was, politely asking Brie if she wanted ice and lemon in her Diet Coke, and resisting all attempts to upend the ice bucket over her snotty little head.

People have a way of getting under your skin and into your head when you least expect it. That's the only explanation as to why when Little Lord and Lady Fauntleroy were finally settled under a sun umbrella in the beer garden, I was sitting opposite them, trying to school my features into something approximating contrition.

"So, I guess . . . ?" As a big introduction to why Daisy and I had been getting off with each other behind his back, it was pretty weak.

"I know, okay? You don't have to pretend anymore." I could see Brie's hand creeping out to touch Charlie's leg, but she didn't say anything. Though if looks could kill, I'd be flat on my back with her tweezers sticking straight into my heart.

"I wanted to tell you . . ." This was so hard. Harder than splitting up with a whole little black book of ex-girlfriends. I never cared about hurting them. But Daisy's taught me how it feels to be the one who gets hurt, and Charlie was always the one who could get my smile back after she'd torn it off my face with her fists and her fury.

Charlie hunched farther down on the bench, elbows on his knees and his eyes fixed on a point somewhere behind my left shoulder. "Can we not do this now?" he said. "In fact, let's not do this at all. I knew what you were; knew it was never going to be me. But I just didn't think it would actually be her and that the two of you would sneak around behind my back."

And even though Brie was sending me fuck-off vibes through eyes that seemed to have turned into laser beams overnight, I leaned across the table so I could grab his arm for emphasis.

"I *wanted* to tell you."

"But it was more fun to string along the tragic gay boy with his pathetic crush. God, I bet you and Daisy just laughed yourselves sick!"

"Charlie-boy, no, of course we didn't."

"I don't mind that you're seeing each other, though I'm still having trouble getting my head around it; it's the deceit," Charlie suddenly blurted out, wrenching his arm out of my grip. "I thought we were friends."

"We are!" I protested, but I couldn't say any more than that. "C'mon, you know we are, Charlie-boy. You've thrown up on my shoes, and you're still alive, aren't you?"

It was the most stupid thing to say because Charlie's face darkened the minute I finished the sentence. Evidently all mentions of the night that he'd declared his crush on me were strictly verboten.

"I think it's totally out of order the way you flirt with Charlie when you know that he's in love with you," Brie suddenly piped up, and Charlie buried his head in his hands.

"Oh God, make it stop," he begged.

"I don't flirt with you," I said automatically. "Well, I do, but I thought you enjoyed it."

But Charlie wasn't coming out from behind his hands anytime soon. Plus, now he was rocking scarily from side to side.

"Well, I think it's mean when you're not going to follow through, and Charlie doesn't deserve it," Brie snapped, her big green eyes flashing with righteous indignation.

It would have been so much easier if I'd fallen in love with her. She was straight and not too bright, and I'd probably have dumped her within a week.

And then I wondered whether things would be simpler if I *was* in love with Charlie. He adored me and he was funny and had impeccable taste in music. If only he had breasts and hips and all those other soft bits in between, he'd be made for me.

I realized that they were waiting for me to say something.

"How do you know I'm not going to follow through?" Sometimes I wonder if I was dropped on my head as a baby, or if all the dope I smoke has permanently addled my brains. There has to be some reason why my foot is constantly wedged in my mouth.

Brie gave me a look that I didn't know she was capable of, and she held it for a count of ten, not blinking. It was the Glare of Doom and its evil death rays could destroy all of Metropolis.

It was so typical of Daisy to just up and leave me to sort out her mess. Daisy. Daisy was impossible to put into words.

She was beyond good or evil. She was something that I couldn't even believe had happened to me. Sometimes when we were lying in bed together and I was breathing the vanilla and lavender scent of her, I wanted to ask her to pinch me because I had to be dreaming.

It wasn't something I could explain to Brie and Charlie. It was private. Not just because of the whole gay thing, but talking about it, making words out of it, might make it disappear. Like it never existed in the first place.

"I'm sorry we didn't tell you," I told Charlie. "But I can't talk about it. It's not fair on Daisy—"

"What's not fair on me?" a voice said behind me, and I turned around and there she was. Bathed in sunlight and lit up with a fiery glow so she seemed to shimmer as she stood there. And I was just another sucker ready to fall down on my knees if she wanted me to.

She started walking toward us, and I had to look away because I hate her and love her in equal measure, and it makes my head hurt.

She placed a hand on my shoulder, and I know she felt me flinch against her palm.

"We need to talk," she said, completely ignoring Brie and Charlie, who wore matching perplexed expressions like we were the last question in *Who Wants to Be a Millionaire*.

"God, you're a crap lesbian," Charlie blurted out, and then remembered that he was meant to be the injured party. "*And* you're a crap friend."

Daisy was now trying to lean against me like we were a touchy-feely boyfriend-girlfriend-type couple. I slid a few inches along the bench and tried to pretend that I hadn't noticed how soft her skin felt against mine. Or how she was wearing a really low-cut peasant top that made her breasts look as if they were trying to mount a bid for freedom.

"I'm a pretty crap everything, Charlie," Daisy said, and I had to give her kudos for not raising her voice. If I'd been having this conversation with her, she'd be hollering and hitting me by now. "But the bottom line is that it's between me and Walker. It's really got nothing to do with either of you."

Well, that took the wind right out of their collective sails. I could see the cogs—or that should probably be cog—whirring in Brie's brain. It probably felt quite lonely in there.

"But I don't understand!" she wailed. "You're gay!"

Charlie had an evil smirk plastered on his face. "You're gonna have to give the handbook back, Daze. And they're gonna revoke your membership."

"There's a handbook? Have you got one? You never showed it to me!"

Daisy looked down her nose at Brie. "And forever we'll remember this as the day that Brie took the word *gullible* to extremes we never imagined possible."

"Well, you might not be a big, honking lesbian anymore," Brie hissed as she and Charlie got up. And as she walked past us, she gave Daisy's poor, defenseless arm a girlie pinch. "But you're still a big, honking bitch."

Daisy didn't even wait for them to get out of earshot before she sat down next to me and said: "Thank God for that, I thought they'd never leave. Come here, you."

And so it came to pass that at 3:15, in broad daylight and full view of anyone who happened to be sitting in the beer garden of The Elephant's Head, Daisy kissed me.

Her lips, as always, made me come undone. But whenever I have Daisy wriggling in my arms, all I can think of is that my meter's running out and I'm only halfway around the block. Is this the last time I get to hold her before she runs, screaming all the way, back to Lesbian City?

"Let's go back to your place," she suggested breathily when we both remembered that oxygen was necessary for our continued survival.

It felt as if the sun had suddenly gone out, even though it was still blazing away in the sky. "You know what, sweetheart? Let's not."

Daisy licked her lips in a gesture that may or may not have been innocent. I never could work her out. "I want to make things up to you. I know I've been a bitch, but I've figured things out. I want to be with you."

It's funny how six little words can feel like the difference between life and death. Or love and hate. Or a lesbian and a girlfriend. I stopped trying to tell my legs to just get up and walk away from her.

"You do?" I sounded so hopeful.

"Uh-huh." She nodded and then nibbled on her thumbnail. "But here's the weird part, and please don't get all huffy: I kinda want to be with Claire, too. How do you feel about that?"

And in the end, it was as easy as getting up, giving her a look so cold that I could have had it directly imported from the nearest frozen tundra, and then getting the hell out of there before I throttled her.

"Well it's true that we love one another."

Brie

Charlie brought me a card today and slipped it in my bag when I wasn't looking. I didn't find it till just before I was due to go onstage, and I decided, what the hell, it's our last night, if I say that Katharina wears Lancôme Juicy Tubes in Sorbet de cerise, then she does. Lavinia says she doesn't, but I'm not sure I trust her. I like her, don't get me wrong, but Lavinia does her makeup like an old lady. She doesn't have any eyebrows, which says to me that she overplucked them in her party-girl days and pencils them in really crookedly. Plus she's never even heard of lip liner.

So, anyway, I'm rummaging in my bag and I find the card. It has a picture of a cute little Westie terrier on the front (Charlie's latest thing is that he's going to get a small dog to love him unconditionally and also as a way to meet other, attractive, dog-loving boys. Who are gay. It's a whole gay thing.) wearing a tracksuit with the words HOPELESSLY DEVOTED TO YOU over its pointy little ears.

Inside he'd written:

> Dearest Brie (you know you're named after a cheese, right?)
>
> Baby girl, I just wanted to say how glad I am that we're friends again. I know I don't tell you this enough, but I love you more than I love anyone, even if that love doesn't involve wanting to get you naked and do unmentionable things to your quivering girl flesh.
>
> I'm sorry that I was such a wanker to you this summer, but maybe I had to be. Because without me, you became the amazing girl that I always thought you could be.
>
> Your Katharina totally rocks and so do you. And if, five years from now, you are still a virgin and Adam Brody doesn't come through like I suspect he will, we'll give it another go. Hey, what are friends for?
>
> So, break a leg tonight (metaphorically speaking) and save a dance for me at the party.
>
> Big smoochy kisses,
>
> Your ever loving, though ever gay friend,
>
> Charlie xxx
>
> P.S.: Walker and Daisy have had a massive bust-up. I'll give you fifty quid if you dare to ask her if this means that she's not bisexual anymore.
>
> Love ya!

Although this summer had some major sucky bits, in the end I think it worked out okay. Me and Charlie are friends, and he's stopped putting me down and calling me stupid. And I made other friends like Tash and Gemma, and we're going to try and get Saturday jobs in Top Shop together so we can eye up cute boys and get staff discount cards.

What else? Well, my dad speaks to me now! He even came into my room the other day to ask me about iPods and mended the wonky handle on my chest of drawers while he was at it. He still has the whole no-touching thing going on, but I think it would be too much for him—to, like, speak to me and give me hugs as well. But he sent off to a whole load of drama colleges, and when school starts back in the autumn, he's going to have a meeting with my personal tutor to discuss "my future goals." Yay! I have future goals. I also get the feeling that he told Mum to back the hell off. I don't get any more snide remarks about my weight or the size of my arse. She still comes into the kitchen if she hears me open the fridge, but now she pretends that she's going to load the dishwasher.

I still don't feel happy all the time. But Charlie says I should aim for about sixty-five percent and that I should stop obsessing about cellulite and getting dryness lines around my eyes, because when I'm a famous actress, I'll be able to afford liposuction and Botox injections.

So this summer hasn't been anything like I thought it would. And now that I'm about to go onstage for one final time, I feel sad, like something really good is about to end. But I s'pose the difference is that there's other stuff to look forward to.

I adjusted my stupid wimple thing that I have to wear for the first act, and smeared on one last coat of Sorbet de cerise for luck. It's not like Lavinia can give my part to someone else.

. . .

Our last performance pretty much blowed. Apart from me. Turns out that while I was doing my makeup and my breathing exercises and getting into character, the others were guzzling down vodka and Red Bull. Even Gemma and Tash. So unprofessional. Charlie threw up in one of the fire buckets at the side of the stage just before his third entrance, and Lavinia was so spitting mad that she almost canceled the wrap party, but she relented at the last moment.

Just as well 'cause I spent a fortune on my new dress.

"So, like, him and Daisy have split up, not like you could ever say they were really going out, and he's all, like, Charlie-boy and just expecting me to follow him round like a freakin' puppy dog . . ." Charlie ranted.

It seemed like he'd been going on and on about Wanker and Daisy forever. Or it felt like forever. Certainly since we started walking down Camden High Street toward Chalk Farm.

He hadn't even told me that I looked pretty, which was just unforgivable.

"So I said to him, 'You can't treat me like shit and then expect me to be all happy 'cause you wanna hang again.' And he said . . ."

God, Charlie was being such a whiny-ass, little crybaby. "Yeah, yeah." I sighed and checked out my appearance in the shop window that we were passing. The new strappy pink sandals really slenderized my ankles.

"Brie! Jesus! You're not even listening to me!" Charlie suddenly wailed, and I was forced to turn around and look at his mopey face.

❀ **Brie**

"What?"

"What do you mean, what?" Charlie was all red-faced, but I think it was from the alcohol. "I'm sorry, is my pain boring you?"

"Well, yeah, actually it kinda is, Charlie."

I didn't know which of us was more surprised. I think it was probably him. "Oh, well then," he said sniffily, and with this big dollop of hurt that I wasn't buying for a second: "Sorry for inflicting my angst on you."

I love Charlie, but sometimes he is a pain in the arse.

"Oooohhhh, Charlie!" I groaned, winging around and bopping him over the head with my clutch. "Grow up, will you? If Walker's getting on your nerves and treating you like shit, then don't let him get away with it, all right? Just don't keep banging on and on about it to me 'cause it's really boring!"

Charlie began to storm off and then stopped midflounce so he could snort with laughter. "Oh my God! I've just become the sidekick in this relationship. When did this happen?"

"You're such a retard." I smacked Charlie on his arse (nice and firm it was, too, even though he does like, no exercise) and he squawked.

"Hey! Don't touch what you can't afford, Brianna."

"Whatever, Charles."

Then he took my hand and squeezed it gently. "He just really hurt me."

"I know, but he's a stupid wanker," I said consolingly. "Bet he fancies you, really."

Charlie looked at me hopefully. "You think so?"

"Nah."

We carried on walking for a bit, and just as we were crossing the Lock Bridge, Charlie said: "Look at the sky, Brie."

Normally I don't walk around and look up at the stars. I

just don't. You don't really get many stars in North London, unless they're the kind who are in *EastEnders*. It has something to do with pollution, I think.

But I looked up, and the sky wasn't black but more of a deep, deep blue, like my MAC Blu-Noir eye shadow, and there were tons of stars, twinkling away.

"I think it's 'cause there aren't any clouds tonight," Charlie said. "It's very pretty isn't it?"

"Yeah. So do you know what any of them are called?"

Charlie put his hands in his back pockets and gazed at the sky. "Let me see. That one over there is called Mavis. And, oh, there's Eric. Give him a wave."

And then Charlie took my hand and started running, even though I can't move fast in high heels.

When we got to Lavinia's place, all the doors and windows were open and people were spilling out into the front garden. She had one of those huge Victorian houses overlooking Primrose Hill, which she told me belonged to her second husband, and she got it in the divorce settlement when he buggered off to Belize with her understudy when she was playing the lead in *Cavalcade*.

Charlie pulled me up the front steps, and Lavinia was standing there with a glass in her hand and lipstick smeared on her front teeth. I was really going to have to have a word with her about that.

"Brie, darling!" she cried, pulling me in to peck the air above my cheeks. "My little protégée is finally here. Come in. Drink champagne, mingle, have fun!"

Charlie stepped up for his air kisses, but she just gave him a snotty look. "Charlie. Well, I suppose you were more or less adequate," she sniffed, and turned away to greet the people behind us.

"Adequate?" Charlie pulled a face at me. "I poured heart and soul into my tragi-comic role as Tranio or Lucentio or whatever the fuck my character was called, and all I get is a sodding *adequate*?"

"You had to be prompted every night," I reminded him as we found the kitchen and Charlie started rummaging through the bottles on the table.

"You're so going to be one of those Hollywood divas who forgets her roots the minute the big time beckons." Charlie laughed. "Bingo!" He picked up a bottle of champagne and began ripping the foil off the top.

"I'll never forget you," I protested, grabbing a couple of glasses from the drain board. "You'll have to come to Hollywood with me and make sure I'm all right."

"Yeah, I can be your personal manager. I'll be the 'people' in 'we'll get your people to call our people.'"

I put the glasses down and tugged the bottle out of Charlie's hands. "Seriously, I'd never want to stop being your friend," I said, entwining my fingers in his. "I don't know what I'd be without you. Don't want to find out either."

"You'd be fine without me," Charlie said, smiling and smoothing the hair back from my face. "I think we've already established that I'm merely your bitch."

But then he was hugging me, his arms wrapping around me so tight that I could hardly breathe. Charlie is the only person who ever really touches me.

I let my hands glide over his back, and he made a funny, snuffly sound and buried his face against my neck. I know. I *know* he's GAY, but just for a second I pretended that he wasn't because he loves me in this really good way, but I'm still not over wishing that he loved me in the other way, too.

Anyway, it was one of the best cuddles ever, and it only stopped when Wanker crashed through the doorway.

"Oh, for fuck's sake, would you two get a room?" He sneered. "He's gay, Brie, sweetie. It's never gonna happen."

I'd have liked to scrub the smirk off his face with the washing-up brush that was on the drain board.

"Don't you be starting with her," Charlie hissed, wagging his finger at Wanker warningly. "And the gay thing didn't stop you and Daisy from humping away."

Wanker took a long pull from the bottle of beer swinging between his fingers. "That was different," he muttered, all his bluster gone now that Charlie had totally called him on it. "Anyway, I thought you promised me that you'd never say her name again, Charlie-boy."

"Oh, please stop calling me that," Charlie snapped, yanking my hand and tugging me past Wanker, who was now slumped against the fridge. "And just fucking grow up!"

Wanker so didn't get the message that he totally wasn't wanted and followed us as we wandered around the house.

Me and Charlie found our way out into the garden, and Charlie collapsed on a little wooden bench and pulled me down to sit on his lap. "Have some more champagne," he suggested, shoving the bottle in my face. "It's got practically zero calories."

"Did we manage to lose that loser?" I asked, peering back at the way we'd come, but Wanker was nowhere to be seen.

We'd almost finished the bottle when Wanker and Daisy wandered out. In the midst of a furious argument. Like, what else is new? But more importantly, like so much more importantly, Daisy was wearing a dress! It was tight and black and vintagey-looking, and she kept tugging at it like it was too small. It wasn't, but when you're used to wearing all your clothes at least two sizes too big, then I guess you need time to get used to clothes that fit properly.

"Why don't you want me?" Daisy was yelling, but she shut up when she saw me and Charlie sitting there, watching them.

"Hey Charlie-boy," Wanker said, and held up two more bottles of champagne. He brushed past Daisy like she was made of air, but she trotted along after him, her eyes all squinty and annoyed.

Charlie slid off the bench onto the ground so Daisy could sit down. Wanker sat at her feet 'cause he's not over her, and she *so* owns his arse.

She nudged Wanker's shoulder with her knee and opened her mouth to say something but was interrupted by Charlie. "It's not fair," he ranted. "I never get to kiss anyone. You and he do nothing else but try and eat each other's mouths off each other's faces. Brie got to kiss Walker when they were doing the play. Well, what about me?"

"He's pissed," I said, like they hadn't already worked that one out. I ruffled Charlie's hair and made a mental note to do a deep conditioning treatment on the bleached bits tomorrow. "Anyway, *you* kissed *me*!"

"Yeah, I'd forgotten about that." Charlie perked up. "But I still feel like I'm lagging behind."

Daisy stopped yanking at the front of her dress for, like, one millisecond. "Rewind just a second. What do you mean you two kissed? In what strange universe did you two end up snogging?"

"I had a momentary sexual identity crisis." Charlie looked like he'd sold his soul to the devil as he flashed this totally evil smile at Daisy. "I hear there's a lot of it around."

She had to let that one go, but I could see her mouthing something at Wanker, who just shrugged.

"It's not fair. It's not fair. It's not fair," Charlie chanted.

"Well, Daisy only got to kiss me," Wanker said, leering at her. "So you two are even."

That wasn't quite right. But I looked at Daisy and dared her to say anything about the time that she committed assault on my mouth. And she looked right back at me and shook her head, and I knew she wasn't going to say anything.

"It's still not fair," Charlie whined, and I was just seriously thinking about whapping him over the head with the empty bottle so he'd either pass out and/or shut up when Wanker suddenly swiveled around and cupped Charlie's face in his big hands and planted him one right on the lips!

I think Charlie only realized what was happening after it was almost over because he started wriggling about like a little fish on a hook.

"There you go, Charlie-boy," Walker said, like he'd just given him a bag of crisps or something. "And now I've kissed all of you. I should probably get a prize."

Daisy shoved one of the bottles at him. Her eyes were like evil rays of death. "How about a smack in the mouth?" she suggested nastily, and Walker flashed her this smile, which was actually more like him just baring his teeth.

"Oh, I think you've already given me one or two of them," he said, and Daisy looked even more pissy.

"You know you're being completely unreasonable about this whole thing," she spat out, adjusting her dress for, like, the gazillionth time.

Wanker was wrestling with the cork from the other champagne bottle, and as he wrenched it out with a loud pop, it spilled all over his hands in this bubbling froth. "Yeah. I know. Normally when I'm going out with a girl, and she wants to be free to get off with other girls, then I'm completely fine and dandy with it," he said, shaking his hands and spraying Charlie with little drops of champagne.

Charlie stuck out his tongue and tried to lick the champagne off his cheeks, then said, "If you two want to argue about stuff that's kinda personal and embarrassing for other people to have to listen to, could you piss off and do it somewhere else?"

"We are not arguing," Daisy snapped, when like, they totally were. "We're having a discussion."

"Which sounds like scenes from my parents' marriage," Charlie pointed out. And even though he was still pretty drunk, he was starting to sound less pissed and more pissed off. "Weird, isn't it, that you couldn't kiss and hold hands, but you don't mind slagging each other in front of me?"

"Nothing to do with you, Charlie-boy."

"Yeah, just butt out of our business," Daisy added, and then they looked surprised like they weren't meant to be agreeing with each other.

Poor Charlie. And in a way, poor Daisy and poor Wanker.

They were just so . . . stupid. I mean, I still had wrong feelings about Charlie, but I managed to build a bridge and get over them, and so should they.

"You're all really dumb," I piped up, and almost wished I hadn't when three pairs of eyes immediately began to glare at me. "Anyway, I don't reckon I'm going to have another chance to do this because it's not like we're good friends or anything so—"

"Oh my God." Daisy sighed, rolling her eyes. "Is she going to get to the point anytime soon?"

I opened my bag and rummaged. "I made a list," I explained, pulling out the sheet I'd ripped from my notebook. "Of questions I wanted to ask you and Walker so I can figure out the whole gay thing."

"You made a list?" Daisy asked hysterically. "She made a list!"

Well, duh. "I didn't want to forget anything."

Charlie propped himself up his elbows. He seemed a bit dazed, like the kiss with Walker and then all the sniping had blown out a large part of his brain. "I've been looking forward to this all night. Go for it, Brie."

I smoothed down the paper, which had gotten a bit crumpled, and squinted to see my writing in the dim light.

"Okay, question number one to Daisy. Were you going to have a schedule to decide whether you were going to see Walker or Claire on different nights? Or were you going to decide on a first-come, first-served basis?" I read out.

Daisy made this weird choking noise and spilled champagne down the front of her dress.

"How am I ever expected to know this stuff if people won't tell me?" I wailed.

"Well, it was a bit of both really," she said very slowly. "Like I see Claire on Tuesdays 'cause we go to this gay club together, but otherwise I was going to take it on a suck-it-and-see basis."

Charlie had a coughing fit. "Do you want to rephrase that?" he spluttered. "Go on, read out the next one."

"Question number two to Walker. Secretly were you hoping that you'd get to watch Claire and Daisy kissing because boys like watching lesbians together?"

"No!" they both shouted, and Walker lay back on the grass and started laughing. Daisy meanwhile was wiping her hand across her eyes and giggling.

I thought they were perfectly intelligent questions. It's not like anything *they* did actually made any sense. "Are you going to take this seriously or not?"

"I'm sorry." Daisy sat up and tried to pretend that she hadn't been crying with laughter five seconds before. "How many questions are there?"

"Well, there's one more. But it's an important one. Question three to Daisy. Are you gay, straight, bisexual—"

"Or just really, really greedy?"

"Shut up, Charlie!"

"What am I?" she repeated. "I'm all of the above. I'm none of the above. I'm a lesbian who likes kissing Walker, even though he hates the ground I walk on. I'm me and I'm still trying to figure out what and who the hell I am. When I find out, I'll get back to you."

And then Walker said in this throaty voice that would have been kinda sexy if it hadn't been coming out of his mouth, "I don't hate you. I wish I did, 'cause then I wouldn't want to do this."

That was the cue for Walker to lean forward, cup his hand against Daisy's cheek, and kiss her really softly on the lips. It was actually quite sweet and made me feel a tiny pang of hope that one day I'd meet a straight boy who would kiss me like I was made of glass and might break.

That lasted for about five seconds, and then the kissing got less sweet and more about slurping noises and hands . . . *Euwwww!* Hands going toward places that maybe they shouldn't be going toward when they're in public.

Charlie obviously agreed with me because he picked up the empty bottle of champagne that was lying next to him and shook it over the pair of them so they were showered with a spray of tiny drops. "Must you flaunt your heterosexuality in my presence?" he asked in a shrill voice as they lifted their heads for a second and then carried on trying to stick their tongues as far down each other's throats as possible.

None of it makes sense really. In a perfect world, Charlie would be my perfect boyfriend. And he'd dress better and we'd have loads of things in common, and not just that we were both into boys. And Daisy and Walker would be going out, and she wouldn't have a girlfriend, too, and also they'd be less up on themselves so me and Charlie could double-date with them.

I tried to say this to them, but it didn't come out right. It didn't come out at all. "I'm falling over my words," I said finally, and Charlie knelt up so he could give me a slightly sozzled kiss on the cheek.

"Which is why I love you. 'Cause you fall over your words and off your heels."

"But it should add up," I complained. "There's four of us. Two boys and two girls, so that should make two couples really, shouldn't it?"

"Well, yeah, it should," Walker agreed, and while I was wondering why he agreed with me, he carried on. "But those two couples could have been you and Daisy and me and Charlie."

"I still don't understand," I said, upending the bottle of champagne so the last trickle dripped into my mouth. "I haven't had sex with anyone yet, and it's already too complicated."

Daisy laughed and put her arm around me so she could squeeze my shoulder. Not in a big, old, gay way but in a way like she liked me. And it felt comforting, like I liked her back. Which, hello! Never gonna happen. "Love is just this illusion that people cling to so that they don't have to be alone," she whispered in my ear. But I didn't believe her 'cause the whole time she was looking at Walker, who was laughing at something Charlie was saying, and her entire face had softened, so that she almost looked pretty.

Besides, I believe in love. And one day it will happen. I know it will. It won't be anything like the love I feel for Charlie, which always makes me feel slightly sad. It will be for someone who can love me back. Who won't be able to live without me and whose face will light up whenever I walk into the room and who'll send me text messages just to say that they're thinking about me. It will be perfect. If there wasn't that kind of love just waiting for the right moment to bring two people together, then what was the point of being alive?

I didn't tell the others that. They wouldn't have understood. Or they'd have made some snarky remarks because they don't have, like, a romantic bone between them.

Instead no one said anything for a while. We just sat back and looked up at the stars shining brightly above us.

SONG CREDITS AND ACKNOWLEDGMENTS

Every effort has been made to seek permission to use the song lyrics quoted in this book, and the publisher would like to thank those copyright holders who have granted us such permission.

Page 3: Charlie
"She's my best friend, certainly not the average girl."
"She's My Best Friend." The Velvet Underground. Copyright © Verve (Polydor).

Page 14: Daisy
"The rumour is you never go with boys and you are tight."
"Expectations." Belle and Sebastian. Words and Music by Stuart Murdoch, Richard Colburn, Michael Cooke, Christopher Geddes, Stephen Jackson and Isobel Campbell. © 1998 Sony/ATV Music Publishing Limited. All rights reserved. International copyright secured.

Page 30: Walker
"Don't you know that you're toxic?"
"Toxic." Britney Spears. Copyright © Jive Records.

Page 44: Brie
"They know how to break all the girls like you/And they rob the souls of the girls like you."
"Awful." Hole. Copyright © Mother May I Music/Echo Tunes (BMI).

Page 69: Charlie
"We don't need reason and we don't need logic/'Cause we've got feeling and we're damn proud of it."
"Speeding Motorcycle." Yo La Tengo. Copyright © Eternal Yip Eye Music (BMI).

Page 87: Daisy
"*She wears sad jeans/torn at the waistband./Her pretty face/is stained with tears.*"
"Like A Motorway." St. Etienne. Copyright © Heavenly Recordings/ Warner Chappell.

Page 104: Walker
"*Hey little apple blossom/what seems to be the problem/all the ones you tell your troubles to/they don't really care for you.*"
"Apple Blossom." The White Stripes. Words and music by Jack White. Copyright © 2003, Peppermint Stripe Music, USA. EMI Music Publishing Ltd, London WC2H 0QY.

Page 122: Brie
"*I'll take the best of your bad moods/and dress them up to make a better you.*"
"Company Calls." Death Cab for Cutie. Words by Benjamin Gibbard, music by Death Cab for Cutie. Barsuk Records © 2000. All rights reserved.

Page 138: Charlie
"*I'm starting to fashion an idea in my head/where I would impress you/with every single word I said.*"
"For You to Notice." Dashboard Confessional. Courtesy of Christoper Carraba. © 2001 Hey Did She Ask You About Me Music (ASCAP).

Page 157: Daisy
"*Your face reminds me of a flower/Kind of like you're underwater/Hair's too long and in your eyes/Your lips a perfect suck me size.*"
"Flower." Liz Phair. Copyright © Capitol Records.

Page 176: Walker
"*Well, if I remain passive and you just want to cuddle/Then we should be ok, and we won't get into trouble.*"
"Seeing Other People." Belle and Sebastian. Words and music by Stuart Murdoch, Richard Colburn, Michael Cooke, Christopher Geddes,